To Margaret,
   with best wishes
      from
   Carol A Jones
      16.6.06.

C. A. Jones was, for many years, a teacher in schools in the South Wales valleys. She is married with one son. After giving up teaching to pursue other interests, she completed a course in creative writing run by Cardiff University. She began writing Sunlight on a Sunday during the final year of the course and is now working on her second novel.

SUNLIGHT ON A SUNDAY

C. A. JONES

Copyright © 2005 C. A. Jones

The right of C. A. Jones to be identified as the Author of the Work has been asserted by her in accordance with the Copyright, Designs and Patents Act 1988.

This book is a work of fiction. Names, characters, places and incidents are either products of the author's imagination or are used fictitiously. Any resemblance to actual people, living or dead, events or locales, is entirely coincidental.

To my family and in memory of my parents who experienced the hardships of life in the mining valleys of South Wales at the beginning of the twentieth century.

Introduction

Month after month - how could they have endured it? Professor Margaret Davies asked herself as she scanned the flat French landscape on a cold November morning. Collecting her thoughts, she looked again into the large shallow trench where some of her assistants were working. As one of Britain's foremost forensic archaeologists she had been called to this World War I battle site where a farmer, whilst winter ploughing, had unearthed some human remains. So far only odd bones and a fragmented skull had been found in the recently turned soil. Was there more?

Gradually the technicians peeled back the layers of earth until one of them exclaimed, "I think we've got a whole one here! Look here's the top of the skull." Then after moving carefully along the trench he started to gently scrape again. "Yes, this must be the foot."

"Leave it there," Margaret shouted. "Take photos at each stage. Can't miss a shred of evidence if we're to have a hope of identifying these remains."

She stepped down into the trench and for a while simply stared at the bits of exposed skeleton to absorb every detail. Then she called the photographer over and pointed out the angles she required. Satisfied that she now had two sets of prints – the one in her mind and the other on film – she took it on herself to carefully expose more and more of the bones. All the time her eyes automatically logged to her memory the least abnormality. She worked very slowly as she scraped the soil around the lower arm region for she hoped to find a small, oval-shaped, aluminium disc. But disappointingly there was nothing.

Looking up at the technician, she said, "Must be an early one. There's no wrist identity disk. No easy means of establishing who he is. Those regulation issue red fibre ones had no chance of surviving this long. Still we might find other things to help us."

She worked patiently, pausing only for the photographs and to put any surviving bits of cloth, leather or metal into small plastic bags. So far, her only real clue was a piece of a belt buckle from which she hoped to be able to identify the man's regiment. Then alongside the thighbone her trowel touched something hard.

More bones, she thought as she carefully exposed the artefact, but it turned out to be a small tin.

"This must have been in his pocket," she said as she carefully brushed off some of the dirt with her fingers. " Perhaps where he kept his tobacco. I think there are numbers etched in the lid but I can't quite make them out. I'll have to wait 'til we get back to the lab. They're very faint whatever they are and I don't want to damage them further."

"Has it got anything in it?" asked the technician as he held open a plastic bag for her to put the box into.

"I doubt it. If it's not airtight then after all this time anything perishable will have had it. Still it had better be opened when we get back in case we miss something."

Eventually the team was able to remove all the remains and pack them carefully for their journey back to England. No other significant clues had come to light. Most of the fragments would be re-buried together, but the skeleton could be interred in a named grave – if it could be identified. Who was this soldier who had died on some dreadful day in the First World War?

Back in the university, the Professor began her detailed examination. She quickly established that the remains were of a white male, aged between twenty and twenty-five. From the pelvis and thighbone she calculated that in life he had been about five feet eight inches tall. She noticed that the right radius was thicker than the left and thus concluded that he was right-handed. There was an unusual thickness to the collarbones and this led her to believe that he had had a job where he constantly used his shoulders and upper arms.

Like someone wielding a pick or shovel, she thought.

Completing her examination of the skeleton, she turned to the tin. After cleaning the outside, she slowly opened the lid. Everything had perished except for a few coins. But she had more luck with the numbers scratched into the top. Under a powerful lamp she could just about decipher most of them. They were in two sets. The first, she thought, could be a regimental number and the second may be the soldier's own army number. But a few digits were incomplete and she couldn't be sure that the numbers she thought she saw were those of the dead soldier.

If I'm right then Colonel Phillips of the War Graves Commission will be able to look up the records and then the remains of this brave young man can be buried properly. I wonder if he was recruited in the South Wales Valleys? Those collarbones could well have come from a miner. Why did this young man join up? He probably had some misconceived notion of soldiers in uniform leading glamorous lives. And what did he end up doing? Burrowing through the ground again – but this time in the dangerous silt under enemy lines.

Chapter One

He hated winter. He had gone down the same track in the dark that morning and now he trudged wearily up it from number nine pit in the black again. It seemed to Dafydd Price that he only saw daylight on a Sunday and then his mother and grandmother insisted that he went to Ebenezer Chapel when he longed to walk the mountains and to be free. Still it was choir tonight and Dafydd loved to sing. He had a fine tenor voice. His steps lightened and his pace quickened as he thought of their newly formed male voice choir.

"Hope Mam's got the water ready," he muttered to himself as the houses came into view.

The row of terraced houses displayed a sameness that any stranger would have found confusing. All were built of pennant sandstone and each had three sash windows and a four-panelled door. Even the paint was the same – a dull, dark brown colour. But to the practiced eye all were different. Mrs. Jones' doorstep was scoured cleaner than the rest. Glyn Thomas liked to whittle in wood and had made an intricate knob for the door. Granny Price had been a tailoress in Aberystwyth before she had come with her husband to the Valleys looking for work. The old man, though young in years, was killed sinking Number Nine pit and his wife had kept the family out of the workhouse by using her skills. It was no wonder that every one knew the Price's house for they had the finest curtains in the street. The three matching pairs were hung, of course, with the pattern outwards so that anyone passing could admire them.

Dafydd pushed open the front door and shouted; "It's choir night. Is the bath ready?"
His mother, Carrie, appeared at the door on the right in the middle of the short narrow passage.

"Of course it is, Dafydd. Do you think that your grandmother and I could forget that it's choir night? Come on, into the back kitchen. Get yourself clean and then you can have your tea. Are those sticks you've brought home with you?" she asked as she noticed the bundle under his arm. "I could do with those to light the fire." Then without pausing she continued, "Where's your Tommy Box? I'll need to fill it for the morning."

Dafydd handed over the sticks and his battered food tin and then disappeared into the small lean-to at the end of the passage, where the bath stood in front of the old range. As he knelt, half-naked, before the steaming water, a wave of weariness engulfed him. But this seemed to wash away as the clear liquid became impregnated with the black dust. As his skin lightened, so did his heart and he began to sing in Welsh one of his favourite ballads – Y Ferch o'r Scer.

> *Mab wyf fi sy'n byw dan bennydd*
> *Am f'an wylyd fawr ei bri;*
> *Gwaith ei charu'n fwy na digon*
> *Curio wnaeth fy nghalon I;*
> *Gwell yw dangos beth yw'r achos*
> *Nag ym aros dan fy nghur;*
> *Der'r seren at a'I'n llawen*
> *Ti gei barch a chariad pur.*

And then, in readiness for choir practice, repeated it, only this time in English.

> *I adore a youthful maiden*
> *Fairer than the morning light,*
> *By her image I am haunted*
> *Through the watches of the night*
> *Better to declare my passion,*
> *Than in silent anguish pine;*
> *Beam upon me, a star of beauty*
> *Promise quickly to be mine.*

He had no idea where Sker was - as far as Dafydd was concerned it could have been anywhere and he would have been surprised indeed to learn that it was a small hamlet on the South Wales coast. He loved the haunting tale of the harpist who was engaged to the Maid of Sker until, when he lost his sight, she cruelly jilted him. Perhaps the young miner was drawn to the song because he too experienced blindness in the blackness underground.

Carrie and Granny Price heard his voice soaring as they waited patiently in the middle room. Every now and then the older one got up and stirred the contents of the large saucepan on the fire.

"This broth will set Dafydd up for the evening," she said. "You clear up after him and I'll make sure that he has a good meal. You know what he's like on choir night. He wants to be gone before he's home. I expect that he'll want to wear those new trousers."

The old lady walked the few steps over to a large chest of drawers standing against the opposite wall. Opening one of the drawers, she pulled out a pair of grey trousers.

"Lucky I had material left from making Doctor William's suit. It was just enough to make these for our Dafydd," she said as she shut the drawer.

Then, as she had done many times before, she ran her fingers over the polished rosewood.

How I scrimped and saved to buy this chest, she thought lovingly as her hand smoothed one of the two half drawers at the top. It contained the few mementos she had of her husband and her long lost parents. On the rare occasion she wasn't busy and was alone in the house, she would take them out and allow the memories to come flooding back, but it was so long ago.

Now, she only dimly remembered the poor farm cottage in the hills above Aberystwyth, where she had lived until she was ten. Then, one spring morning, her father had taken her to the hiring fair in the town. She could still hear her mother's sobs as they walked away. She knew now that her mother was right to weep, for it was a very long time indeed before they saw each other again. In the early morning light, father and daughter trudged down the tracks, then through the streets to the market place behind the ruins of the castle. The little girl was frightened.

"Dad, where are we going?" asked Megan.

Her father couldn't answer for his throat was choked with sadness and anger. But what else was he to do? He couldn't feed them all. She had to go but he was determined that he would get as good a place as he could for his young daughter.

The fair was noisy as people thronged about looking for labour of all descriptions. Adults and children stood in lines waiting to see what fate would bring them. Some of the men and women had been there before but for many of the younger ones this was a new and bewildering experience.

"Looking for a good strong worker, Mister," shouted a man.

"Want a shepherd?" asked another.

Frightened, young children simply stood there not knowing what to do nor say.

Megan's father had led her to a grass bank and said, "Now climb up onto that step and stand up straight."

Was Megan going to be lucky? He prayed that she would be. He couldn't see his first child, this innocent young girl, end up as little more than a slave. He managed to prevent her being taken on by one man who was already the worse for drink. But it was getting late. If he took her home, he knew that he would not be able to go through this again. He had to find someone to take her into service. At last a well-dressed gentleman approached.

"I want a scullery maid," he said, looking the girl up and down. "Is she used to hard work? Can she light fires?"

"Yes, sir," replied her father. "She's been brought up to do most things in the house and she sees to the animals as well."

The man laughed. "I've no animals to look after but a large draper shop to run. Turn round girl. A bit small, but I suppose she'll grow. She'll do." Then looking at her, he said in a softer voice, "You'll start in the kitchen but, who knows, if you prove your worth then when you're older you may even work behind the counter."

The two men talked and it was agreed that Megan would get her keep and one shilling and six pence a week. Her father didn't think that he that he could do any better for Megan. He hugged her briefly, told her to work hard and then watched as his confused and frightened daughter went with the stranger. This time he allowed the tears to roll down his cheeks too.

Then he turned and with a heavy heart he made his way back up the hills.

Not many memories remained of that walk through the streets of Aberystwyth. They were locked away in the inner reaches of Granny Price's mind, too upsetting to be disturbed. She simply remembered clutching her small bundle, which contained all her possessions, until her fingers ached and following the man's black coat through the town.

At the shop, the draper's wife looked her up and down and wasn't that impressed, after all she was a small child.

"We'll try her, I suppose. What's your name, girl?"

"Megan" was the almost inaudible reply as the tears spilled out of the youngster's eyes and down her face.

"Come, come, there's no need for this. Cook will give you something to eat and you can warm yourself by the range in the kitchen. You'll feel better then."

The woman took hold of the girl's hand and led her quickly down a long passage to the kitchen.

"Mrs. Bowen, here's your new scullery maid. Her name is Megan, but Megan what I don't know. Look after her and find out more about her. I've other things to see to at the moment," she added as she walked away.

"Come here, child," said the cook softly after her mistress had left the room. "Over to the fire. You must be cold and, come to think about it, hungry too. I bet that you were up since before it was light and haven't had anything to eat since. You look as if you could do with feeding up. There's not much flesh on you"

So Megan's time in Aberystwyth began. Her new life was so different from the old that for the first few months she was an unhappy, frightened and bewildered young girl. One day she was the eldest of a large family, living all together in a one- roomed cottage and the next she was the lowly scullery maid in a large house. Even now, after all these years, Granny Price still couldn't bring herself to relive those first few months away from her parents and brothers and sisters. She shuddered as she remembered how she had wept every night as she crawled wearily into her lonely bed. If she woke in the night, there was silence. There were none of the noises she was used to. Children murmuring in their sleep, father snoring, the rustle of the straw mattress as her mother turned over… If she was cold there were no siblings to keep her warm for they had all slept entwined together in their bed in the corner of the cottage just like a litter of kittens. Only the kindness of Mrs. Bowen made her life bearable in those first few months.

Gradually Megan had adapted. The house became familiar to her. Hunger was a thing of the past and as she grew stronger so her tasks became less onerous. She worked hard and eventually the draper's wife, perhaps realizing Megan's worth, had taken her under her wing and trained her as a tailoress. She made clothes for the ladies and gentlemen of the town, using fine materials and adapting the new styles that eventually percolated through to this isolated West Wales community.

And there wasn't the constant battle to keep my sewing clean, thought Granny Price with a sigh, for there was no penetrating black dust in Aberystwyth – only the sea air.

Megan now belonged to the town and when she reached the right age, it was inevitable that she would meet a young man and fall in love. Rumours were rife about the exciting young mining communities in the south and it was perhaps no surprise that the young married couple ended up in the valleys.

"Come on, girl," Thomas had said to her. "I know that you have a good job but the harvest has been bad and there's not much here for me. We couldn't get married for years. Me living in the farmhouse and no cottage. There's nothing here for us, but down there…" his eyes had shone with excitement and she couldn't refuse. Her mistress had tried to make her change her mind.

"Megan, do you know what you are doing? You have a good place here. Some of the ladies of the town ask that you and only you make their dresses. Stay here. Don't go with him. You'll meet someone else."
But of course she didn't stay and so the newly married Megan Price entered the next stage of her life.

It was not easy in the early days in the new coal mining villages, but Megan and Thomas were used to hard work. All that mattered to them then was that they were together. They ended up in Morganton and, like all the other newcomers, rented a house from the mine owner.

This one, Granny Price thought. A smile played on her lips as she remembered the lodgers she had taken in to help pay the rent. Single men who worked hard in the week and played even harder on a Saturday night. It was always the same story when they came looking for lodgings. She'd answer a knock on the door and see some stranger standing on the doorstep. Sometimes she'd find it difficult to understand the man for he could have come from anywhere, even from Scotland. Whoever it was, the request was always the same.

" Have you a bed, Missis? I'm a good God-fearing man. Don't drink. You'll have no trouble from me. "

"Well," she'd reply if she had room, "I'll take you in if you promise to cause no bother."

They always did but thinking of her own childhood experiences she didn't have the heart to throw them out onto the streets. After all some of them were little more than boys.

The new mining communities were really frontier towns. There was a preponderance of men, supposedly there to make their fortunes; but the temptations of the alehouses were far too strong. It was a brave woman, indeed, who walked Queen's square on a Saturday night. Fighting was common and these drunken brawls often ended in injuries that were as bad as many received underground. In those days she had thanked God that her husband remembered his chapel roots and how, as founder members, they had helped to build Ebenezer chapel. Too often she saw men squandering hard-earned money on drink and their children going hungry.

The valley towns grew at a pace. Men were needed, not just for the mines, but also to build houses, lay roads, on the railways, in the shops… It seemed that the demand for labour was insatiable. Rooms for rent were at a premium and it was common for a house to have two sets of lodgers – the day shift and the night shift. The man that worked in the day slept in the bed in the night and the night worker used the same bed the next morning.

A little laugh escaped the old lady's lips as some of the arguments over the beds came back to her.

"Get up you lazy bugger. It's my turn now. I've just come off nights. Get out."

"What's the time? Oh no, I've slept through the hooter. I've lost a shift and I've got a head like a bucket."

"I don't care, get out before I drag you out."

Hearing the shouting, Megan Price would call up the stairs, "What's going on? Do you want me to come up and sort you out?"

But for some reason she never had to and if later in the day she glanced in the bedroom it was no surprise to see one in the bed and the other on the floor still sleeping off the excesses of the night before. Her only thought would be about the rent and if, after last night's beer drinking, he had enough money left to pay it.

Gradually things settled down. The houses snaked across one side of the valley and the spoil tips desecrated the other. The Prices had a family that they were able to feed and clothe – until, that is, the accident. Higher wages were paid to the shaft sinkers for the work was very dangerous. A growing family needed more and more money.

"Thomas," her mind cried, "I couldn't stop you taking that job. We'd have managed."

No husband, one son already down the pit but four other children to support. She fell back on her sewing. Yes, as it turned out, it was indeed her lucky day when the draper from Aberystwyth chose the young Megan Price to work for him.

Chapter Two

"My you do look smart, Dafydd," said Carrie when she came back into the middle room after tidying up in the back kitchen. "The cloth in those trousers looks really fine. Have you had enough to eat?"

"Plenty, Mam. Where's Dad? Is he coming to choir tonight?"

"Yes, he'll be there but you know that he can only climb the trip to the main road once in a day. He went up to the Welfare Hall this afternoon to read the newspapers and he'll go from there to Ebenezer."

"Right I'm off then," said Dafydd as he tied his white scarf around his neck and put on his flat cap.

"Have you got your song book?" asked Granny Price.

"Of course I have, now don't fuss. Thanks for the trousers," he shouted as he went out.

Carrie and Granny Price looked at each other and smiled. Now that the other two boys were married, there was only Dafydd left to concentrate their affections on and he could do no wrong in their eyes.

Striding down the street, Dafydd's mind was already singing. Sure-footedly and in the dark, he quickly climbed the steep, rough hill to the main road. There the gas lamps lit his way as he walked on the newly laid pavement.

These flagstones will be far better in the rain – no more mud and puddles, he thought as he listened to the click clack of his boots.

"Caught you up. Thought it was you in front of me," said Will Jones as he matched his step to Dafydd's. "Hope there's a good crowd at practice tonight."

"I expect so, if those in front are anything to go by, Will."

As Dafydd and Will neared the chapel, they saw the lights burning in the vestry and men disappearing through the open door. The two friends followed them down the steps at the side of the building and once inside Dafydd looked around for his father.

"Emlyn is over there, lad," said Idwel, the baker, who was sitting near the door. "On the front bench with Tom."

"Thanks," said Dafydd as he spotted his father and started to make his way over to him.

The room was filling up rapidly. Every one knew each other and many acknowledged Dafydd as he passed. He had to stop to talk to some of them and it took him a few minutes to reach the front of the vestry.

Emlyn Price smiled at his son; "I see that you've made it then."

"Now you know that I wouldn't miss choir, Dad."

"How were your mother and grandmother?"

"Fussing as usual. Mam was concerned about you. I told her that you would be all right as long as you took your time."

"Aye, son, I can't walk as fast as I used to."

Like most miners of his generation, Emlyn had silicosis or "the dust" as miners called it. Working underground since the age of twelve, he had constantly inhaled a fine coal dust that had penetrated his lungs. As he had aged his breathing had become more and more difficult, until he could no longer work. Now at the age of forty-five he was a broken man. One step at a time had become his motto as he struggled up and down the valley streets. He wondered if he would be able to walk up the mountain in the summer – his wife simply hoped that he wouldn't deteriorate too quickly for she knew what lay in wait for him. Far too often she had seen old miners fighting for their every breath and so she had no illusions.

In the vestry the men chatted to each other until the conductor, John Parry B.A., called them to order. He was always referred to as this since it was almost unheard of for anyone from the mining communities to have been to university and his opinions carried a great deal of weight in the town. Like many, he had come to Morganton because of a job. He was the headmaster of the local elementary school and this was another reason for many to hold him in awe. Here in the vestry to the choir, however, he was simply the conductor for both he and his singers had a common aim – to sing well and to enjoy it.

They had sang Clychau Aberdyfi (The Bells of Aberdovey) and Llwyn On (The Ash Grove) when John Parry B.A. said, "We'll have Y Ferch O'r Scer. Dafydd Price you shall sing the first verse and then the rest of you join in for the next. Now remember this is a melancholy piece, so softly please."
Emlyn listened with pride as his son sang for it was generally agreed that Dafydd had the finest voice in the choir. At the end of the piece, for a moment, there was an appreciative stillness before hands busied themselves with music sheets as the men waited for their conductor. But, instead of announcing their next piece, John Parry talked to the men about a very important event and the part they were about to play in it.

It was an excited crowd that left the vestry at the end of choir practice. They were going to compete in the National

Eisteddfod of Wales and they'd only been a choir for a short time! Emlyn and his son walked with some of the older men. Dafydd's endless chatter made them smile because in his excitement he asked and then answered his own questions. He was still talking when he and his father parted company with the rest of the group as they turned down the trip towards Edmund Street.

"The Eisteddfod, Dad, fancy competing in The National Eisteddfod. Will we be ready in time? Of course we will. Only practice, it'll take. Imagine if we win!"

"Now don't get carried away, lad. Remember we're a new choir and we have to enter other competitions first."

"Oh I know that, Dad, but you must admit we have a chance of getting there with John Parry B.A. in charge. An educated man like that knows what he's doing and he was one of the adjudicators at the Bridgend Eisteddfod last Boxing Day."

"Calm yourself, son. If you keep on like this you'll wake the street up."

As usual, Carrie had waited up for them and she was surprised by their noise.

"What's all this about? Lower your voices. Your granny's gone to bed."

"Mam, the choir's going to the National Eisteddfod."

"You'll sing nowhere if you don't give your voice a rest, my son. Now go to bed. You have to be up early tomorrow."

The excitement stayed with Dafydd until he eventually fell asleep in his tiny bedroom at the front of the Price's small terraced house.

Chapter Three

The next morning as the first hooter blasted through the town, Dafydd got up and went down stairs to the back kitchen to put on his working clothes. The same filthy garments he had taken off the night before. Carrie and Granny Price were already up preparing for the busy day ahead. His breakfast of bread and dripping and a mug of tea were waiting for him on the table.

"Hurry up, Dafydd, you're going to be late," said Carrie.

"Yes, Mam," came the reply.

It was the same every morning. He left the house at the last possible moment and often had to run the final few hundred yards to get to the pit before the second hooter went off. He hated the mine. Yet he had no choice. He had to work and in these valleys that meant a job in the pits. It wasn't the physical work of digging out the coal. He was a strong lad with big shoulders. He could manage that easily. The valley women hated the dust, but that didn't bother him. He loathed the blackness that seemed to trap his soul. He wanted to be free to breathe the fresh air, to see how the landscape changed with the seasons, and above all to be able to hear the song of the birds.

"Boy, you've only just made it. One of these days you'll get up early and give us all a surprise. What was it last night – some fancy woman I bet?"

Dafydd smiled in answer to the liftman as he pushed his way into the already full top cage as the men on the lower deck waited below the surface.

"How many of you are in that cage?" shouted the banksman.

"Don't fuss," said one of the miners. "We're in, aren't we? Lower us down."

The men hung on to the handrail of the open lift as it lurched its way to the pit bottom.

Today's Friday, Dafydd thought as they descended. Only half a shift tomorrow and then I can do what I like. If it's fine on Sunday I'll go for a walk up the mountains.

The image of the hills was enough to lighten his mood as they waited for the miners on the bottom tier to get off. Then he braced himself for the jerk as the cage descended the last few feet.

"Come on, boys. We haven't got all day," said one of the miners at the back as Dafydd hesitated at the bottom. Another collier gave him a push of encouragement and then, as a gang, the men walked through the long main tunnel to the coal- face.

"Still working the two foot six seam?" asked the collier on his right. "Ours is nearly finished and I've heard that over in Number Eight they're starting on a two foot one."

"We've got a bit to go yet," replied Dafydd. "The two foot six in our area is OK for a while yet, but I wouldn't want to work anything less. I can swing the pick all right on my knees but I'm not working on my stomach all day for anyone."

"You might have to," the man grunted. "The overman in Number Eight said that they want our steam coal so badly that we'll have to work anything."

"And what about all this fighting in Europe," said another who liked to show off the knowledge he gleaned from the newspapers in the reading room of the Welfare Hall. "It was bad enough when it was only the Turks and the Bulgarians at it but now Russia and Serbia have put in their four pennyworth. Somehow or other we'll get dragged into it. You mark my words. Then we won't be able to cut the coal fast enough."

"No," said Dafydd. "The tunnel I'm working in is low enough. If there is war then I'll be a soldier. Anything must be better than crawling on your stomach all day."

As the gang passed openings in the rock wall, men peeled off into the smaller tunnels. It was soon Dafydd's turn.

" Here's my road. See you at the end of the shift," he said as he disappeared into a side opening, immediately lowering his head. Before long he was bent double as he negotiated the narrow four feet high tunnel to his part of the coalface. In the flickering dim light and on his knees he began his day's work.

Back home, Carrie and Granny Price were also sorting out their day's tasks. Only Emlyn, in his condition, was allowed the luxury of a lie in.

"Emlyn, I'm off now," Carrie called from the bottom of the stairs. "When you feel up to it make yourself some breakfast."

She knew that it was not easy for her husband to do anything now, especially first thing in the morning. She could hear him coughing as he fought to clear his chest of the phlegm that had accumulated in his lungs over night. She couldn't stay to help him get out of bed for it was one of her days at Rock House where she washed and ironed for the colliery owner and his family.

Carrie opened the door of the front room, where her mother-in-law was already sewing.

"I'm off now. I'll call in the Co-op on the way home and get a piece of meat for Sunday."

She buttoned up her coat against the cold wind and fastened her shawl securely round her head and shoulders and walked out into the street.

"Hello, Mrs. Price," said a small boy as he kicked a stone along the rough ground.

"How's your mother today?" she asked.

"Not so bad," he said. "Says she'll get up this afternoon, if the coughing stops."

I hope he's right, Carrie thought as she walked on.

She made her way up the hill, following the path that had been worn by countless others before her. She was glad to leave the rough ground and walk on the new pavements of the main road.

I wonder when they'll be laid in our street, she thought. They'll be a godsend and no more wading through water and rubbish. A set of steps up that hill is what we could really do with though.

The shops were opening up and she passed Morris the draper admiring his window.

"Has the old lady finished that coat for my customer?" he asked.

"I think it's nearly ready, she said something about bringing it up this afternoon."

"Good. Mrs. Morris wants a dress altered. Says it's too tight because it has shrunk in the wash. She won't have it that she's put on weight. Eats too much of Idwel's bread." Then as if to himself, he continued wistfully, "If she ate to live like me not living to eat as she's doing then she would have a lovely figure."

With a sigh, he returned to his window and Carrie couldn't help smiling as she walked on for she had heard rumours about Morris the draper and she always thought that there was some truth in them. Further along the street Carrie saw the baker loading up his cart with the bread he had baked in the early hours.

"How are you, Mrs. Price?"

"Late, Idwel. Good-looking loaves. Always a lovely smell from fresh bread. Can't stop."

At the end of the road she turned up a hill on her right and climbed as quickly as she could to the large house at the top. She walked in through the side gate and made her way round to the scullery door.

Opening it she called out "It's only me."

"Come in, Carrie," said Mrs. Lloyd, the cook. "There's tea in the pot. I'll pour you a cup."

Carrie Price hung her coat and shawl on the hook on the back of the scullery door and walked into the warm kitchen.

"It's a cold one out there," she said as she sat down at the scrubbed wooden table. "I saw one of Annie Thomas' children in the street this morning. Annie's not very well but what can you expect? Working as a coal picker. Out in all weathers, standing at that belt, throwing out all the slag."

"Yes," said Mrs. Lloyd. "An awful job but what else is there? Is it three children she has? Husband killed in that cave in."

"There'll be three orphans there before long. You mark my words," said Carrie shaking her head. "They'll be for the workhouse unless her sisters can take them. But I don't suppose that they find it easy to make ends meet. No one does. Oh! Is that the time? I'd better get on or I won't finish today."

"You may be right there. We've a visitor from Bristol. Madam's niece. Father owns some ships and she is very posh. You should see the clothes she's brought with her. Mary said that they filled the wardrobe and she is only here for a few days."

Then, recollecting that there was work to be done, the cook got up from the table and made her way over to the big range.

Carrie went back into the scullery and pulled out the big copper. Then she took a bucket and went to the range in the kitchen and filled the pail with the hot water from the boiler. She carried the full bucket back to the scullery and tipped the contents into the tub. To and fro she went until the boiler was empty. Then she had to fill the range boiler up with cold water so that later there would be more hot water to meet the needs of the house. In the scullery she tested the temperature of the washing water with her finger.

Too hot, she thought. I'd better put some cold in.

She walked back to the stone sink with her bucket to fill it up yet again. At last she was satisfied and could concentrate on the washing.

Mrs. Lloyd was right, she thought. There is a lot more here than usual. Some fancy things too. I'd better start with the sheets to get them out on the line. It's a good job that it's fine today for the drying. Cook doesn't like wet clothes hanging about her kitchen for too long.

Washing, rinsing, wringing, it didn't seem anytime before Carrie was called to the table to have her midday meal with the other servants. The remains of a cold meat pie, some lamb, bread and cheese were soon eaten and of course the food was all washed down with hot cups of tea. The latter was particularly welcoming to Carrie who had just come in from hanging clothes on the line in the cold east wind. But, as she ate, she couldn't help but think that there was more meat on the table for this one meal than many families she knew had to eat in a week.

The main topic of conversation was of course the new houseguest. Mary, the young maid, certainly admired her clothes.

"You should see her dresses. Ball gowns, really low cut and ever so tight! What she wants them here for I don't know. Oh I wish I could wear clothes like that though I suppose I'd need to lose a good few pounds, even if I had the money to buy them."

George, the only male servant and who referred to himself as the butler but who really was a general factotum, was as usual taking an avid interest in the conversation.

"She wouldn't be allowed to wear them in America," he said grandly. "I read in the Times newspaper that The Modesty League over there is trying to get tight dresses banned."

"Quite right too, I don't know what the place is coming to," said Mrs. Lloyd. If they had such laws here, she thought, then you and your mates wouldn't be able to leer at women. She'd heard tales about George and his friends and not very nice ones at that.

Carrie laughed to herself as she listened to this other world. It was so easy to forget the harsh realities of life in this comfortable haven.

The afternoon passed quickly as there was still much to be done. Luckily the weather kept fine and Carrie was able to dry most of the sheets and towels out of doors. Smaller items she put on the clothes racks that were suspended from the scullery ceiling. These worked on a pulley system and whilst they were relatively easy to haul up when full of pillowcases and petticoats, it was a different matter when laden with wet cotton sheets. At last there was no more to be done until tomorrow.

"That's me finished, Mrs. Lloyd," she said as she put on her coat and large shawl. "I'll have to hurry to catch the Co-op before it closes. I'll be back in the morning to do the ironing as usual"

"Right, Carrie. Let me get your money. You'll want it for the shops."

The gas lamps were lit by the time Carrie got to the main road and some shops were already closing, but the butcher still had carcasses of meat hanging on hooks on either side of the door. She looked in the window and saw a piece of belly pork.

"Yes, that'll do us nicely," she murmured to herself. Not too fat. I'll stuff it with sage and onions just as Emlyn likes it."

She opened the shop door and walked inside.

"You're just in time, Mrs. Price. I was about to get the meat in. You're late this evening."

"Yes, there was extra washing at Rock House. They have a visitor."

"So I heard, very pretty too. Have you seen her?"

"No, but I expect I will at some time. I mustn't keep you gossiping if you're closing. Like me you'll want to get home. I'll have some belly pork, please."

"I'll get it from the window for you," he said as he turned and stretched over the marble slab at the top of the window and picked up the joint of meat.

"Where shall I cut it? Here?" he asked pointing to half way down the joint.

"Yes, that's about right. That'll be plenty for Sunday and some left over for Monday."

The transaction was soon completed and at last Carrie was able to make her way home.

When she arrived, she found her husband and son sitting at the table tucking into the remains of yesterday's broth. Granny Price appeared from the front room.

"I was just finishing off hemming a dress," she said. "I can't do anymore. My eyes are not like they used to be. It gets harder to see in the light of the oil lamp. How are they at the big house?"

The women sat on the wooden armchairs on either side of the grate and gossiped together as their men ate. At last, Emlyn turned towards them.

"When are you two having something to eat?" he asked.

"I'll clear up out the back kitchen first after Dafydd and then we'll have something. I've had food at Rock House today so I'll not need much. These days, all Mam seems to eat is bread and dripping and drink cups of tea with plenty of sugar. Don't worry about us." Then, changing the subject, she asked, "Have you been up the Welfare Hall today?"

"Yes. Interesting article in the paper by a man who was on the first ship sailing through the Panama Canal. Fancy being able to sail directly from the Atlantic to the Pacific. No more going round The Horn."

Carrie dutifully nodded her head in agreement, neither knowing where Panama was nor understanding the significance of the canal to world trade.

"Oh I'd love to sail in a ship and see some other countries," said Dafydd, taking an interest in the conversation. His day had been particularly hard. There had been a small roof fall near where he was working and two men were trapped. He had immediately volunteered to join the small rescue team. The colliers knew that they had to work quickly but carefully. A further fall could trap them all. When it was his turn to crawl into the opening that they had made in the fall, Dafydd had to push his fears to the back of his mind. He hacked out rubble and shoved it behind him for the others to clear. He tried to keep his thoughts on the trapped men, but the longer he was in the hole, the more difficult it became. Just as his skin began to crawl with fear his pick struck air. The men were pulled out safely. The rescuers praised for a job well done. But Dafydd couldn't dismiss the incident from his mind.

If I'm caught by a fall and get out alive then I'm not going down that pit again, he vowed to himself.

"What did you do today, Dafydd?" asked Carrie.

"Cut coal, Mam, the same as usual."

He didn't say anymore because the Senghenydd disaster was still a very raw wound in the mining communities of the South Wales Valleys.

Chapter Four

The next morning began with a repeat performance of the day before. Dafydd just about managed to get to the pit on time, Carrie made her way up to Rock House, Emlyn struggled to get up from bed, and Granny Price got on with her sewing. But it was Saturday!

"What you doing tonight?" asked Dafydd's mate Will Jones as they left the colliery at the end of the half shift.

"Going up The Royal Oak with some of the others. Are you coming?"

"Yes, but I'd better not be as drunk as last week or I'll get thrown out onto the streets."

"We'll look after you, don't you worry," said Dafydd with a big grin on his face.

The two laughed knowingly together as they made their way home.

Carrie arrived home at the same time as her son.

"What's that you're carrying, Mam?"

"Some left-overs from Rock House. I told Mrs. Lloyd that I would take them to the Thomas'. Times are very hard for them now. They could do with something tidy to eat. I saw one of the boys yesterday. He looked so small and pinched. But before I go there I suppose I'd better feed you."

In the house, Granny Price had prepared Dafydd's bath and was in the middle room putting out some food.

"I'd have done his bath, Mam," said Carrie.

"I'm not too old to do things like that, you fuss too much. Did you see the visitor? I went up to Morris the Draper to take back that sewing and she'd just been to the shop. A real lady he said."

"Well she has lots of fine clothes," said Carrie, thinking of all the ironing that she had done that morning. "We'll probably see her in chapel tomorrow. No doubt she'll come with those from the big house."

"Is that for me?" asked Dafydd as he came into the room and saw the food on the table. "Who's that you're talking about?"

"The visitor at Rock House. She's very pretty I've heard," said his granny with a smile.

"Is that all? I thought it was something important like the beer wagon hadn't got here."

"That's all you think of," said Carrie. "Don't you get drunk tonight!"

"Don't worry, Mam. I've got more sense than some of them. Besides you don't give me enough money," he teased.

Like many of the men in the valleys Dafydd, as Emlyn before him, handed over his wages to his mother. She in return gave him pocket money to spend in whatever way he wished. The remainder of his money and the earnings of the two women just about met the family's living expenses. There was no money to waste and Dafydd was well aware of this.

The young men of the village preferred The Royal Oak to the recently built and much grander Morganton Hotel. The former was one of the first public houses to be established in the community and the licensee Rhys Davies and his wife had long experience in handling and limiting the excesses of the young miners. The pub was in the middle of the terrace of houses and shops on the north side of Queen's Square. It was a double fronted building with the same rectangular sash windows as the miners' cottages. The only indications of its function were the semi-circular sign over the front door, on which were written the words Royal Oak Inn and the name Rhys Davies, and the large wooden board between the two front windows. This again had the name of the pub in large letters as well as Rogers of Cardiff, Celebrated Ales. Inside on the ground floor was one large room that was dominated by a central bar. The younger men gravitated towards the left of this whilst the older ones congregated around the open fireplace on the right hand wall. The atmosphere in there on Saturday nights was warm and friendly. It was a place where the men could forget their harsh life underground and, encouraged by the beer, dream of better things.

Dafydd met up with Will Jones on Queen's Square and the two walked into the Royal Oak together. The rest of their mates were already at the bar.

"Hello, Idwel," said Will as he stood aside for the baker to pass. "You're out late tonight."

"None of your cheek, young Will. You know that I don't bake on a Sunday," retorted Idwel as he made his way back to his friends at the table by the fire.

There was a good crowd in the bar and Will had to shout to get the barmaid's attention.

"Can we have some service here, Sally?"

"I'm serving as fast as I can. As usual, you've no patience, Will," she called back.

"We can't stay here all night," said Jack Davies, who was standing next to Dafydd, as he looked around for an empty table. "There's one in the corner. Go and grab it, Dafydd. I'll bring your pint over when we're served."

Dafydd walked towards it, kicking at the sawdust as he went. He didn't have to wait long before the others joined him on the hard benches around the well-worn table.

"Did you know that the Morganton Hotel has twenty bedrooms?" was Jack's strange opening gambit.

" Of course we do," said Will. " What's the matter with you. Anyway they need them. A lot of travellers stay there."

"That's not all," went on Jack mysteriously. "There's a group of women there and for your information lads they are quite free with their favours. Provided of course that you grease their palms"

Seeing the smirks on their faces, he knew that he had their attention. Then he surprised them further by saying, "How much money have you all got?"

"What do you want to know that for?" asked Dafydd.

"Well I thought that one of us could try out one of those women."

"You don't mean…"

"Of course I do. Put our money together, draw lots and the winner could go over to the Morganton Hotel and meet one of the "ladies" in the bar."

In their excitement, it wasn't long before they were spilling their coppers onto the table. But who was going to win?

The Morganton Hotel was about two hundred yards away on the opposite side of the street. It was a large three-storey building with two entrances. The one led to the reception desk and the other into the saloon bar. The lads exuberantly pushed the second door open and looked around for an empty table.

"Follow me," said Jack Davies confidently as he strode across the room and pulled out a chair at a table towards the back. "We'll be all right here," he added as he sat down. "Not too obtrusive if you know what I mean."

They nodded their heads in unison but whether they understood was another matter. Eventually after some re-jigging of chairs they were all squashed around the table.

"No wonder we don't come here very often," grumbled Will. "Not much room here."

"Stop moaning, go and get us some beer. Dafydd, you go with him," commanded Jack who seemed to have taken sole charge of the proceedings. "Now where's our money?"

The excitement hadn't left the group and they exuded an air of expectation as they waited for their ale. Their eyes darted everywhere. They couldn't see any women. Under normal circumstances they wouldn't have expected to because it was only those females of dubious character that would enter such a place and not many in the valleys wished to be tarred with that brush.

"Where are they?" asked Will.

"They'll be here. Have some patience, Will Jones. They're probably entertaining," said Jack knowingly.

Just then the door leading to the stairs and the reception area opened and in walked what appeared to be a very fashionable woman.

"That's one," whispered Jack.

As if one, they all turned to look at her.

"Don't all stare at her," he hissed.

"I don't know why they are allowed to stay here," said Dafydd sanctimoniously.

"It's good for trade, boy. That's why."

"What do you mean, Jack?"

"Look at the number of the so called pillars of the community that are in here tonight. You wouldn't normally see them here. There's some money passing over this bar. Think of the licensee's profits and he gets a cut of those women's earnings. It'll be the same every night until they move on. But they'll be gone when the wives hear rumours about what's going on and start asking questions. You can imagine the wife of the manager of the Coop demanding to know what the attraction is up that hotel. Some of these men would be far too scared of their wives finding out what was going on here, even if they were innocent, so they'd stay home for a bit. The women's trade falls off and they go on to the next place."

The lads all nodded their heads as if they knew this sequence of events all along but they almost jumped when Jack said, "Right boys, it doesn't look as if that one's busy at the moment so it's our turn. Who drew the lucky straw?"

Dafydd stood up reluctantly and then, after some encouragement from the others, edged nervously towards the woman.

"Go on!" Jack whispered loudly from behind him.

As he approached, although his stomach churned, his mind registered curious details. Her dress was cut a little too low, her lips and cheeks were too red and her hair was not quite neat and tidy. She was attractive but in a coarse sort of way and she was certainly older than she appeared to be from a distance.

"And what can I do for you, young gentleman?" she asked.

"How much?" was the almost indistinct reply as he stood there inwardly shaking.

"Two shillings, she said quickly. You can afford that, a strapping lad like you."

She watched carefully as he counted out the coppers into her eager hand. Satisfied that it was the right amount, she quickly slipped the money into a pocket hidden in the folds of her skirt.

"It'll be a change to sample a bit of young flesh," she said as she took hold of Dafydd's arm and began to walk to the door. He had no option but to follow her.

The other lads watched the proceedings with a great deal of glee and only just stopped themselves cheering when Dafydd was yanked through the door.

The unlikely couple climbed the stairs - the one with alacrity, but the other lagging behind.

"Come on," she urged. "Don't you want what Rosy has to offer?"

What have I been talked into? Dafydd thought desperately.

But it was too late. He couldn't go back because the boys would remind him of his shortcomings forever. He had to go through with it whether he wanted to or not.

They were walking along the first floor landing when a small man came out of one of the bedrooms and with his head bowed scuttled passed them.

Good grief! That's Morris the draper. I wonder what his wife would say if she knew?

And for the first time a smile played on Dafydd's face. Then without warning Rosy stopped at the next door, opened it and pulled him in behind her.

The room was larger than any bedroom he had seen before. The gaslights hissed softly as he looked around. He saw a wardrobe spilling with clothes, a large, mirrored dressing table covered with all sorts of bits and pieces and a washstand with a fancy jug and basin on its marble top. Then his attention was drawn to the centrepiece of the room - the large brass bedstead. As he looked at it, his stomach churned.

"Come over here," said Rosy as she sat down on the bed. "Help me unhook my boots." She lifted her skirt to expose her ankles and then tantalizingly she edged it up further, showing her long legs. Still, very unsure of himself, he walked towards her and getting down on his knees began to unfasten her shoes. Somehow his shaking hands managed to get them off and just as he looked up she hitched her skirt higher to reveal this time her silk garters.

"Now my stockings," she whispered as she guided his hand up her leg. "That's right, pull those down first."
He felt her smooth legs and wanted his hands to explore further but he was still too afraid. Sensing this, she leant towards him in that low cut dress. His eyes were drawn towards her bosom and then, realizing what he was doing, he jerked his head away. Nothing was lost on Rosy.

"And now my lovely," she said quietly, "You can help me with my frock."
She got up from the bed and turned away from him.

As if in a dream, Dafydd rose to his feet and undid the buttons. Still facing away from him, she allowed the dress to fall off her shoulders and then slid slowly to the floor. He looked at her bare back in amazement for he expected to see a white petticoat like the ones he had seen so often amongst the sewing in the front room. He gulped for he so wanted her to turn round but, at the same time, was afraid for his experience was limited to stolen kisses on a mountain path.

Sensing the fear, Rosy said gently, "Close your eyes."
Automatically he did. Stepping out of the dress, she turned and faced him.

"Don't open you eyes," she commanded as, with a practiced hand, she undid his trousers and explored inside them. It was as if the connections had finally been made in Dafydd's mind. He looked at her, let his eyes travel down her naked body and, now in no doubt of what was to be done, he took command of the situation and pushed her onto the bed. Rosy knew that there would be no gentle caressing, nor did she want any, for this was young blood out for his first real kill – something she had not experienced for a long time.

"At last," she murmured as she opened her legs and felt the push of him inside her.

The others were no more than a job but he was different - young, handsome and ripe for the taking. She gasped as he plunged further and then faster. Hungry for an experience that was lost in time, she matched his rhythm. Again, again, her mind shouted, and then, lost in the pleasure of the act, she cried out as they both gave themselves up to the inevitable climax.

Spent, they lay back on the bed and gradually his eyes closed as he fell asleep. A little later, Rosy slipped out of the covers and began to tidy herself. She replenished the face paint, pinned her hair back into some sort of order and dressed. Then she went back to the bed and shook the young man.

"Come on my lovely, you have to go. There's time for one more after you. Wake up."

Slowly, Dafydd came to his senses. The room, the woman, what have I done?

Then he jumped up.

"Where's my clothes," he muttered. "What's the time?"

"About half past eleven," replied Rosy.

"I'll have to go. Mam and Granny Price will hear me coming in and if it's after midnight it's Sunday and heaven help me!"

He threw on his clothes and rushed out of the room, down the stairs and out of the hotel. All the time he could here Rosy's laughter getting fainter and fainter.

Outside in the street, Jack was leaning against a lamppost waiting for Dafydd.

"Hey!" he shouted as his mate rushed past him. "Why are you in such a rush. Is the Devil after you?"

Dafydd stopped, turned round and said, "I might have guessed that you'd be waiting. Here to gloat?"

"Hold your horses, I only wanted to make sure that you were all right. Did you enjoy it?"

Dafydd saw the grin on Jack's face. What could he say? Once he had got over his inhibitions, of course he had.

With a broad smile he replied, "I don't think that life will ever be the same again."

Chapter Five

"Six days shalt thou labour..."

Sunday, no pit, thought Dafydd as he got out of bed and looked out through the curtains. There was frost on the slates, the sky was clear, and it was cold outside but calm. He gazed across at the hills on the other side of the valley.

That's where I'm going. Climb the old track and go round the top of the old quarry. Get some fresh air into my lungs. Have to get out of morning chapel though. I'll say I'll go this evening. It'll be dark then anyway and I'm not going out with the lads after what they got me into last night.

When he appeared downstairs, Carrie greeted him with "You're up then. Late last night weren't you."

"Yes, Mam, we were all at the Royal Oak."

"Not too drunk I hope but you don't look the worst for wear," she said peering at him closely as she put his customary breakfast of bread and dripping on the table.

"It's a lovely day and a pity to waste it. I thought that I'd walk up the mountain this morning and go to chapel this evening."

"You make sure you do. It's the Reverend Evans tonight and we want a full congregation. Mind you're back in time for your dinner. I've got a nice piece of belly pork. I'm going to stuff it, just as you and your father like it."

Leaving the house Dafydd walked down the same track as he took to the pit, but at the bottom he turned right and followed the river until he came to some stepping-stones. Crossing over these, he climbed effortlessly up the steep side of the valley. Some of the grass was still in the shade and crunched under his boots. There were no houses on this side, only tramlines that took the waste up the mountain to be dumped on the conical shaped tip at the top. Eventually, he reached the ridge above the quarry and looked down on the lines of houses on the opposite side of the valley. He could pick out all the familiar landmarks – the pit in the bottom, the main road, every one of the chapels, the Welfare Hall, and the Morganton Hotel.

Never again, he thought as a smile played on his lips and, as if to erase last night from his mind, he turned his back on the valley and walked on. Although his eyes looked at the landscape and his ears listened to the sounds of the birds, all he really saw was that low cut dress and what it attempted to conceal as Rosy's laughter echoed in his head.

Throughout the day, his thoughts returned to the night before and more than once his mother asked if he felt all right for his lack of attention made her think that he was sickening for something. But he had eaten his dinner so there couldn't be much to worry about. When evening came the family dressed in their Sunday best and walked up to the main road where they joined nearly everyone else in the community as they made their way to the various places of worship along its length.

Ebenezer was different from the other nonconformist chapels in the town. For a start it was not as large. It had no balcony but a single floor with a vestry below. It was not a sombre arena where the minister preached hell and damnation but a light airy church where the whitewashed walls complemented the highly polished pews. It had obviously been built with love and care.

All who entered that evening were in their Sunday best. The men dressed in suits and stiff collars, the women in long skirts and dark coats. Most of the congregation was seated when there was a flurry of activity in the vestibule. The party from Rock House had arrived. The colliery manager and his family walked grandly down the aisle to their pew at the front, followed by every eye in the place. The service could now begin.

"There she is, Mam," hissed Carrie. "See her at the back, that's Mrs. Lewis' niece, the visitor."

Expectantly the worshipers waited. The door to the minister's vestry opened and out walked the Reverend Evans. Importantly, he climbed the few steps to the pulpit in front of the pipe organ and looking down on the packed congregation he announced the opening hymn. The organist played the first few bars as the people got to their feet. The singing filled the place. Many of the men belonged to the male voice choir and automatically slipped into different parts as they sang. As usual, Dafydd's voice could be distinguished from all the rest, but this time he had some competition.

At one point in the hymn, as the men were singing softly, a new, sweet soprano voice was heard. It had to be her, the visitor, for there was no other stranger in the congregation. Dafydd was spellbound. All through the long sermon he stared at the back of her head. Surely if she could sing like that, she must be the most beautiful girl in the world. Her voice went round and round in his head and for a part of the last hymn he pretended that he had something in his throat so that he couldn't sing. He stood there and listened and from all that sound her voice homed in on him.

At the end of the service, the congregation stood as the Reverend Evans made his way down the aisle. They then waited respectfully until the Colliery manager and his family followed. All eyes were on the young lady. Dafydd's expectations were not unfounded and to him she was indeed the loveliest woman he had ever seen. He tried to hurry his family out of the chapel in the hope of getting another glance of her but there were neighbours to be acknowledged and gossip to be listened to. His mother and grandmother could not be hurried and by the time they got outside, the party from Rock House had disappeared.

It seemed forever before Dafydd could get to sleep that night.

"I don't even know her name," he kept repeating over and over to himself. "What's the point, I'll never get to speak to her. She's not ever going to look at the likes of me. She's only here on a visit anyway. I'm just plain daft thinking of her like this."

But however much he scolded himself, he couldn't get her out of his mind and when sleep did come she filled his dreams.

"Dafydd, Dafydd get up! You're going to be late."

So the new week began.

Chapter Six

On Monday morning at Rock House, Louisa arrived at the breakfast table at the same time as her aunt.

"Had a good night, Louisa?"

"Yes, thank you, Aunt Sarah. I've slept well since I've been here. It must be your feather bed."

"Well it doesn't get much use these days. It's so good to have you here. It's a pity you can't stay longer. With your uncle tied up in the colliery all the time, it gets quite lonely. There's very few around here we can socialize with. I suppose there's the doctor, the Reverend Evans, the manager of the Welfare Hall and one or two others. Your visit makes a nice change for me."

"Cheer up, Aunt Sarah, remember we are all going to Dyffryn House for the ball. That'll be exciting."

"Yes, we'll all enjoy it. It's bound to be a grand affair. I was so pleased when the invitation included you. I'll be able to show off my pretty niece."

"And I, my very attractive aunt."

They both laughed happily together as the conversation turned to balls and dresses.

There was only eight years difference between the aunt and her niece. The former was the youngest child of a large family and her sister, Louisa's mother, the eldest. Over the years the two had grown very close and as far as Louisa was concerned, it was a sad day when her aunt married and left Bristol. So it was not surprising that, about an hour later, the pair were in Louisa's bedroom admiring a beautiful satin dress.

"Look at these!" exclaimed the aunt as she touched the tiny pleats that criss-crossed the bodice. "And the neckline, it's so low. The waist is tiny too. Oh there are silver tassels on the sleeves. I've got to see it on you. You must try it on."

It wasn't many minutes before Louisa acceded to her wishes and put the gown on. She would indeed be the belle of the ball in that ivory frock offset by her dark brown hair and her laughing blue eyes. After all this was the purpose of her visit to Dyffryn House. Louisa was now of marriageable age and the mother and aunt wouldn't miss an opportunity like this to find her a suitable husband.

Louisa's family belonged to the upper middle class. Her father, with his roots in trade, had made a fortune with the expansion of The British Empire and could now add the title "ship owner" to his name. They lived in a grand town house in Bristol where every whim was attended to by a retinue of servants. The parents were determined that their only daughter would marry well. Both Louisa's mother and aunt hoped that her beauty would entice one of the aristocracy and they had heard that the Marquess of Bute and his family had been invited to the ball. So Louisa was actively encouraged to accept the invitation.

"You know how you love to see your Aunt Sarah," her mother had said. "You can combine the two. A week, or longer if you wish, at Rock House and then the weekend at Dyffryn. Of course your father will buy you a new dress for the ball. I hear that some of the latest fashions from London have arrived in Bristol. Let's see if there is something suitable."

It was settled, for like any fashionable young woman, Louisa loved new clothes.

The morning had started earlier and with more urgency at the Price's household. There was Dafydd to get off to work, the house to be cleaned, the sewing for Morris the draper's customer to be finished and the chickens to be fed.

Carrie spent Mondays at home. Her first task, after her son had gone to the pit, was to get rid of some of the grime that continually invaded her house. The coal dust got everywhere. Not only was it brought in on Dafydd's shoes and clothes but it was also blown in through every crack by the wind. She wrapped herself up in a voluminous pinafore and attacked the dirt. The back kitchen was the worst but it was bound to be, for this was where Dafydd bathed. He came straight in there in his working clothes, black with the muck from the pit. She scrubbed and sanded the flagstones, wiped down every conceivable surface before turning her attention to the grate. Out came the black lead and the brushes and she rubbed and polished until it gleamed.

She had just finished black-leading the grate when she heard movement in the middle room and surmised that Emlyn had got up. She took off her pinafore and, to keep as much dirt as possible from the rest of the house, she hung it on a hook behind the back door.

"How are you feeling now?" she asked as she walked in. "Ready for breakfast."

His only reply was another bout of coughing.

"Have a nice cup of tea. You'll feel better then."

She fussed over her husband as if he was a child and, comforted by her attention, gradually he become more relaxed and his breathing eased.

He managed to eat a little and then typically said, "I can't stay here all day. There's the chickens to see to. There should be some eggs."

"Good, I'll make a rice pudding. It always tastes better with an egg mixed in."

Emlyn took some grain from an earthenware jar in the bottom of the cupboard and picked up the bucket full of peelings, old cabbage leaves and stale bread from behind the back door. Carrie watched him as he painfully climbed the half dozen steps to the garden.

The chickens had heard that it was dinnertime and were anxious to get out of the shed. They clamoured around his legs as he emptied the pail onto the bare earth and scattered the grain. To begin with, the old cockerel surveyed his kingdom. A patch of ground fourteen feet by twenty, a tumble down hen house and half a dozen hens. Then he too got on with the important business of the day and foraged amongst the food.

There were some eggs and they were indeed a welcome addition to the household's food supply. Most of the families in the street kept chickens and some reared rabbits for the table too. Despite plenty of work in the pits, the poor wages meant that it was a constant struggle to keep the large families fed. Emlyn carried the eggs carefully down the steps and gave them to Carrie to put away in the pantry – a cupboard under the stairs with a few shelves and a stone slab that remained cold even on the hottest summer's day.

When Carrie had finished cleaning the rest of the house, she carefully tidied herself up and then went into the front room to help Granny Price with the sewing.

"What do you want me to do?" she asked.

"Finish this hem off, then I can cut a dress out. You've been a long time cleaning."

"Yes, I don't know, that dust gets everywhere. I wish we had a bigger garden. Have you seen what Elsie Jones has done? She's built a shed in the back, put a range in it and makes the men bath there. Some say that she stays in it herself in the day and only uses the house to sleep in and on Sundays of course."

"You'd certainly keep the house clean that way, Carrie love; but what would you do about the chickens?"

Laughing, the two women went back to their sewing only stopping now and then when one or the other remembered a bit of gossip that had to be told. The time passed quickly as they worked together and they were both surprised when they heard Emlyn come back in for his diner.

"I don't know, gossiping again," he said. "Who have you been talking about this time? I hope that you've got something good to say about them."

"Now, Emlyn, don't tease. You know that we've been sewing. Sit in here with Mam while I see to the dinner. Tell her what you've been reading about in those newspapers in the Welfare Hall. Why you're interested in other countries I don't know. We've got enough troubles of our own to worry about."

Chapter Seven

Week faded into week until it was Christmas. As far as Dafydd was concerned, the only respite from the toil was choir practice and the promise of competition stirred his mind. The choir's first battle was to be on Boxing Day in Pontypridd at the Market Hall. John Parry B.A. had brought the poster to Ebenezer and had put it up on the chapel's notice board. Dafydd read out the notice to his father.

"A Grand Eisteddfod, Dad, at the Market Hall, Pontypridd on Friday, twenty- sixth of December 1913. Look whose adjudicating the choirs - Mr. David Parkes, Mus. Bac. (Oxon) F.R.C.O., and L.R.A.M. I've never seen so many letters after a name. Wait there's more. Composer of the Elected Knight and Director of the Bridgend Eisteddfod. Wasn't that where John Parry B.A. judged last year? That must give us a chance."

"Aye, son, but don't count your chickens. We'll have a lot of competition. Who's the other adjudicator?"

"A Mr. W Howells F.T.S.C. from Porth. At least he's from the Valleys. Let me see what else it says. The Eisteddfod proceedings are to commence at half past ten in the morning. Dad, we'll have to catch the nine o'clock train to get there in plenty of time."

"What! And get to Ponty before half past and only five minutes walk from the station. The half past nine train will be early enough."

Dafydd looked back at the notice board. "Wait, there's a grand concert for the winners at half past seven in the evening."

"Don't bank on going to that, son. If we get placed we'll be doing really well."

But as far as Dafydd was concerned their tickets to the concert were already booked.

John Parry realized that his infant choir had little time to prepare properly for the Pontypridd Eisteddfod but they had to start somewhere. Besides he had two weapons up his sleeve, the choir's enthusiasm and Dafydd Price's voice.

If we can bring it off, he thought, we might get a highly commended or even a third. They'll learn a lot from the experience and it'll show in the next one we enter. But am I being too ambitious about The National?

There was a new purpose to the choir at the next practice. There were only four weeks to their first competition. The men agreed that there had better be two practices a week and the last one on Christmas Eve. No one minded however many times a verse or even a line was repeated. All eyes watched the choirmaster's hand. As it began to move mouths opened and as it fell the sound swelled – perfectly synchronized. Bang, bang – the voices silenced.

"Not quite right, gentlemen. Listen to the piano. Mr. Davies, play that line over please."

The pianist thumped out the notes.

"Right, let's try it again. Remember the rise in the middle and then I want you to fade away at the end. Are you ready? Now watch me. One, two, three."

And so it went on, practice after practice. The same force drove all the singers. For their own self-esteem and to establish their choir, they needed to achieve some sort of recognition at their first Eisteddfod.

The thought of the competition completely overshadowed everything and for the first time Dafydd was impatient to see the end of Christmas Day. The house was packed with family. Emlyn and Carrie took great pleasure in seeing their three sons under the same roof. The two older ones were married with families of their own and Granny Price indulged her great grand children with stories of another life after, of course, they had all put on the new clothes she had made as Christmas presents.

The sewing had been carefully put away and Emlyn and his three sons sat and talked in the front room.

"How's the choir going, Dad?" asked Ivor the eldest.

"Not bad, there's usually a good crowd at practice and of course John Parry B.A. knows what he's doing."

"Not bad, Dad. Haven't you told them that we've got the Pontypridd Eisteddfod tomorrow."

"I had heard," said Ivor. "It's all round the village. How do you think you'll do?"

"If we perform well then that's enough this time, but your brother expects more than that," answered Emlyn with a smile. "How's work?"

"Could be better," said Arthur. "They're opening up narrower seams. None of us like working them."

Dafydd, not wanting to listen to talk of the pit, said, "I'm getting hungry. I'll go to see how long dinner is going to be."

The table in the middle room was dressed in the best tablecloth – brought out only for weddings, funerals and Christmas.

"Oh, look at those plates," exclaimed one of Carrie's daughters-in-law as she helped lay the table. "Those are new, aren't they? Where did you get them?"

"They're a Christmas present to myself. Madam told Mrs. Lloyd to give me extra because of the visitor. I needed more dishes. Bought them from the cheapjack. You know, his cart was on Queen's square last week. I heard that he stayed at the Morganton hotel. He must be coming up in the world."

"The Morganton Hotel, you say. Do you know what's been going on there? May from the Co-op told me. Whispered it when she was slicing the bacon. Didn't want some of the other customers to hear."

With that the younger woman lowered her voice and repeated to her mother-in-law what she had been told.

Every now and then the two women forgot themselves and bits of the conversation could be heard. Dafydd happened to enter the room just as his mother said more loudly "Not Morris the draper! If Mrs. Morris knew…"

His stomach dropped. He stood there, did they know? But his sister-in-law, realizing that he was there and not being very happy about discussing such things in front of the young man, changed the subject.

"That's a nice smell coming from the oven, Mam. Is that for dinner?"

"Yes, it's a chicken. The old cockerel had had his day. He was big and fat after the amount he used to eat. There'll be plenty for all of us."

Early on Boxing Day, Carrie was brushing Dafydd's jacket. "Mam, doesn't he look smart. But you're ready far too soon, Dafydd. Your father isn't dressed yet."

"He'll have to hurry up. We've got to catch the nine o'clock train to Ponty. It's the first train today, only Sunday service, and there's no half past nine. It had better not be packed. Tell Dad to get a move on."

"All right, I'll go and see if I can hurry him up for you."

Carrie couldn't help smiling at her mother-in-law as she left the room. Everything had to be done in double quick time this morning. Her son was so excited.

Upstairs, Emlyn was just about ready. Like Dafydd, he had dressed in his Sunday best. When Carrie poked her head around the door of their bedroom she saw him standing in front of the dressing table carefully parting the remains of his hair. He stood in the only empty space for into that small room had been crammed a double bed, a wardrobe, dressing table and washstand. No wonder there was barely room for him to dress.

"Emlyn, your son's waiting for you. He's so excited."

"I only hope that he won't be too disappointed. You know that we haven't got much of a chance. They're all backing the Ynys Wen lot to win. They say that no one can touch them."

"When will you be back?"

"Oh, early evening. Probably catch the five o'clock train. Might even be earlier. I suppose that I'd better go down to him now and take him off your hands. We'll walk slowly to the station."

Luckily they met some of the others on their way down the trip and Dafydd's exuberance was reigned in. Of course they were too early but so was John Parry B.A. Excitement or nerves, or a combination of the two meant that no one was late. They wandered around the platform laughing and joking with each other to hide their nerves until at last the signal went down and they heard the hissing of the train as it pulled into the station. There were a few people on it but, since this wasn't a working day, there were plenty of seats for the choir.

Pontypridd station, even on Boxing Day, was busy. Coal trains on their way to Cardiff, Penarth and Barry. Empty trucks sat in sidings waiting for locomotives to take them up the valleys to be filled again with the black gold. Passenger trains arriving and leaving, going south to Cardiff and beyond or north to the valleys and the mountains. The men tumbled out onto the platform and followed John Parry B.A. They marched like an attacking army down the steps and out of the station. They passed the Sardis Road chapel, crossed over to Mill Street and on to the Market Hall.

"Competing choir, are you?" asked the official at the table in the entrance foyer. "Name please."

"Ebenezer choir," replied a few of the men in unison.

"Yes, I see it," said the man as he put a tick against a name on the list in front of him.

"You'll be fifth on. Nine choirs competing today. Good entry. If you go through and sit with the others on the left-hand side, the adjudicator will explain the procedures at the start of the competition."

In they trooped and sat down on the hard wooden benches. Dafydd looked around at the other competitors. They seemed to fall into two groups. There were some that were silent and looked worried and others who were chatting quit unconcernedly amongst themselves. He couldn't help listening to the pair in front of him.

"At least we're inside today. Not like in the Rhymney Valley Miners' Eisteddfod. Remember that!"

"Aye! What a day that was. It bucketed down and that tent, or marquee as they called it, was full of holes. Water dripping down my neck and me trying to sing."

"What about the outside. We had to wade through six inches. And after all that we weren't even placed."

"Fixed they said it was."

The two nodded their heads wisely together and for the first time it began to dawn on Dafydd that Ebenezer choir might not win.

Just then the people in the front stopped talking and looked expectantly towards the stage. The silence spread through the competitors but the lad couldn't see any reason for it. Then his eye caught some movement to the side as someone climbed the steps onto the platform. The figure swept into the middle of the stage. All looked expectantly towards him. His commanding presence left no one in doubt that it was Mr. David Parkes, the adjudicator.

"Good morning, gentlemen. I've been told that all the choirs are present and so we'll begin the proceedings." He cleared his throat and then read out the instructions. "Each choir, in its allotted order, will come on stage and can begin its rendition, after my signal of course. There will be a pause between each item for Mr. Howells and myself to make notes. At the end of the last performance we will retire to the committee room to make our decision and, when we have reached it, we'll come back here to give our verdict." Looking up he asked, "Are there any questions?"

No one dared to put a hand up. After waiting a few seconds, Mr. Parkes strode from the stage to the adjudicators' table half way down the hall. There he made a show of getting himself comfortable, of making sure that he had sufficient notepaper and even had an official climb onto the stage to see that nothing obstructed the view.

"Gentlemen, we are ready. Will the first choir take the stage please?"

The competition had begun.

At the end of the third choir's performance, Dafydd thought to himself, we're going to win this.

Then they announced Ynys Wen. On a signal from their conductor, as of one they rose from their seats and in correct order marched onto the stage. Perfectly lined up, they waited for the baton. They were all in winged collars and black bow ties. Even their suits appeared to be the same. Dafydd's mouth dropped. He hadn't seen anything like it.

"That's what they wore when they won at the Park Hall in Cardiff," someone whispered in front of him.

There was worse to come. Their singing was magnificent. And all this just before it was Ebenezer's turn. It was enough to demoralize anyone. At the end, Ynys Wen marched off the stage in perfect reverse order back to their seats. A few minutes later "Next choir" rang through the hall.

"We must look a right shambles, Dad," Dafydd whispered as they got onto the stage.

"Don't get disheartened. You are here to sing. Watch John Parry B.A. and give it your best."

To the listeners, there wasn't a great deal of difference in the singing. Ynys Wen was slightly crisper, perhaps a little more responsive to the baton of their conductor, but Ebenezer sang with heart. In what seemed to be seconds the choir's turn was over and they were making their way off the stage. All heaved a sigh of relief as they sat down. Only John Parry realized what a gamble he had taken and one he thought he had lost when he saw the effect the last choir had had on his men. But the colliers were made of tougher metal and as he sat down the words not bad, not bad at all went through his mind.

The remaining choirs sang and the adjudicators left the hall. Men chatted amongst themselves trying to guess the verdict. All had their favourites and few were impartial.

"Well done, men," said John Parry as he circulated amongst his choir.

"Were we all right?"

"Of course you were. You rose to the occasion magnificently."

"We didn't disgrace ourselves then?"

"No, not at all. You should be proud of yourselves."

At last there was movement at the back of the hall. The noise subsided and Mr. David Parkes marched down the central aisle and onto the stage. His eyes swept the audience, commanding everyone's attention. Inevitably the adjudication was long and complicated.

"He wants his four pennyworth," came a loud whisper from near the back.

The adjudicator's head swivelled immediately in the right direction and a whole section of the audience tried to avoid his glare by sinking lower in their seats.

At last he said, "And now to the awards. "Highly commended today is the Tonypandy Male Voice Choir."

There was a polite round of applause as its conductor walked to the stage to receive the rosette and certificate.

"Dad, I thought that we'd have got that," said Dafydd disappointedly.

"We acquitted ourselves well. We've nothing to be ashamed of. Don't fret."

But the lad was too disappointed to be placated. He didn't really listen to the announcement of the next place.

"Clap, Dafydd, clap," Emlyn urged.

Then the adjudicator's voice was heard again. "I award second place to a choir I haven't judged before. They are obviously a new group and they have more to learn, but they sang with great vigour and the tenor parts were particularly well executed. Will the conductor of Ebenezer choir come forward please?"

"It's us! It's us, Dad, we've come second."

"Yes, Dafydd. Thanks to you and John Parry B.A."

Chapter Eight

In contrast, Christmas at Rock House was uneventful. Problems at the colliery meant that Sarah Lewis spent many lonely hours. She tried to make the best of them. The gardener had placed a pine tree in a wooden tub in the hall and she decorated it with bows and ribbons that she had bought at Morris the drapers.

"Are you going to put candles on the tree, madam?" asked Mary, the young maid.

"Of course, we'll light them on Christmas Eve. See I have them here in this box. Look what else I've got."

"Oh!" gasped the girl as she saw the beautiful glass balls that nestled in the bottom amongst layers of tissue paper.

"Get me my sewing basket. I need some white thread to hang them on the tree."

The day of the twenty-fourth had been particularly lonely. Sarah's husband was out till late and the servants were busy preparing for Christmas day. The memories of the Dyffryn House ball served only to feed her poor spirits. She remembered that Louisa's excitement had been infectious.

They were met at the station by the horse and four and then driven in style through the lanes to the village of Saint Nicholas with its thatched cottages and then up the long gravel drive to the house. Although it belonged to her husband's cousin, she had only been to Dyffryn once before. She'd forgotten how beautiful the grounds were, even on a damp winter's day. How grand the house was with its wide staircase and its oak panelling. The porcelain, cut glass and silver in the dining- room, and the silk curtains and oriental rugs in the drawing room emphasized its opulence. But what Sarah marvelled at most were the flowers. In the middle of winter there wasn't a room without them. They'd been chosen specially to blend in with the décor. Her hostess, though, obviously didn't think that there was anything special in that.

"I give a list of the colours I want in each room to the head gardener and he chooses the flowers accordingly," the lady of the house had remarked. "If you'd like to see the greenhouses then I'm sure that Reginald would only be too pleased to take you round them tomorrow. The gardens are his pride and joy."

The ball had been fun despite the fact that her husband had left them largely to their own devices. Whilst he talked of coal and ships with the other middle-aged men, she and Louisa had danced the night away. There were plenty of unattached young males who, if they couldn't dance with the niece, were more than happy to partner her attractive young aunt. There were many suitable prospective husbands but Louisa moved from one to the other without indicating a preference.

And when the two ladies chatted on their way up the stairs in the early hours, she had said, "They were all so friendly, Aunt Sarah."

"Do you want to see any of them again?"

"Of course."

"Who?"

"Not who but all of them," said Louisa with a smile as she closed her bedroom door.

The following morning, after a late breakfast, Sarah had wrapped herself up against the December weather and set out to explore the grounds. Walking across the croquet lawn in front of the house, she met her host Reginald Cory.

"Cold morning," he had said quite informally as he acknowledged her.

"Yes," she had replied, "But I couldn't possibly go home without a walk in your magnificent grounds."
She smiled to herself as she remembered the obvious enthusiasm in his reply.

"I'll escort you, if I may. Then I can tell you all about our plans. We're not finished yet, but I don't suppose a garden ever is."
There was so much to see and so little time.

"Lawns and flower beds you've seen aplenty, but what do you think of this?" Reginald had asked as they entered the Moorish Courtyard with its stepped crenellations and horseshoe arches. "A touch of southern Spain, don't you agree?"
Encouraged by her delight he had taken her to the Pompeian Garden. There, from the sunken lawn, she had admired the colonnades and fountain. Walking on a little further they came to windows cut in the yew hedge.

"Look through there, that's the outdoor theatre. We'll have plays there in the summer."
His enthusiasm had no bounds. He told her how he and his landscape- architect, Thomas Mawson, had travelled Europe looking for inspiration.

"Come in the spring to see the bulbs and again in the summer for the bedding plants and the roses," he had urged her as they had entered the greenhouses. One section was full of flowers and it was obvious where the cut flowers for the house came from.

That walk was such a treat, she thought. We must visit when the weather's warmer. Surely my husband can leave the colliery for a few days. Yes, she would go again in the summer when the roses were in bloom.

The thoughts of Dyffryn did nothing to lighten her spirits for they served only to remind her of her loneliness. There was one consolation that Christmas Eve – her husband came home early from the colliery and they lit the candles on the tree together!

Christmas dinner at Rock House could only be described as a very staid affair. They were only a small party for who was there to invite in Morganton? Inevitably the Reverend Evans had lingered too long over grace and this no doubt caused the cook to fret over the food. Sarah had chosen the menu with care. Nothing exotic, since she couldn't imagine her guests appreciating Salmon with a Mousseline Sauce or an Asparagus Vinaigrette – even if it had been in season. In any case, she wasn't sure that Mrs. Lloyd could have handled such dishes. Instead her instructions were to prepare a cream of barley soup, to be followed by baked haddock with a sharp sauce. Poultry, she felt was not appropriate for such substantial men and had chosen a sirloin of beef but she was determined to have a choice of puddings so that she at least could have one of her favourites – a chartreuse jelly. She needn't have worried for her husband and the minister became so involved in an ecclesiastical argument that they really hadn't noticed what they were eating – though the Reverend Evans had managed to eat plenty. The other guests seemed to enjoy the meal but since they held the two men in such awe, they had contributed little to the conversation around the table.

Again Sarah couldn't help comparing her dinner party with the supper at Dyffryn House. There the long table, decorated with frosted holly leaves and other greenery, had been laid with every conceivable cold dish! Arranged down the centre were the puddings – pastries, fruited jelly, custards, raspberry cream, blancmange, charlotte rousse... They looked so appealing and tasted divine. The young men were very attentive and made her feel special. So much so that she wished that she had had a free choice in whom she married but the match had had to be an appropriate one.

She didn't want for anything in the material sense but would she ever find true happiness? If it wasn't religion, it was coal. Had the colliery's output increased? What was the latest price for a ton? How long did the ships have to wait in the Bristol Channel before they could dock to load up? And so it went on and on. True, her husband had given her some lovely Christmas presents. He had sent to Cardiff for the matching diamond earrings and necklace. Sarah had worn them with her new evening dress on Christmas night. They had impressed Mary, if no one else.

"Madam, they're beautiful" the maid had exclaimed as she fastened the necklace. "You look a picture."
But the mistress had yet again slept on her own for as soon as their guests had departed her husband had said, "It's late, go to bed my dear. I'll be up soon. I've a small matter to see to."
An hour later she had fallen asleep.

On Boxing Day, the servants, true to custom, visited their families and lunch was a cold affair since the cook would not be back until the evening. There was a light covering of snow and this prevented Sarah from going for a walk. She longed for some company for, although her husband was in the house, she saw little of him between meals. He locked himself away muttering about some navy contract he hoped to win. She was glad when the servants arrived back as their chatter relieved the silence.

The following day the holiday was over and life returned to normal. That morning, Sarah's maid was full of Ebenezer choir's splendid performance.

"Came second they did and against all that competition. Of course the Ynys Wen choir were first. But much more experienced. Won before, many times. They said that Dafydd was the best singer out of all of them. You know, madam, Carrie Price's son. The winners all had winged collars and bow ties. Everyone said that they looked smart. Our boys want them now, but they cost too much."

"Slow down, slow down," laughed her mistress. "What are you telling me? That the choir needs small items of dress that they can't afford?"

"Well they want to be as good as the next but Carrie will tell you. She's here today to do some washing."

Carrie Price duly explained that some of the men of the choir had been so inflated by their success that they had convinced themselves that there were only the bow ties between them and winning.

"Does Morris the draper stock them, Carrie?"

"I suppose he must do. The shop is full of everything; but what call has he got for bow ties around here?"

"How many would they need?"

"You'd have to ask John Parry B.A., madam. He's the only one who would know."

It wasn't long before a note was dispatched from Rock House with a request for the choirmaster to join the colliery owner and his wife for dinner on the following evening.

John Parry arrived in good time for dinner at Rock House.

"Thank you for your invite, Mrs. Lewis," he said on entering the drawing room.

"It's a pleasure to welcome you here, Mr. Parry. Unfortunately my husband will be a little late. He's trying to persuade the navy to take our steam coal but drawing up the contract is proving to be more difficult than he thought. He did say though that we were to start diner without him. I do hope that you are hungry."

"I certainly am," he replied with a smile. "I usually eat alone so it is very pleasant to be invited out for dinner."

Three places had been laid at one end of the long dining table. The two sat opposite each other, leaving an empty chair at the head. Mrs. Lewis soon found that she was attracted by the choirmaster's cultured Welsh voice and by his easy manner. They talked about many and far ranging topics. She had not felt so alive for a long time. He certainly wasn't the stern academic of his reputation. Time and time again he made her laugh as he lightened even the most serious matters. His tale of the Pontypridd Eisteddfod was a mixture of both pride and humour. He was certainly very proud of his choir's achievements and no one could doubt that. His sympathetic account made her wish that she had been there.

"I think it was the bow ties and winged collars," he teased. "They certainly impressed Dafydd Price. Luckily when he started to sing he forgot about Ynys Wen's fancy dress and let the music fill his mind."

"His mother tells me that the men want to buy some now, but they can't afford them."

"True, they seem to think that you get extra points for dress."

"We would like to encourage the choir and my husband has agreed to fund a supply of collars and ties – if that's all right with you?"

John Parry couldn't believe what he was hearing. This would be just the thing to add confidence to their performance. They could march on stage feeling that they were as good as anyone else. Which in all truth they were. It was soon decided that he would collect numbers and sizes and report back as soon as possible. They were still talking animatedly when Mr. Lewis, the colliery owner, arrived home.

"I must apologize, my dear, for being so late. Especially when we have a guest but that navy contract is proving to be very difficult." Then turning to the butler he continued, "I'll dispense with the soup, George. Just bring me the meat course."

"Will that be enough for you, dear? You've had a long day at the colliery."

"Quite enough thank you. The two of you won't have to wait too long for me then. Carry on with your discussion." But from then on the conversation was much more serious.

Morris the draper's shop had two big windows facing the main road. It was only last year that the new large glass panes that went right into the doorway had replaced the smaller, more conventional ones. He was very proud of his display and often boasted that if you didn't see it in the window then you wouldn't find it in the shop. There were antimacassars and table runners, net for curtains and bales of cloth, women's and men's underwear, shirts and blouses, ties and socks… On a fine day, there were even towels hanging from hooks outside. He employed two female assistants, as he liked to call them, and of course Mrs. Morris oversaw the whole operation. The shop girls were inevitably young and pretty.

"Must set a high standard," he'd say. "If people are buying nice things then they like to be served by attractive shop assistants."

He didn't take into account the fact that most of his customers were miners' wives who were more intent on making their money go as far as they could than admiring the appearances of those who served them. As long as Mrs. Morris was there then all he could do was look and then only surreptitiously. When she wasn't then that was another matter. But the girls soon became adept at avoiding him, especially in the back storeroom. Their best defence was to say:

"I thought I heard the shop bell ring. It must be a customer."

And he would be gone for, when it came down to it, there was nothing more important than making money.

"Good morning, Mrs. Lewis, and a happy new year to you. It is very good to see you here. What can I do for you?"

"I'd like some wing collars and bow ties, please."

"For your husband, of course. I have his size in my book. How many collars, two or three perhaps?" he asked hopefully.

"No, Mr. Morris. They are not for my husband. They are for Ebenezer Choir."

"The choir!"

"Yes they need them for competitions so I want a collar and black bow tie for each singer. I have a list of the sizes here."

Morris the draper swallowed hard, he couldn't believe his luck. The only trouble was that he didn't have anywhere near

65

that number in the shop. There were some winged collars but no bow ties.

"We don't have much call for these items," he heard himself saying.

"Does that mean that you haven't any in stock?"

"No, I've got some but I think that I might be a bit short. The traveller calls on a Wednesday. I'll place the order with him and the extras will be here next Monday. I can parcel them all together and send them up to you then."

"That'll be fine. When they come in, don't deliver them to Rock House but take them to Mr. John Parry and charge the cost to my husband's account please."

"Certainly, Mrs. Lewis." Morris was never one to miss an opportunity and his next words were, "Can I get you something else? We've had new lace in – made in Brussels I'm told."

At about a week later, at breakfast, George brought the morning post into the dining room at Rock House.

"For you, sir," he said handing over a number of envelopes. "And for you, madam."

"I see that you have a letter, Sarah. Who's it from?"

"I'll open it after breakfast, but I recognize the writing. It's Louisa's."

"I'm afraid I can't stay to hear her news but you can tell it to me at dinner. I will make an effort to get back in good time tonight."

Once her husband was safely out of the house, Sarah pulled a smaller envelope out from underneath the larger one. She felt her fingers tingle for she recognized that writing too. It was the same hand that wrote the list of wing collars and black bow ties.

Chapter Nine

Winter turned into spring and the days lengthened. Dafydd came home in daylight and nearly every Sunday the weather was fine and he could go for walks on the mountain, but he was no longer alone for he had acquired a companion. Since that fateful night in the Morganton Hotel, Jack had taken him under his wing and had decided to oversee his friend's education. There was only one subject on the curriculum – women.

"It's like this see – there are some that do and some that don't. You have to know who's who," said Jack as they walked along in the spring sunshine. "Some are too afraid of their mothers, fathers, chapel or whatever else to let you have more than a kiss. And there are others who want it as much as you and me. The trick is recognizing the signs."
Dafydd nodded wisely in the hope that Jack would continue for his encounter with Rosy had opened up a whole new vista to him.

"Hold her hand, then after a bit put your arm over her shoulder. If she doesn't pull away and seems to settle into your side then you've got some hopes."

"But what next?"

"Well suggest that you come for a walk up here but it's a bit open for anything serious. Not many of them want to come up this far anyway. Too much of a climb, but there's always that group of trees behind the old railway sheds. Lots of bushes there too. Quite private and if it comes to rain then there's shelter handy. Yes that's always a good spot.

"A good spot for what?"

"Dafydd, boy, I didn't think that you were as green as that! Now imagine that you are out walking with a girl and you manage to end up down there. Get yourselves in amongst the trees and give her a kiss. No peck on the cheek mind. You'll see that the rest will come natural like. But be careful or you'll end up married to her. Now you know what I mean?" Dafydd nodded but didn't show any enthusiasm for such an outing.

"Look, man, said Jack in exasperation, "You've started with Rosy, just build on it. I know that it was her job but remember what it felt like. It'll be just as good the next time. Believe me, I know."

Jack, recognizing Dafydd's naiveté, thought, it'll have to be arranged for him. I know, I'll set him up with May from the Co-op. She'll make him understand. Not one for mincing words that one, or for wasting time. Jack's mouth twitched into a smile as the pair walked on in silence.

Dafydd felt sure that none of the girls he knew would venture down to those old sheds with him. In his experience all they wanted to do was to parade in their Sunday best up and down the main road. That's what they called walking out.

But Jack's experience of women was very different from that of Dafydd. Jack grinned as he thought of his own initiation into the adult world. His upbringing was chalk and cheese to that of his friend. There was no mother in the house. She had died when he was young. He was the youngest in the family and after his brothers and sisters had left home, his father had more or less allowed him to do what he liked. He was often in trouble at school and Carrie used to try to keep

Dafydd away from him then. But when Jack had gone to work in the pit, he had to listen to the over-man. Jack was good-natured and didn't shirk his share of the work. But away from the colliery, he retained his spark of independence and it wasn't unusual for his old devilment to surface. He was the natural leader of the lads of his age in Morganton.

After Jack's youngest sister had married, the old man got into the habit of bringing women home – especially when he was drunk – and he was none too careful about what his son saw and heard. Some of these girlfriends fancied a bit of young blood and Jack was well developed for his age. If his father knew he didn't seem to object for he never mentioned it.

Jack's initiation had come one evening when he was just fifteen. It had been a typical Saturday night. His father had come home from the pub with a woman in tow. Jack had caught a glimpse of her as she and his father had lurched noisily across the landing. They were in such a hurry that they didn't close the bedroom door behind them properly. Jack knew this because he'd been listening for the click of the latch and he seized his chance to see what was going on. He had heard enough bumping and creaking in the past, this time he was going to see what really happened. He crept along the landing, got down on his hands and knees and pushed the bedroom door open a couple of inches. He waited but neither of them noticed so he gently pushed again. Now he could see into a slice of the bedroom. His view was dominated by a pair of women's legs paddling in a sea of cloth. His eyes travelled upwards and he swallowed hard for she was just about to remove the last vestige of clothing from her top half and out tumbled a pair of very generous breasts. The effect on Jack was electric. Oh how he wanted to reach out to them.

The woman turned towards the bed and in a loud whisper said, "Move over, lazy bugger. Move over and make some room for me."
There was neither movement nor answer. Realization dawned on her.
"You've passed out on me, after getting me in this state! You won't get me back here again, you bastard."
With that she turned from the bed, bent down to pick up her clothes and as she started to straighten her eyes met Jack's.
Jerking the door open, she saw him on his hands and knees and started to laugh.
"Get up, boy, trying to learn something were you?"
As Jack stood up her attitude changed for there was no comparison between this lad approaching manhood and that fat slob sleeping it off on the bed.
"If you want to learn then I'll show you," she said as she grabbed his shoulders and pushed him across the landing. Before he knew it he was on his bed with her besides him and somehow those full breasts were begging to be touched.
There was nothing special about what followed as experience now told Jack, but it was the first time. A smile lit up his face as he remembered how clumsy he had been but she hadn't minded. Just wanted to get on with it and seemed satisfied at the end. She'd come back for more the next week and had made certain that the old man was well oiled. She said that he was asleep before his head touched the pillow and was in with me as quick as a wink. Thinking of those two round breasts still has an effect on me. Aye, he thought, she taught me a thing or two. I suppose it's my turn now with him. Dafydd is too innocent for his own good.

Prompted by these thoughts, Jack turned to face his mate and asked, "Haven't you ever really fancied someone, Dafydd boy?"

"Never thought about it. Walked out with one or two, but nothing serious."

He didn't mention Louisa. He had found out her name from his mother and she still filled his dreams. He knew what Jack would say if he told him - "Out of your league, boy. Find someone of your own class and forget her." But why should he? He could dream couldn't he? He had to have something to think about down that dirty hole. Especially now that Mr. Lewis the coal owner had signed that contract. The over-man had come back from seeing the under manager of the pit with the news.

"The Navy will take all the coal we can mine," he'd said.

But Dafydd knew that it meant working the smaller seams and he couldn't force himself into those tunnels. Luckily in his part of the pit the two foot six was still yielding well, but for how long? He couldn't bear to think of what might happen when it showed signs of running out.

There must be something that I can look forward to, he thought, and then it came to him – the Cymanfa.

His mood lifted as he remembered some of the other singing festivals that were traditionally held in Hebron. As many as possible crammed into Morganton's largest chapel with the choir in pride of place in the centre of the balcony. Right in front of the conductor, John Parry B.A. Everyone was agreed that there was no one better to lead the singing.

We'll out sing all the other Cymanfas, that's for sure.

And with that fighting thought he turned his attention back to Jack and his tales about women.

"I'll arrange a double date for us one Saturday night."

"Right, yes," agreed Dafydd for there couldn't be any harm in going out in a foursome. But little did he know what Jack had in mind.

Chapter Ten

John Parry had worked with the Ebenezer choir throughout January and February and now he could hear the difference in their singing. The men had grown in confidence and he wanted them to make an impact at the Morganton Cymanfa Ganu (singing festival). Representatives from chapels in the other valleys would be in Hebron on that day and they'd report back every detail to their congregations. The Cymanfas inspired great rivalry. Some of the lads in the choir had even wanted to wear their winged collars and bow ties. He had had a hard job in persuading them that black bow ties were not quite the dress for chapel.

    He wondered if Sarah would be there. In his mind he had long given up calling her Mrs. Lewis and she had simply become Sarah. Of course she will, he told himself, but in the company of her husband. It was becoming more and more difficult for him to meet her with any degree of equanimity. He had dined at Rock House on a few occasions now and each time he had fallen more and more under her spell. He had been invited again that evening but he looked on his proposed visit as a mixed blessing. He so wanted to see her but each time he did his desire for her increased. He had to keep reminding himself that she was the wife of the most important and influential man in the community and as such out of his reach. Little did he realize that she reciprocated at least some of his feelings, but whether this arose out of neglect and boredom or out of true affection was another matter.

On a cold March morning Sarah sat at her small, ornate writing desk in the corner of the drawing room at Rock House. It was time that she replied to her niece's letter. Picking up her pen, she began to write.

> Rock House,
> Morganton,
> March 1914.

Dear Louisa,

    Thank you for your last letter. It was so good to hear from you so soon and to know that you are able to come to stay over Easter.

    Your visit will coincide with the Cymanfa Ganu or singing festival. This is quite an event here and the towns in the valleys compete unofficially, of course, for it is suppose to be in praise of God. Everyone taking part seems more concerned about out-singing the other communities. Even the Reverend Evans speaks about the likely winners. There's some unofficial betting on this year's outcome and if it wasn't for his position I'm sure that he would wager some money too.

    The conductor this year is Mr. John Parry. Remember when I wrote to you last, I said that he had been to dinner. He has had a great deal of success with Ebenezer's Male Voice Choir and they are singing a special anthem at the festival. He's very talented and such a pleasant dinner companion since he is so knowledgeable. Last time he came we played a duet together.

Pausing, Sarah remembered how sympathetically he had played – never showing off his obvious superior accomplishment. She acknowledged that for the first time in many months she felt that she mattered for her own sake and not because she was the colliery owner's wife. Sighing audibly, she returned to her letter.

> *Your uncle is as busy as ever despite the fact that he secured the navy contract. Now he's worried about the quality of the coal that is mined. They'll take only the best steam coal and apparently perfectly good fuel is being poured onto the tip. Before the contract he would have sold it as house coal, so I'm not so sure that he's doing the right thing. All I know is that he is back to spending most of his time at the colliery.*
>
> *So you can see that I'm really quite lonely and will be very glad of your company. You must tell me all about your latest suitors. Has anyone proposed yet and if they have did you accept? What it is to have the attentions of so many young men.*
>
> *You must bring news of the latest fashions too. It's such a backwater up here and I've worn these dresses so many times. Bring some details and I'll see what can be made up in the locality. Morris the draper seems to be able to get most things and the washerwoman's mother-in-law can sew anything. I'm not even going to be able to get to Cardiff, let alone go on a visit to London, with your uncle so busy. I'm sure that some new dresses would lighten my spirits.*

She looked up again as she pictured herself in a new dress. A pale green taffeta or a lilac silk would be nice. She hoped that Louisa would bring some patterns with her. Then hearing the clock strike eleven, Sarah put pen to paper again so that her letter would catch the mid-day post.

> Write to tell me when to expect you. I'll send George to meet you at the station. I must see cook now about tonight's dinner. I've invited Mr. John Parry so that he can tell us more about the singing festival. I have impressed on your uncle that we have a guest for dinner but I suppose that he will be late as usual. Write soon with your plans.
> Your loving aunt,
> Sarah.

Sarah folded the letter, addressed an envelope and rang the bell.

"Yes, madam," said George when he appeared in the drawing room.

"For the twelve o'clock post," she said as she held out the letter, " and tell Mrs. Lloyd that I'll be along shortly to discuss the preparations for this evening."

"Very well, madam."

As the butler left Sarah got up from the desk and walked over to the large bay window. Gazing through it, she saw and yet did not see the hills in the distance for her mind was so unsettled. Writing to her niece had awakened memories of happier times when she too had been the centre of attention. When life was full of parties and young men. When shops had silks, lace and ribbons in abundance. When the latest fashions were discussed and followed avidly. And now, she sighed, this, as her eyes registered the drams snaking their way up the mountain to the spoil tip at the top.

What have I got? She asked herself as she turned and glanced around. A fine home – yes. Everyone admired her taste and she had to admit to herself that she had a very elegant drawing room. She was glad that she had taken such trouble in furnishing it, even ordering some of the pieces from Liberty's of London. Her eyes stayed for a few seconds on her favourite item – her John Broadwood semi-grand piano. She had brought it with her from Bristol and sometimes, playing it was her only escape from loneliness.

Yes, I live in the best house in the neighbourhood, as befits the colliery owner and his wife. Two large bay windowed rooms on either side of the oak front door, then the dining room, study, kitchen…she ticked them off in her mind. A sweeping staircase leading to the first floor and the bedrooms. A narrower flight linking the back stairs to the second floor and the servants' rooms. Oh yes, a grand house indeed. All I want is someone to share it with. I would never have believed anyone if they had told me on my wedding day that I would become a poor second to a colliery – a dirty dark pit! He only shares my bed when some physical need overtakes him and that is less and less frequently. Discarded before the age of thirty – surely I'm not that unattractive.
Walking over to the marble fireplace, Sarah peered into the large gilded mirror. Turning her head this way and that, she registered satisfaction with what she saw.

If only he would pay me a little attention sometimes, she sighed. Surely he can find some time for me. Is the colliery that important?

To prevent any more self-pity, she turned away and walked out of the room and down the hall towards the kitchen to discuss with the cook the details of that night's dinner party.

And this time, she thought, the food will be far more interesting.

That evening Mrs. Sarah Lewis dressed with even more care than usual. With her hair piled high, her long neck enhanced by a choker of soft pearls and dressed in a gown that emphasized her full bosom and narrow waist, she was confident that her beauty would appeal to any man. But whom am I dressing for, she asked herself as she looked in the long mirror, my husband or the choirmaster? Reluctantly, she had to admit that it was the thought of John Parry that made her heart skip.

Just then there was a tap on her door and as she turned to answer it, to her surprise in walked her husband.

"I'm here as promised. I know that there's not much time but I'll be dressed for dinner." A quick kiss on her cheek and he was gone.

He had made the effort to get back for dinner but she didn't know whether to be pleased or disappointed - if he had been late she felt certain that the start to the meal would be much more relaxed and enjoyable. Deciding that only time would tell her that, she took one last admiring glance at herself in the mirror and then made her way downstairs to make sure that all was ready for her guest.

In the kitchen, Mrs. Lloyd had the dinner well under control. She had just checked on the food in the oven when one of the young maids came in.

"That's it, the table's right at last. First the napkins weren't folded to madam's satisfaction and then she thought that there were some smears on the wine glasses. I ask you,

George had washed them all specially for this evening. But no he had to go round and polish all of them again! And she was so particular about those menu cards she's made. Never seen those before!"

"It's for dinner à la Russe," said Mrs. Lloyd, showing off her newly acquired French phrase. "Now are you certain that you know how to serve."

"Yes, you've told me often enough. I must listen carefully to what I'm asked for and then put the food from the dishes on the sideboard onto a warm plate. Larger portions for the men."

"That's right, George will carve at the sideboard too."

In the dinning room, Sarah was taking one last look. The spring flowers from the greenhouse had been put into small vases and were now arranged with some of the cold dessert dishes down the centre of the table. Cutlery and glasses sparkled on the white tablecloth and the sideboard was prepared in readiness for the hot food. Satisfied that everything was in order, she made her way to the drawing room to await her guest.

Chapter Eleven

Avon View,
Clifton Gardens,
Bristol.
March 1914.

Dear Aunt Sarah,

Thank you for your letter. I'll be arriving on the seventeenth. I'm taking the mid- morning train from Bristol and should get to Cardiff in the early afternoon. The connection for the valleys will get me into Morganton at four o'clock. Send George in good time in case I've misread the timetable. Mother is allowing me to travel on my own. I won't have a maid accompanying me. It will be quite an adventure. I only hope that I'll find a porter easily at Cardiff. I have to change platforms there and I'll have a lot of luggage.

Life has been quite busy these last few weeks. I've been to a number of balls and before you ask, yes I have met some handsome men. All of course very well connected and one or two of them are even interesting company. But there is no one special yet, I'm afraid.

At this point Sarah's thoughts began to wander. Images of dancing partners flashed through her mind. Yes there was one she had liked – if not loved. But he didn't meet with her parents' approval. Sighing she turned back to her letter.

> *I must tell you about the meeting I went to last week. Mother didn't approve because it was about votes for women. I don't think that she has told father! Every time he reads about the Suffragette Movement he mutters something about upsetting the natural order of things. Mention Mrs. Pankhurst and he has apoplexy. But they are quite right. Why should we be second-class citizens? We ought to be able to vote. Lots of us could play a useful role in society – if only we had the training. Sometimes I quite despair when I think of the future. Married off to some one I'm not in love with to enhance the family name and to produce the requisite heir. No, Aunt Sarah, I'm not ready for that – if I ever shall be.*
>
> *I hope that you don't think me too shameful but it's not just the meeting. Since my birthday, I have accompanied mother to some of her afternoon soirees and I've been amazed by what is acceptable to her friends. There's talk of husbands' mistresses and wives' lovers. All is taken as being normal! I certainly don't want that sort of life.*

Sarah couldn't help smiling at this as she thought, little do you know. Some men are fickle and others married to their professions or businesses. What's a wife supposed to do?

> *How is your Mr. Parry? He sounds quite pleasant and I know how much you like to play the piano. It must be nice to have an appreciative audience. I remember that Uncle used to sit and listen to you playing when you were still in Bristol but it seems that*

he is far too busy now. I'm intrigued by your explanation of the Cymanfa – if that is how you spell it. You know how much I like to sing and, if the songs are in Welsh then, I can always listen to the choir. Of course I'll come with you. I'm really looking forward to the festival.

  I must close now as I've promised mother that I'll accompany her to one of those endless teas. Don't forget to send George early.
With much love,
Louisa.

On the seventeenth, Sarah waited eagerly for her niece to arrive at Rock House.

  "Oh it's so good to see you," she said as she held out her arms to welcome Louisa. "How was the journey on your own?"

  "It was fine. I found a porter easily at Cardiff and as soon as I got off the train at Morganton I saw George waiting for me. Do you like my new hat?"

Louisa spun round so that her aunt could see this latest creation.

  Laughingly Sarah replied, "Of course I do. Go and take your coat off and then we'll have tea in the drawing room. I know that the cook has made some of those griddle cakes you liked so much last time you were here. I can catch up on all the news then too."

Some minutes later they were sitting on the sofa in front of a large coal fire, drinking cups of tea, eating cakes, and all the time happily chattering to each other.

  "And what about Mr. Parry?" asked Louisa. "Did you play another duet with him?"

"Not when he dined last time. But both he and your uncle were equally insistent that I played and sang. I don't think that I had ever had such an attentive audience. I must admit though, that Mr. Parry is very interesting. He is determined that the Cymanfa will be a success. It's as if the town's reputation is at stake.

" Didn't you say that he's a fine conductor? I wouldn't worry. When are you going to introduce him to me? Will I see him before the Cymanfa?"

But to deflect her niece's obvious interest in the choirmaster, Sarah said "Everyone wears his or her best for it. Some of the women even manage to have something new and they'll be very interested in our outfits. Have you brought something special to wear?"

It was just the right distracter and the conversation turned effortlessly to dresses, coats and hats.

In the Price's household, the two women were also talking about clothes. Granny Price was glad to have finished the last garment needed for Sunday.

"That's the tenth blouse like that I've made," she said as she fastened off the thread. "I think it's the lace that they're fancying. It does look nice sewn in a V from shoulders to waist. I don't know where Morris the draper got it from. He says it is hand made in Brussels. More like it came off a machine in Nottingham. But there we are, he'll say anything to make a sale. Have you got your clothes ready, Carrie?"

"Yes, I'm going to wear my best skirt and that blouse you made me. You know, the one with Brussels' lace."

And with that the two women burst out laughing.

Sunday proved to be fine and mild.

"With good weather like this, we'll have a rousing Cymanfa," remarked Emlyn to Carrie over breakfast. "The chapel will be full all right. You had better be in Hebron early tonight or you won't have a seat."

"Yes, but it's a big chapel. We'll be there in plenty of time anyway. Most of us from Ebenezer are going to sit on the side balcony. Then we'll have a good view of the choir and the rest of the congregation."

"You and Mam only want to see what the women are wearing. It'll be who's had new clothes, or did you see so and so in that old coat."

"Stop teasing, Emlyn. You know we go to listen to the singing," replied Carrie indignantly but secretly acknowledging that discussing what people were wearing was one of the pleasures of the event.

Hebron was packed. People had been queuing long before the caretaker had opened the doors. Men, women and children – all decked out in their Sunday best. What a sorry sight it would have been in the rain but instead the good-natured crowd waited patiently in the late afternoon sun. At last, they moved slowly inside. Some took the narrow stairs on either side of the vestibule up to the balcony, whilst others streamed down the two aisles. It wasn't long before the chapel was full and people were looking for seats.

"Can you move up, please?"

"That's it, children, squeeze together so that there's room for Mrs. Jones."

"I think we'd better put a few chairs in the aisle. Fetch some from the vestry," said one of the deacons to the caretaker. "We'll soon have to close the doors. I suppose, though, that some can sit on the stairs if they only want to listen to the singing. They won't see anything from there."

"The women won't like that. They'll dirty their best clothes. I'll see how many chairs I can squash into the aisles."

At last the people were in but one pew remained empty. The party from Rock House entered the chapel and walked carefully down the now narrowed aisle and took their seat. Carrie and Granny Price stretched their necks to see what the ladies were wearing.

"There's Mrs. Lewis. Doesn't she look elegant with that fox fur? And that hat! I wish I could have a closer look. Miss Louisa must be dressed in the latest fashion. Try and see, Mam. Perhaps you can make something like it for some of your customers."

"It's no good. I can't make it out from here. It's my eyes. You'll have to tell me about her outfit when we get home."

Just then a hush fell on the congregation as the door to the minister's vestry opened and out walked Hebron's minister followed by his colleagues from the town, including the Reverend Evans. Bringing up the rear was John Parry B.A.

"Look he's got a black cloak on," hissed Carrie. "Doesn't he look important, Bachelor of Arts he is."

The ministers took their seats to the side of the pulpit and the choirmaster entered it. He looked up at his choir on the balcony in front of him, gave an indication with his hands and as one the men stood. A brief nod to the organist and the first few bars of the opening hymn filled the chapel. The choir sang the first verse and then John Parry looked at the congregation. He gestured for them to rise and Emlyn's prediction of a rousing Cymanfa was fulfilled.

After it was all over, people gathered outside the chapel as they waited for friends and relations. All praised the singing.

"Best Cymanfa ever," said one knowing lady. "Bound to have beaten the other valleys."

The colliery owner, his wife and guest waited too. Mr. Lewis wanted to thank the choirmaster for all the hard work he had put in.

"John Parry, over here," he shouted as he saw the very man come through the chapel door.

Picking his way carefully through the crowd, but always acknowledging the praise, the choirmaster eventually reached the party from Rock House.

"A great effort, well done," said Mr. Lewis as he shook John Parry's hand.

"Indeed it was," said Mrs. Lewis adding to the praise. Then turning towards Louisa, she added, "I don't believe that you have met my niece."

"No. I don't think that I've had that pleasure but I think that I've seen you in chapel on a previous occasion."

"The singing was magnificent, Mr. Parry," said the young lady. "I particularly enjoyed the soloist. What a fine tenor, who is he?"

"Dafydd Price, a local lad."

"You mean Carrie's son," said Mrs. Lewis with a smile. "You know, Louisa, Carrie who comes in to do the washing. Is that him coming out with some of the other men? Look at the people rushing to congratulate him. There's Mary, my maid, hanging onto his arm."

"I'll go and fetch him so that he can hear your praise for himself," said the obliging choirmaster.

"Dafydd, come here lad," he called as he walked back towards the chapel door.

At last John Parry gained the young tenor's attention. Dafydd struggled through the happy crowd as they heaped compliments on him until he reached the choirmaster's side. He was surprised to hear that the colliery owner wanted to see him.

"Well done, lad," said Mr. Lewis immediately.

"Oh yes indeed," enthused his wife.

"You have a lovely voice," added Louisa as she held out her hand towards him. "Congratulations on your singing." Dafydd took her hand awkwardly and looked into her eyes. He knew then that at this time in his life, there was no other woman that he desired more than the young lady in front of him. Embarrassed, he muttered something about finding his mother and Granny Price and disappeared back into the throng.

"Overwhelmed by the praise, I'm afraid," explained the choirmaster apologetically.

"Not to worry, Mr. Parry, he did very well indeed. Probably given us the edge over the other towns. Will you join us for supper?" asked Mr. Lewis magnanimously.

"Thank you, but another time perhaps. I feel rather tired now after all the excitement. I need to unwind. I wouldn't be very good company."

Louisa watched her aunt as the two men talked. Was there a moment of disappointment on her face? She couldn't really tell but John Parry with his good looks and pleasant manner was certainly a man to be admired.

Over supper, the talk inevitably was of the Cymanfa.

"I'm sorry that you were not able to join in more," said Sarah to Louisa. "But it's a Welsh affair."

"Don't worry, Aunt Sarah, I enjoyed the singing. No wonder you are taking an interest in that choir, they are a joy to listen to."

"Yes Ebenezer's choir is your aunt's hobby at the moment. But to be fair, they practice hard and show great improvement. They deserve our support."

"We haven't done much. Just spent a few pounds on collars and bow ties. I just show an interest. Anyway you know how fond I am of music."

And the choirmaster, thought Louisa as she listened to her aunt's defensive reply. Then not wishing to embarrass her, the niece changed the subject by saying, "Well, Uncle, what did you think of my new hat?"

"Very nice, very nice I'm sure. But you had better ask your aunt. I'm no judge of such matters."

So for the rest of the meal the conversation turned to more acceptable topics for Sarah. The two ladies discussed the latest fashions whilst the gentleman, superfluous to this talk, sat back contentedly and allowed his thoughts to turn yet again to the colliery.

At last, after all the excitement and the inevitable post mortem, Dafydd was alone in his tiny bedroom. But he couldn't sleep. His mind was full of Louisa. As far as he was concerned, there wasn't another woman who came anywhere near her. He had actually touched her, looked into her eyes and she had spoken to him! Whatever his mate said, no one in Morganton would do instead of her.

Jack had been true to his word that Sunday on the mountain and had arranged a number of double dates for the two friends. May from the Co-op was always one of the young women but inevitably she ended up with Jack for the evening.

Dafydd smiled as he remembered his mate's wink as he whispered, "Next time your turn," and then Jack and May had disappeared behind the old sheds. As yet, there had never been a next time. True there was always another girl for him. The last few times it had been Mary, the maid from Rock House.

Pretty, nice enough and I enjoyed the kissing and cuddling, he thought. Would have gone further too if she had let me. Glad now though. I don't want to be mixed up with another woman. Then he scolded himself – Dafydd Price, pull yourself together. She's a lady and not for the likes of you. Take Jack's advice. Show more interest in the local girls.
But, when the young miner eventually drifted off to sleep, he dreamt that Louisa was in his arms.

Chapter Twelve

For a while, life in Morganton returned to normal. The next big event – The Welsh National Eisteddfod – was some months away. Dafydd's week was mapped out for him – work, choir practice, Saturday night out with the boys and chapel on a Sunday. The Saturday nights were becoming more difficult. He wanted a quiet drink and a bit of a laugh with the lads but Jack had other plans for him. Seeing that his friend hadn't made any progress as far as the girls were concerned, Jack vowed that this weekend he'd make a big sacrifice and let Dafydd go out with May. She'd show him a thing or two and then he'd be more interested in the local women.

"Don't be too late now," said Carrie as she saw her son to the door.

"I won't, Mam. Going up the Royal Oak with the boys."

"I heard that you are courting Mary. She's always asking after you when I'm at Rock House."

"Taken her out a couple of times. That's all. Nothing in it so don't you go imagining things."

Carrie smiled at him as he left the house. He could do a lot worse, she thought. She's a good worker when she puts her mind to it and she'll always have a job with Mrs. Lewis.

Dafydd met Jack on the hill.

"I was just coming to call for you. Change of plan. You take May out tonight. She's waiting for you outside The Welfare Hall," said Jack as soon as they met.

"But I was…"

"No buts about it. Come on. I'll walk with you."

"Hello, May," Dafydd stammered when they met up with her. "What do you want to do?"

"Let's go for a stroll," she replied tucking her arm in his. "Night, Jack," she called over her shoulder as they walked away.

"I thought that you and he were courting," said Dafydd.

"Perhaps, perhaps not. Nice to have a change. Don't you think so? You've got lovely muscles, Dafydd Price," she said as she played with his arm.

The young man gulped. How do I get out of this, he thought.

"We'll go down this way," she said as she led him into the lane between the Co-op and Morris the drapers. At the bottom, she turned right and after a few yards they came to a gap in the Co-op's back wall.

"In there," she hissed as she pushed him into a large doorway. They were behind the shop's storeroom.

"No one comes down here in the night," she whispered. "Now Dafydd Price, come here."

Taken aback, the young man did as he was told. She reached up and pulled his head towards her. She kissed him hard on his lips and then forced her tongue into his mouth. Gasping for breath, he pulled away from her.

"What's the matter?"

He didn't know what to reply. This wasn't what he wanted. May was pretty enough and she did have beautiful eyes but she wasn't the girl he dreamt about.

His reluctance though, didn't put her off. Her hands travelled down his body to the area between his legs. He felt himself responding to her touch and at the same time wondering how far this was going. Experienced as she was, she knew that if she continued, then, like any other full-blooded male, his body would eventually defeat his mind. Her fingers were now trying to undo his buttons and he felt his resolve breaking. He bent his head towards her seeking her lips. He smelt the lavender water that May had dabbed on her neck and he forgot Louisa. May's firm breasts pushed into him and he knew that he desired her just as much as she wanted him. Eager hands pulled away clothing and then he was inside her. For the next few minutes, no one else mattered and at the end, as he held her to him, he muttered, "May, my pretty May."

As they stood locked together, Dafydd tried to rationalize what he had done. Was it wrong? He was in love with Louisa. But then he remembered May's lovely eyes and he realized that he'd make love to her again if he had the chance. He went to lift her chin up to kiss her gently when he had heard a noise. His whole body froze.

"What's that?" he whispered.

"Sh," said May as she listened.

Then he could feel laughter ripple through her body as she buried her face in his jacket, trying not to make a sound. At last she pulled her head away and whispered in his ear.

"It's him, Morris the draper. Going out the back way. He's off to the Morganton Hotel for a few drinks with his fellow shopkeepers, or so he tells his wife. Off to see the barmaid, is more like it. Haven't you noticed her new clothes lately? I'll give you two guesses where they've come from and for what. I pity him if Mrs. Morris finds out."

Dafydd couldn't help smiling to himself as he thought, so the old bugger is at it again. There must be plenty going on in Morganton that I know nothing about.

Then he realized that the interruption had dissipated the magic between them and moving away from May, he said

"Come on, let's walk. You can tell me all the other bits of gossip that I ought to know about."

In the month before the Eisteddfod, choir practice became the most important item on the agenda.

"No! " shouted John Parry B.A. as he stopped the choir yet again. "Lighter and softer. Think of the meaning of the words."

Sarah smiled from her seat in the gloom at the back of the vestry. She had slipped in without anyone noticing her. They were all so intent on the music that they hadn't registered the door opening.

A hard taskmaster, a perfectionist, she thought as she stared at the conductor. But the men respond magnificently to him. Oh I do so hope that they do well, but they must.

She listened with appreciation as they went through their pieces. At the end she heard John Parry say, "Thank you, men. That was a distinct improvement. We're nearly ready."

"Aye," someone shouted. "We're not going all the way to Bangor for nothing. If we don't come back with the cup Lizzie will swear that I've been carrying on with another woman. Choir practice indeed, she'll say."

At this they all burst out laughing and the party split up good humouredly, well pleased with their progress.

"They sound very good, Mr. Parry," said Sarah as she emerged from the gloom.

"Oh, it's you, Mrs. Lewis. I didn't realize that you had come in."

"I didn't want to disturb you. But I thought that perhaps you could do with some help over the arrangements for the journey. I don't know how to put this other than to say have you sufficient funds? Can my husband and I help with the rail fares or the cost of the accommodation?"

"Very kind of you both but we are being put up by people in the area. We'll only be away for two nights. Travel one day, compete the next and back home on the third. I know though, that there's some difficulty with the rail fares. But the men are so independent. I'll tell you what I'll do, I'll make a few discreet inquiries to see if some of them can't manage and get back to you."

After this, the conversation moved on to other things and it was noticeable that neither wished to end it. At last, however, Sarah moved towards the vestry door, for she knew that her husband would be home in a short while.

"I did so enjoy the singing," she said as she held out her hand. "You won't forget to get in touch with me about that other matter?"

John Parry took her hand and replied, "Of course not."

The small group of ex-miners who congregated most days in the Welfare Hall had more than usual to talk about. The newspapers were full of the political situation in Europe and, nearer home, the latest escapades of the suffragettes. These men had a better idea of what women were capable of than the politicians. Many knew first hand what power a strong woman can wield. It might be the man who worked in the colliery but it was the wife who ruled the house and often, in their community, brought up a young family on her own when her husband was killed underground or died early from respiratory disease.

"You mark my words," said Emlyn to the rest as they sat around the table in the committee room. "They'll get their own way. It's only a couple of months ago that those suffragettes tried to break into Buckingham Palace. Then last month, that woman, Emily Davies, got trampled by the King's horse in the Derby. You wait and see what they'll do this month."

"As long as Doris doesn't join them and go on strike, I don't care. Food on the table when I come in, is what I want," said one of the others.

This remark caused some laughter but generally they felt that if women wanted the vote, let them have it. It was no big deal to the miners for there were no divisions in their lives. Both sexes had jobs to do and it was debatable who worked the hardest – the man underground or the wife at home. She coped with bringing up a large family on subsistence wages and all the time battled against the coal dust. Water to be boiled for the tin bath, clothes to be washed, the house to clean, and always in an environment that rapidly bred dirt.

The European situation, however, could not be dismissed by a clever remark. Since the murder of the Archduke Ferdinand of Austria on June the twenty eighth, the articles in the newspapers had become far more serious and now Austria-Hungary had declared war on Serbia.

"What do you think, Tom? You were in the army. Will we be drawn into this mess?" asked Emlyn of the man sitting next to him.

"Don't know but I'm glad I'm not in it now. I wouldn't want to be fighting at my age. With a bit of luck they'll sort it out between themselves and we won't be affected."

But he was to be proved very wrong indeed.

In early August, the German army swept through Northern Europe, occupying Luxemburg on the second, declaring war on France on the third and invading Belgium the next day. In response to this the British Government declared war on Germany on the fourth of August 1914.

In the reading room, the men were of the opinion that it couldn't last long.

"It'll be short," said Tom, who had rapidly become the authority on the fighting. Armies can move quickly these days. Look how the French and Germans are racing for the Belgium coast."

But by the end of September he wasn't so sure for the British Expeditionary Force was entrenched near the Aisne as it fought off the Germans.

Surprisingly, international events quickly affected the small community of Morganton. The first disappointment came at choir practice. John Parry B.A. had to tell the members of Ebenezer Male Voice choir that the Eisteddfod had been cancelled.

"But why, Dad? After all that practice and the fighting is miles away, across the sea. Why?" asked Dafydd as he and Emlyn walked home.

"I know, Dafydd. It's a long way off but we must support the country. Lots of the competitors may have joined up and there'll be problems that we don't know about. It's cancelled this year but the war will soon be over and we can enter again in twelve months time. We'll have months to practice and then we'll have a much better chance of bringing home the cup."

A few days later, Dafydd suffered another blow. The Navy in war needed as much steam coal as it could get and the coal owner, always with an eye to making money, gave instructions for the two-foot seam to be opened and worked.

Meanwhile, it seemed only natural for the choirmaster to share his disappointment with his patron.

"I felt that we had a real chance, Mrs. Lewis. The men had worked so hard. Put heart and soul into it. They were excited too about the trip. For many of them it was going to be quite an adventure," said John Parry as he sipped tea in the drawing room of Rock House.

"I agree with you whole-heartedly. The choir makes a beautiful sound. I've really enjoyed listening to them at their practices. But you mustn't give up – there's always next year."

"You are right, of course. It's just that it's such a disappointment."

For some minutes, the two drank their tea and ate some dainty sandwiches whilst they both thought of what might have been.

"A cake, Mr. Parry?" asked Sarah holding up a plate.

"Thank you, I'll have this one if I may."

Again there was silence until Sarah said, "I'm having difficulty with the timing of a piece of music. I just don't seem to be able to get it quite right. I wonder if you could help me?"

"Certainly, shall we take a look at it now?"

"That indeed would be appreciated but have you had enough to eat? Or may I pour you another cup of tea?"

"I've had more than enough, thank you. Let's have a look at the music."

The two moved over to the semi-grand piano where Sarah sat and played the piece through. Listening carefully, John soon saw where she was going wrong.

"I'll play this part for you," he said as he pointed to a section of the music. "Shall we change places?"

He played the difficult section through a few times, always explaining what he was doing. When Sarah returned to the instrument, he was full of praise for she almost had it. Without thinking, he bent over her and with his right hand played the few bars that were still slightly mistimed. Just then, Mary entered the room to clear away the tea dishes. The two at the piano were so engrossed in the music that they didn't notice her. But she gave them a very knowing look as she left with the tea tray.

Before the afternoon was over, it was agreed that John Parry would come to Rock House on a more regular basis in order to improve Mrs. Lewis' piano playing. But in the kitchen, a very different interpretation was being put on this innocent pastime.

"Didn't notice me at all," said Mary. "I clattered the plates but they didn't even look up."

"Not with the best china," admonished Mrs. Lloyd." I don't want any broken dishes. And don't you go spreading rumours. John Parry B.A. was only helping Mrs. Lewis with her music. You know what a pleasure she gets from it."

Chapter Thirteen

The Welsh Echo

Yesterday, August 5th, Field Marshal Earl Kitchener of Khartoum issued orders for the expansion of the army. He is to raise a fighting force composed entirely of volunteers. Each man will sign up for a maximum of three years and must agree to be sent to serve anywhere in the world.

South Wales Gazette

September 10th 1914
Join the 10th (service) Battalion
(1st Rhondda)
at Pontypridd Market Hall.
Every Day from 9a.m.

Your Country Needs You!

D. Watts Morgan M.P.

Posters appeared throughout the valleys encouraging the young men to enlist. Kitchener's face seemed to look out at people from almost every shop window and the M.P.'s message urging men to join up at Pontypridd was on every notice board. No one believed that the war would last long. To many it was a chance to see a bit of the world. The brutality of war was beyond their comprehension. They just saw the glamorous life of a man in uniform – little did they know how far from reality was their idea of army life. The young men of Morganton were no different.

"I can't stick it any more, Jack. That two-foot seam has finished me. I'm joining the army with you."

"But why, boy? You've a good home. Now that Dad's gone I'm on my own. I'm going to sign up and see a bit of the world. You know what they say – all the women like a man in uniform."

"My minds made up. I'm coming with you. I don't want to die down that dirty hole."

"Well I don't suppose that I can stop you. But I wouldn't want to be in your shoes when you tell your mother."

On Saturday the two friends caught the two o'clock train to Pontypridd and then walked through the busy town to the Market Hall. They were surprised by the queue. In just two weeks in August Kitchener's first call to arms had raised one hundred thousand men throughout the country, and the response was no different here in South Wales. They joined the end of the line and immediately Jack started speaking to the man in front of him.

"Didn't expect to see so many. Hope we won't have to wait long."

"Me too. Couldn't get here any earlier, been in work. Wanted to join up for some time but never got round to it."

"Same here," said Jack. "Want to see a bit of the world. Seems like a good chance. This war is not going to last long and they'll send us somewhere else then."

The man nodded in reply as they edged a few paces forward. The crowd laughed and chatted as they waited but when the men came within a few paces of the door they fell strangely silent. Inside the hall, the atmosphere was very different. There was a quiet purpose as the officials saw to their task and the recruits lost their bravado.

Dafydd stared at a big poster proclaiming in huge letters –

YOUR KING AND COUNTRY NEEDS YOU.

He almost jumped out of his skin when a voice barked at him, "Name?"

"Dafydd Price" was the automatic and somewhat frightened reply.

"Address?"

"Twenty three Edmund Street, Morganton."

"Age?"

"Twenty"

"Occupation?"

"Occupation" Dafydd repeated hesitantly.

"Job, boy, job."

"Miner, sir."

"Right, over there for your medical. Join that queue."

And before he knew it Dafydd was lining up with others for a cursory look over by the doctor. He stood there stripped to the waist with his bracers hanging down behind.

"Stand against that pole. That's it, feet together, head up - five feet ten inches. Now your chest."

The frock-coated doctor looped a tape measure around his chest and then bent over him to listen to his heartbeat through a stethoscope. Dafydd had been weighed, measured and pronounced fit - all in a matter of minutes.

"You'll do. Over there to sign up," said the Doctor pointing to another well-dressed figure sitting at a large table covered with papers. "Next."

Two minutes later, Dafydd was in the army.

"You've seven days in which to clear your affairs. Report back here at nine next Saturday morning. From here you'll go to your barracks", said the N.C.O. "Understood?"

The young miner nodded.

"Off you go."

He followed the one in front through the door and found himself back out on the street clutching his papers.

A few minutes later Jack appeared besides him and said, "Signed up then, boy. We're off a week today."

But Dafydd was strangely quiet. He had done what he had set out to do but now that he had signed up he was afraid of facing them back home.

That evening the two friends met up at The Royal Oak.

"Have you told them?"

"No, I'll tell them tomorrow just before chapel. They're never late so they won't have much time to argue. Think of it, only one more week underground."

The family's reaction was predictable but there was nothing they could do about it. He'd signed up. He was old enough and he was determined to go. Emlyn tried to console the two ladies.

"It's only 'til the end of the war and it'll be over by Christmas. He'll be back home then. He'll have satisfied his

wanderlust. He'll get a job back in the pit, settle down and before you turn round he'll be married."
But Granny Price was too old and too wise to be taken in. War meant fighting, men injured, men killed and one of those could so easily be her grandson.

The first few weeks were indeed an adventure for the two young miners. They learnt army routine, how to aim and fire a rifle, and hand-to-hand combat. They were used to the harshness of life underground and down the pit their lives had always been regimented. They got up by the hooters, did what the over-men told them, walked long distances to the coal face... Now they rose with the bugle, obeyed the sergeant and drilled on the parade ground. For some recruits conditions were better in the army than at home for at least they were well fed.

It was at this time that Dafydd learnt a surprising fact about his friend. It was the day the previous batch of volunteers was being shipped out to France and realization dawned on their group that they would be next. Jack had been unusually quiet for some hours and that evening he told Dafydd his secret – one that the latter could hardly believe. Jack Married!

"She told me about the baby that last week at home. I couldn't just walk out on her. I know what it's like to be without a parent. Besides I didn't want another man bringing up my child."

Dafydd didn't know what to say. He just nodded as he tried to take in what he had been told.

"We went to Ponty, to the registry office. Ran away like. No one knew until we came back and then only told her mother. Said we wanted to get married before I went away. Now when the baby comes it'll be all right."

Dafydd still didn't say anything but it didn't seem to matter as Jack just carried on.

"If I don't come back she'll get a pension and the child will have my name. Promise you'll go to see her if anything happens."

Dafydd nodded again, still not knowing what to say and then it struck him – who was she?

"Jack you haven't said who you've married!"

"Haven't I? It's May, May from the Coop." Then more slowly as if he couldn't quite believe it, " She's my wife now."

He was silent again until he suddenly asked Dafydd, "Did anything happen that night?"

"What night? What do you mean?"

"That Saturday you went with May. I know I told her to but I've always wondered."

Now Dafydd understood what he meant. How could he say the truth? It obviously bothered Jack that someone else may have made love to May.

"She taught me a bit about kissing," replied Dafydd carefully. "Then Morris the draper came out of his back door and May told me about what was going on between him and the bar maid. We went for a walk after Morris had gone and I learnt a lot about the goings on in Morganton."

Jack seemed to be satisfied with the answer, but Dafydd wrestled with his conscience. Not only had he misled his best friend, but also he knew that May's lovely eyes and the smell of lavender water might tempt him again.

At the end of November it was their turn to leave for France. They were on their way to war at last

"We've got to be careful now, boy, or we'll be split up. We can't have that can we? You make sure that you do as I say."

Dafydd nodded thoughtfully for it hadn't crossed his mind that they could be parted and now that the big adventure was upon them, he looked to his friend for support. But he needn't have worried; Jack was determined to keep them together since he felt partly responsible for Dafydd joining up. He also knew that his friend wasn't as yet wise enough in the ways of the world to survive easily on his own. Fortunately at this early stage in the war, the army was keeping together the men in the same draft and they were all shipped out at the same time. At long last, they were off to war – their great adventure. Everyone vastly underestimated how things were going to change. Nothing could have prepared them for their new life on the battlefields!

When they arrived in France they spent a few days encamped near a village a few miles behind the front lines. It was almost like being back at barracks. The recruits could hear gunfire in the distance but the sound was muffled and hardly intruded into their daily routine. War didn't seem too bad. On their fourth day it all changed. For the first time they encountered men returning from the battlefield.

It was late afternoon and they had been busy training since first light. They had shot at targets, loaded and unloaded rifles, spiked stuffed sacks and crawled for what seemed like hours on their stomachs. At last they had been allowed to stand down.

"Oh! That was bloody hard," said Dafydd as he sank gratefully to the ground.

But Jack was still on his feet and staring into the distance.

"Look, look over there. There's a column of men."

Dafydd got back up and peered in the same direction.

"They're slow, aren't they?"

Then they heard a cry, "They've wounded with them. Wounded are coming in!"

With others the two friends rushed to help the men. It was then that some of the horrors of war were brought home to the new recruits. The sight of the able bodied was bad enough. They were caked in mud, their clothes ripped and their eyes dull. They were exhausted and could hardly put one foot in front of the other. But that was nothing to the sight of the wounded! Some still managed to stand with the help of makeshift crutches. Others were half carried by men who themselves looked as if they were going to drop. Their bandages were so caked in blood and dirt that only the odd lighter patch indicated what they were. Not even their exhaustion could mask the pain in their eyes.

After such sights, the recruits had little sleep that night and early the next morning they were moved up to the front. As they marched, the green fields on either side of the road slipped further and further away until they saw nothing but churned up earth. The road degenerated into a muddy track and the noise of battle grew louder. They looked wide-eyed at some of the strange sights.

"Jack, are those dogs?" asked Dafydd. "They're coming out of holes in the ground. I thought they were rabbits but they're too big for them, and foxes aren't that colour."

"You're right. They are dogs, living underground! Well, I never!"

They marched past the dugout kennels of the French dogs that were used to carry messages on the battlefield. This complex was the beginning of the vast system of trenches and dugouts that was to be their new home. The realities of war hit them with a bang as they halted at the entrance to the reserve trench.

"Down that gap," shouted the sergeant as he pointed to an opening in the side of the bank in front of them. Dafydd's eyes were drawn inexplicably to the top where there was tier upon tier of sandbags.

"Line up inside on the right and keep your heads down."
They were in a trench, about five feet wide, complete with wooden linings and duckboards but open to the elements.

"You'll spend the rest of the day and night here. Tomorrow you'll be moved up."

Over the next few hours they learnt the ropes as they mingled with some of the outgoing veterans. At base camp they had been instilled with the image of perpetual conflict. Words like guns, mortars, rifle fire, and raids were barked at them. In some parts of the line there was constant shelling, enemy snipers fired at anything that appeared above the parapet, and nightly raids were organized across no-man's land to attack the enemy positions. But, to their surprise, it wasn't the case here.

"No, we get a bit of peace," said one of the experienced men. "There's no firing at breakfast or come to that in the evening. It's live and let live. We all have to eat, even the Hun."

Another butted in then, "You wait till you smell the bacon in the morning – lovely." And his nose quivered in anticipation.

"Saxons across the road," continued the first soldier. "Don't want to fight more than we do, so we go careful like. You'll get the hang of it. Live longer that way."

"If you want my advice," said his mate. "Don't volunteer – unless of course it's for sanitary man. Best job in the company. Left alone, only have to look after the latrines. Back from the line too."

At this, Dafydd and Jack looked at each other in amazement. Cleaning the latrines! Surely that was a punishment, not a perk. But at least they rested easier that night – despite the cold and discomfort. The veterans had managed to push the picture of the battle weary troops and their wounded to the back of their minds. The next morning, the smell of bacon cooking in the trench did indeed overpower the war reek of chloride of lime. After breakfast, they were hurried through the communication trenches to the next line.

Here they were divided into groups with an experienced junior N.C.O. in charge. They were now ready to relieve the soldiers in the front trench.

"Stick to me," whispered Jack as they were being sorted. "Quick, slip behind those two. We'll be all right, and he grabbed Dafydd's tunic and pulled him after him.

"Stand still over there," yelled the sergeant but he was too late. He glowered as the two looked back at him innocently from their new positions.

"Right, you lot," said their corporal. "Down that trench there to our bay. Follow me."

They emerged in a part of the fire trench some 25 feet long, separated from the next section by a 12 feet thick buttress.

"Now listen to me. Rule number one – keep your heads down at all times! The Saxons are all right but they'll shoot at anything that appears above the parapet. We do the same to them. See those loopholes over there, they'll be manned all the time and if you see a Hun shoot!"

The men nodded in unison as each grappled with the realities of war.

"If you want to see what's going on, use a periscope. That's this," said the N.C.O. as he picked up a strange "L" shaped object. "You push the top above the parapet and you look through this end bit. Right, who's going to try it?"
Without hesitation, Jack took the instrument and slowly pushed it up above the sand bags.

"What do you see?" asked Dafydd.

"Barbed wire and then mounds like these."

"That's the Hun's lines," the corporal said. "Any movement?"

"No, Corp, not that I can see."

Thus their first eight-day stint in the line began. Their group soon knitted together. They had to, living in such a small space and soon each was contributing, in his own way, to the welfare of the others. Rotas were organized for brewing tea and fetching rations. They looked after their mates' belongings, defending them from scroungers in a world where possession was nine tenths of the law. They shared food parcels and supported each other emotionally. In attacks they cared for their wounded until medical help arrived – often going against orders to push on. In a sense they became a trench family, bound together by their shared experiences and supporting each other in terms of both their emotional and material needs. This was very necessary for there was no such support to be found in the formal military structure of the British Army. It was a comfort to all when at the end of each day they were able to sit down, eat their rations, have a smoke and chat. For that precious hour the line was quiet.

"All I do is itch," said Dafydd one evening, trying to push his arm further up his back. "I'm being bitten everywhere."

"Come here, lift your shirt up. Let me see if I can catch it," said a mate. "Only another two days and we'll be at the end of this stint. Can have a bath, a change of clothing and with a bit of luck get rid of these buggers."

"You've got me itching now," complained Jack. "If we're not molested by the Huns we are by these bloody lice. I'd jump in the river back there if it wasn't so freezing."

The winter was both cold and wet in the trenches. The temperatures were just about bearable but the near continuous rain made life almost impossible. At one stage the ground was so waterlogged that the walls of the front line trenches came tumbling in around them. The mud was so bad that life in their bay became more than Jack was prepared to put up with.

"I can't slop around in this anymore," he said as he peered at the slurry in disgust. "Look, corporal," and with that he pulled his right foot out of the clinging mud. The grey slime covered his boots and as he lifted his foot so it hung in ribbons as if unwilling to lose contact with the rest.

"We can't even walk without slipping. There's no grip so how can we brace ourselves to fire the machine gun? We can't stand! We can't sit! You get a cup of tea and it's half mud."

"The Hun must be the same, Jack," said Dafydd. "It rained all night on him too."

"He must be as fed up as us then," and with that Jack scrambled up the side of the trench, over the sandbags and stood up in full view of the enemy. He didn't see what else he could do.

"Get down, you idiot!" yelled the corporal. "Get back down here! You'll get yourself killed!"
But Jack looked through the barbed wire into the enemy lines and didn't see a soul.

"Come up here," he shouted. "Come up here. You can stand on solid ground. There's no one around. No one's shooting."
Before long some of his mates joined him and then others from the other bays.

"Look over there," one shouted.
The Germans were out on top too. Both sides were walking in full view of each other. No one fired for they had a new common enemy – the mud. They were all cold, wet and filthy. How Dafydd longed for the tin bath in front of a roaring coal fire.

Some days later, Dafydd wrote home.

Dear Mam, Dad and Gran,
We've had a strange few days here. It rained cats and dogs and our trench was flooded. We couldn't live in it and we were out on top until the weather cleared up. It's all right, we weren't in any danger. The Hun was soaked too so we've been sitting here looking at each other. But as soon as it dried up a bit we were sent back in.
Nothing else to tell you. I'm O.K. just a bit damp. Thanks for the parcel. We shared it all around.
Dafydd.

P.S. Jack wants to know if you've seen May and how she is.

"That's all he's written!"

"Don't fret, Carrie, love. At least you know he's safe."

"Yes, Mam, I suppose so. But why did he have to go?" The tears spilled from her eyes. The old lady got up stiffly from her chair and went over to comfort her daughter-in-law.

"Come, come. Don't upset yourself. You know what they're like at his age. Won't listen to reason. Long as he's safe that's all that matters. Why don't you go to see how May is? Then you'll have something to write back to him about."

Carrie nodded and managed to say, "I'll call at her mother's on the way home from Rock House."

"Cup of tea here for you," Mrs. Lloyd shouted as she heard Carrie come in through the scullery door. "Had any news of Dafydd?"

"A letter came this morning. Short as usual. Never tells us how he is. Wrote about the war that's all."

"Still you know that he's all right."

"I suppose so, that's what Mam says too." Then finishing her cup of tea she pushed her chair away from the table. "I'd better see what the washing is like."

"There's a lot," said Mrs. Lloyd. "The master was taken ill a couple of nights ago."

"No! What's the matter?"

"Heart, the doctor says. Working too hard, if you ask me. George said that the Navy's going over to oil ships. You know he's always reading things in the paper. He says who's going to buy our coal if the Navy doesn't want it. If that's the case I don't know what's going to happen to the pit and the men will be out of work."

"It must be a worry for Mr. Lewis. No wonder he's ill. Poor Mrs. Lewis, she must be very upset."

"Oh yes, she spends a lot of time just sitting by the side of his bed. Up there now but George says that there's been no change over night."

The two women were silent for a few moments as they both thought of the mistress at the side of her sick husband.

Mentally shaking herself, the cook said, "This is no good, we've work to do, Carrie."

"Yes, I'd better start if there's a lot of washing."

She left the kitchen and went into the scullery to get out the big copper.

Upstairs, Sarah was sitting at her husband's bedside.

You're so pale, she thought as she gently pushed damp strands of hair from her husband's forehead.

He must have felt her gentle touch for his eyes opened.

"Would you like some breakfast?" she asked. "You have to build up your strength."

He nodded slowly and then whispered, "I'll try. To please you."

Then his eyes closed again as Sarah walked quietly out of the room and down the stairs to the kitchen.

"Make a tray up, Mrs. Lloyd. Something light. We must get him to eat. Where's George? I want him to fetch Doctor Williams. There's no improvement that I can see."

The cook, noticing the tears welling up in her mistress' eyes said, "You go back upstairs, Mrs. Lewis, and I'll send the tray up with Mary. George will go right away for the doctor."

Sarah climbed the stairs slowly. That pit will be the death of him, she thought. He's done nothing but worry since that letter came from Bristol with the news that from now on the Navy is only going to build oil fired ships. First it was getting the contract, and then there was all the work involved in retaining it and now it looks as if he will lose it anyway.

At the mid-day meal in the kitchen, the main topic of conversation was the state of the master's health.

"She'll be a widow before long, you mark my words," said George.

"Now, now!" scolded the cook. "He's just drank half a cup of my beef tea and I'm going to make a chicken broth for this evening. A bit of rest and good food and he'll be back on his feet again."

The butler shook his head but didn't say any more for he saw the look on Mrs. Lloyd's face. He knew more than the rest of them because he had overheard the doctor and the mistress talking at the bottom of the stairs.

"It's too early to say yet, Mrs. Lewis. We'll see what the next few days will bring. Bed rest, a light diet and no talk of the colliery."

But George had heard it all before and didn't see any hope in what had been said.

They ate the rest of their meal in silence. Every one was subdued, for the gravity of the master's illness had cast a shadow over the household.

On her way home that evening, Carrie, as she had promised her mother-in-law, called at May's mother's house.

"It's nice to see you, come in. We have a visitor," called out Nellie Evans to her daughter as she ushered Carrie into the middle room.

"Hello, Mrs. Price, how are you? Have you heard from Dafydd?" asked May who was wedged in the old wooden armchair by the fire.

"You look well. How long before the baby?"

"Only a few weeks now. But did you get a letter?"

"Yes, but not much in it, as usual. They seem to be all right. Wanted to know how you are. That's why I've come. I can write back and say that all is well by the look of you. I've got some other news too"

"What's that?" asked Nellie who was always interested in the latest gossip.

"Mr. Lewis the coal owner is very ill."

"When was this? What's the matter?"

"A few days ago, heart attack. He hasn't really improved."

"Well that must have been a shock for Mrs. Lewis. She's much younger than him though."

Ignoring the second remark, Carrie replied, "It was. She spends a lot of time by his bedside. They are very devoted."

"That's not what I heard," said May from the fireplace.

"What do you mean?" demanded her mother.

"I was told that John Parry B.A. spends a lot of time at Rock House."

"Mrs. Lewis is interested in the choir. They both like music. They play the piano together, that's all. So don't you go spreading any rumours," said Carrie indignantly.

But that's not what the maids say, thought May as she kept her own counsel. Changing the subject she asked, "Did Dafydd tell you about the mud? I don't know how they survive in such awful conditions."

The three women discussed the war, but after a few minutes, Carrie excused herself.

"I'll have to hurry as it is. There was a lot of washing today and I've got Emlyn's tea to make."

Chapter Fourteen

The men might identify with the conditions under which the other side lived but the generals never forgot that they were the enemy. Trench warfare was beginning to be defined. Thus as soon as conditions allowed, the orders came down the line to start up the night raids again. The soldiers knew this was the case as soon as the sergeant appeared in their bay.

"They're after volunteers again," said one of the men as soon as he saw the sergeant. "I wonder what it is for this time?"

"Gather round, you men," called the N.C.O. "There'll be a big raid tonight. High Command needs intelligence on the deployment of enemy troops in this area. The mortar boys will soften the Hun up first. Then we go in. We've got scouts to cut the wires and they'll direct us in. We want identification of enemy troops and information on the state of their defences"

"Have we any choice?" whispered the same man to his mate.

"Speak up, man. Let's all hear what you've got to say."

"Um. Do we take prisoners, sergeant?"

"I take it from that, Jones, you're volunteering. Prisoners are always useful. We might get extra information from them. Besides, they would be proof that you actually went on the raid. Wouldn't they, soldier?"

"Yes, sergeant."

As expected the whole bay volunteered. The artillery co-operated and for once the bombardment ended just as they were about to cross into no man's land. The scouts led them through gaps in the wire that had been created by the mortar bombardments, and this meant that a number of them could cross together. But this was the easy part - the worst was yet to come.

Will the Hun keep his head down long enough? Dafydd asked himself as he crouched his way across. By now his eyes could pick out the sand bags on top of the enemy's forward trench. We're nearly there. Where the hell are the bombers?

As if on cue, two throwers and two carriers scuttled past him and hurled their grenades high into the air and over the parapet. As the grenades exploded the men charged. They killed some Germans and captured others. The scouts managed to get these and their equipment back across no man's land to the British trenches. So far everything seemed to be going to plan. Then the patrol came under fire from enemy soldiers further down the line.

"Time to go, men," shouted the sergeant. "Get out all of you, get out!"

"Jack, never mind him. Come on, get back!"

"It's your lucky day, man," said Jack as he pushed the terrified German roughly to the bottom of the trench and followed Dafydd.

By now the land was erupting around them as the enemy gunners got their range, they weaved their way back through the wire just as a mortar exploded no more than twenty yards away. They were flung to the ground as debris flew everywhere. Within minutes they were struggling to their feet, oblivious of the lacerations they had received.

Got to get back, got to get back, the words went over and over in Dafydd's mind as he lurched forward towards his own lines. He felt someone grab hold of him and support him as he struggled on. Some British soldiers had left the relative safety of the trenches and were bringing in the wounded.

The two pals had got off lightly. The explosion had dazed both but they didn't have any real injuries. Cuts and bruises would soon heal but in daylight a cut on Dafydd's cheek looked deep and nasty.

"Sergeant, come and have a look at this," yelled the corporal. "I think it needs stitching."

"Mm, you may be right there. Get yourself sorted out at the Dressing Station and be back by yesterday."

Dafydd had been cleaned up and stitched when a shuffling line of men came in. At the front was the only sighted soldier. On his shoulder rested the hand of the man behind him. Dafydd saw that this was the pattern along the whole line. Some men had heavy bandages across their eyes. Others just looked unseeing down to the ground.

"Poor bastards," said Dafydd to a man near him. "What's happened to them?"

"Mustard Gas," replied the man. "The Huns have a new weapon."

It wasn't many weeks before the cry of "Gas!" would send shivers down Dafydd's spine as he struggled to pull on his newly issued gas mask.

The Germans manufactured the poison in makeshift laboratories near the battlefield. It was a vicious substance that blinded and burnt but it didn't always reach the right target. If the wind changed direction then the gas could be blown back across the lines from whence it came and so it was an unreliable front line weapon.

Back at the bay there was something to celebrate – Jack was a father. The mail had come through, only three weeks late this time!

"It's a boy. I'm a dad," he yelled as soon as he saw his friend.

"Read it, read it," he continued as he thrust the letter into his mate's hand.

The excitement wiped away the shuffling line from Dafydd's mind as the two of them celebrated the big event. That night he saw again the hidden side of Jack's character. It was relatively quiet. They had managed to eat their rations undisturbed and were sitting on upturned boxes chatting quietly, when Jack carefully pulled a card from inside his tunic. Catching a glimpse of it, Dafydd realized that it was one of those postcards he had seen with some of the other married men.

"Who's that for?" he asked.

"May of course."

"It's a nice card."

"Yes," and then more quietly so that Dafydd could only just make it out, "Roses for love and white heather for luck."

As spring progressed into summer the weather became dryer and life in the trenches was marginally more bearable. At least there were times when clothes were reasonably dry and the mud caked over as the water table level receded. But Dafydd didn't look at the landscape that he had envisaged in his dreams back in the valleys. Trees were blackened stumps on the edges of dark craters, which, more often than not, were filled with oily water. Paths were trodden mud and only if they were lucky were there duckboards to cross the worst of the muck. There were no birds to listen to, only the thump, thump, thump of the eight-inch howitzer or the rattle of machine guns. There never seemed to be any quiet. Somewhere within ear shot there was always the sound of gunfire. He, like the rest of his comrades, had become inured to sights that would have brought tears to the eyes of even the most hardened collier. German dead grotesquely staged around a gun post after a mortar attack didn't even merit a second glance. If they had been British perhaps Dafydd might have paused but even then he would not have felt any pity. Self-preservation mattered more than anything and his uppermost thought would have been – it's not me!

Like most British soldiers, Dafydd adapted to trench warfare. They'd been lucky in their part of the line for the Saxons had no more enthusiasm for combat than they did. So apart from the raids, the ordinary soldiers on both sides tended to keep to the unwritten rule of live and let live. If a soldier did anything silly like sticking his head above the parapet then that was a different matter. He was then fair game for the snipers. However, one spring morning, a big white board was hoisted up from the enemy's forward trench. Jack was at the loophole watching the line.

"Corp, come and have a look at this." He shouted and then read out slowly "Goodbye Tommies. We are being relieved by the Prussians. Give them hell."

"What does it mean?" he asked.

"That's put the kybosh on it," said the N.C.O. "The Prussians fight, really fight. They're some of the fiercest troops in the German army. No more easy life for us now."

At Brigade headquarters, the news was greeted with as much dismay and plans were hastily put together to counteract the expected onslaught. The army was short of shells and so they couldn't bombard the Prussians out of their trenches. Instead it was decided to blow them up from underneath. Tunnel warfare had become an acceptable battle tactic at headquarters.

Ex-miners were the obvious soldiers to tunnel under the enemy trenches and plant the bombs. Unfortunately, timing fuses were notoriously unreliable. If they were lucky, the miners got out before the enemy trench blew up. The ex-miners in the battalion were called upon to use their old skills. Thus Dafydd and Jack were once more on their knees, with picks and shovels in their hands digging their way underground. This time it was near the surface and through unstable layers of mud and rock not in the sedimentary strata of South Wales that had been laid down in the mists of time. Each painstakingly dug yard had to be shored up and even then the whole tunnel shook when a stray shell landed nearby.

"We'll cop it one day," said Dafydd as they paused and peered uneasily at the shaking boards.

"You might be right there," replied Jack. "All we can do is get through this as fast as we can and hope that nothing happens. Lucky this is fairly loose and easy to cut. I'm stripping to the waist, I'll be able to work quicker," and with that Jack started to pull his shirt up over his head.

"Bugger it's caught in this tag. Why we have to wear a string round our neck with a piece of cardboard on it, I don't know. They make such a fuss if it's mucked up, I'd better take it off."

"I'll do the same," said Dafydd as he took off his shirt and vest and threw them with his tag in a heap behind him. "Give me your clothes and I'll put them on the pile. We'll pick them up on the way back."

In the dim light, Jack hacked away whilst his mate came behind shoring up. Others passed timber down the narrow tunnel and scooped out the debris. They hadn't much further to dig when suddenly there was a tremendous bang and a curtain of mud and rock cut off Dafydd's vision. Boulders crashed into him pushing him down to the floor.

He yelled "Jack! Jack!" as he was engulfed by the maelstrom.
Mud flowed into his open mouth silencing the cries for his friend who had been buried by the worst of the slide.

"Get them out!" came the cry as the soldiers scrabbled with their bare hands in the dark.

"Where's the lantern? I've got a boot here! Someone help me pull."
A light appeared, as did extra hands that scooped out the dirt as fast as they could.

"Pull" came the shout. "Pull!"
Straining with effort, the man yanked as hard as he could and another dug frantically with his hands searching for the other foot.

"I've got it!" he yelled.
Together they pulled. There was no time to be careful. If they didn't get him out now, he would suffocate. Thankfully, there was some movement. Sensing it, they made one last great effort and as they tugged the body slid towards them.

"Pass him down, get him outside."

Not knowing whether they had rescued a corpse or not, the soldiers handled the body gently. Eventually they laid him down on open ground. One cleared his nose and mouth and bent over his face. Yes, he was breathing but only just. He was alive. Wrapped in a blanket, the still figure was stretchered to the nearest first aid post. There the stretcher-bearers left him as near to the large white bell tent as was possible. The ground was littered with the wounded.

At last it was his turn and he was carried inside. The doctor and his orderly were able to work unhindered on their unconscious patient. After ensuring that his airways were clear, the M.O. began his examination of his body.

"Just as I thought, his arm is broken," he said as he felt along the bone. "Got some splints?"

"Yes here."

"Hold him steady as I put this back into place and then we'll strap it up."

The two worked together quickly and efficiently. Broken ribs were bound, deep cuts stitched and the worst of the dirt cleaned off the young soldier's body. At last, they were finished but he still hadn't regained consciousness.

"I don't like the look of this," said the doctor as he examined again a nasty lacerated area on the head. "He's had a huge blow here. He could have a cracked skull. Time will tell I suppose. Do we know who he is?"

"No, there's no disc. There's nothing on him. All we know is that they brought him in from the Welsh Regiment."

Just then the orderly noticed a movement.

"Doctor, I think I saw his eyes flicker."

"You're right, he's coming round. With a bit of luck he might not be so badly injured after all. Hello, soldier, you're OK now. A few broken bones, but nothing that won't mend. What's your name, lad?"

"Jack, Jack," and then the eyes closed again.

There was nothing else to be done.

Stretching his aching back, the doctor said, "That's all we can do here for him. He'll have to be hospitalised. Tell the regiment where we've sent him and that his name is Jack something or other. They can sort out the details and pass them on. That's it then. Get him shipped out as soon as you can. On to the next poor blighter, I suppose."

A short time later, the still unconscious soldier was stretchered to a waiting ambulance and then with the other badly wounded he began the journey to the hospital that the army had set up in an old house some distance from the battlefield. Narrow tyres, rudimentary suspension and well-rutted roads all worked together to weave a nightmare for these badly injured soldiers. Involuntary cries were wrung out of even the most battle hardy as the vehicle lurched forever onwards. But to the young soldier lost in some other world, nothing mattered.

In the relative peace of the hospital he regained consciousness and over the next few weeks his broken body mended. But he spent long hours first lying on his bed and later sitting in a chair subsumed in his own thoughts. In the night, like many in the long row of beds, he cried out as he relived the horror. Always the same words escaped his lips.

Hospital routine worked around him. He did what was asked but always without any interest and in silence. He ate because he was told to. If no one said "Come on, eat up" the food was left on the plate. If he wasn't encouraged to wash, he didn't. To change his dressings, he had to be told to lift his arm or turn on this side or that. Nothing could be taken for granted.

"Hello, Jack. How are you today?" asked the doctor on his rounds. "Yes, your arm seems all right. Open and close your fingers. That's it. Now squeeze my hand. Tighter."
The patient listlessly followed instructions but there was no "How am I doing?" or "It doesn't hurt as much." He didn't utter a word and the expression on his face didn't change.

"Good man, now for your chest. Any pain when you breathe?"

Again, there was no answer. The doctor had to content himself with his own observations. He could see that the patient's body was healing, but his mind was another matter.

Turning to the nurse he asked, "Are there any details yet on who he is? If we had some we might be able to pull him back into this world."

"Nothing sir, they've been on to the regiment again but they're in the middle of that push on Festubert and men are going down like nine pins."

"If that's the case, we can't keep him here. In a short time we're going to need every bed we have and more. Arrange for him to be shipped back home. Send him to one of those rest places they're opening up. Back to Wales if you can wangle it. Something there might strike a chord. It must have been that blow to his head," the doctor muttered to himself as he walked on to the next bed.

The young nurse followed him. She was already hardened to the sight of the badly wounded although she had only been in France for a few months. She, like others of her generation, was a necessary part of the war effort. It had started in the Crimea, when women staffed front line hospitals and now in the twentieth century their presence in war was both needed and accepted. Being some distance away from the trenches she had not as yet faced the worst horrors but others, who had trained with her and posted nearer the battlefield, spent many nights picking their way through the debris of war to help bring out the wounded. And a stray bullet was no respecter of gender.

Chapter Fifteen

"Has the post come, Mam?"

"Been and gone, Carrie, but nothing for us."

"Oh, I wish he would write, just for us to know that he's all right."

"Has May heard from Jack?"

"No, I met Nellie on my way home. She said that May is so tied up with that baby that she spends all her time with him. Everything else seems to have gone out of her head."

"There you are then, the two of them haven't written," and then changing the subject Granny Price asked, "How was it at the Big House today?"

"No better, Mr. Lewis is still in bed. Doesn't seem to improve. John Parry B.A. called to find out how things were. Didn't stay long though according to Mrs. Lloyd."

"That's interesting, heard any more of those rumours that's been going around about him and Mrs. Lewis?"

"Now, Mam, don't you start too. But Mary the maid swears that there's something going on. I haven't had a chance to talk to Mrs. Lloyd when she's on her own. She'd know but wouldn't say any thing in front of the other servants. Madam is a very attractive woman and years younger than Mr. Lewis. If you ask me, he's always been tied up too much with that colliery. Paid all his attention to it and not given enough time to her."

Granny Price smiled to herself. She had achieved her objective and deflected Carrie's mind away from Dafydd. But deep down she wasn't sure that he was safe and breathed a sigh of relief when the postman passed their door. She was afraid for her grandson when there wasn't a letter – for they hadn't heard from him for weeks. But what would the news be if the postman knocked the door? A note from Dafydd or something much more sinister?"

News on all fronts was bad for the mining village of Morganton. With the colliery owner ill, there was uncertainty about the future of the pit on which their livelihoods depended and anyone who looked at the newspapers in the reading room of the Welfare Hall knew that the war was not going to be over for some time.

Emlyn had forced himself to climb the trip to the main road. He now had to stop every few paces to catch his breath – especially when walking uphill. And what were there but hills in this steep sided valley? His condition was obviously worsening, but something drove him to the reading room every day. He stood in front of the large wooden easel, which housed the newspapers for he felt that the reports of the war were his only link with his son.

Thank goodness the women didn't see them, he thought as he read the account of the Battle of Aubers Ridge. So many killed in such a short time. In twelve hours eleven thousand casualties! Oh, Dafydd, how I pray to God that you are safe. According to this, General Haig has sent them in again!

Emlyn didn't want to read anymore but his eyes were drawn back to the paper.

After four days of artillery barrage, on the night of May 15th, the

> *British infantry attacked the German lines. We can report that, after attack and counter attack over the following twelve days, the army has taken a length of the enemy's trenches. However, casualties were high on both sides.*

Emlyn slumped into the chair that stood besides the easel.

There's no hope for him. No hope, he thought as he allowed the tears to trickle down his cheeks. How long before the telegram comes? What will Carrie do? She'll be beside herself. Dafydd is our youngest and her favourite. And Mam? Hasn't she seen enough in her life?

It was an effort for Emlyn to compose himself but eventually he struggled to his feet, closed the newspaper and left the building.

Once outside, he started to walk towards Ebenezer. The chapel had always played a big part in his life but he didn't go through the front door to sit and pray for his son wherever he may be, instead he walked down the path to the vestry door. Once inside he sat on one of the old wooden benches and listened as, in his mind, Dafydd's voice filled the hall.

"Emlyn, Emlyn are you all right?" asked John Parry as he sat besides the old collier. "Is the dust bad today? You've been sitting here for some time."

"No worse than usual, Mr. Parry. I came here to listen to Dafydd. He loved the choir and he had such a magnificent voice."

"Had, Emlyn? Have you heard?"

"Oh no, it's me. I shouldn't read the newspapers. The news is so bad that I wonder if he survives."

"I know, my friend, I know."

The two men sat there in silence for a few minutes. From those few words, Emlyn knew that the choirmaster cared deeply about the fate of his son. He had always respected John Parry B.A. but simply because of his position and his education. Now he saw how much the choir members had come to mean to their conductor. He appreciated the genuine concern that the choirmaster felt for Dafydd, fighting for his survival on some battlefield in Northern France.

Without much enthusiasm, Sarah sat down at the breakfast table. She missed the physical presence of her husband, even if of late his contribution to any conversation had been small. He had always been in too much of a hurry to do little more than eat. But anything was better than seeing him lying listlessly on his bed. If there was an improvement in his condition, it was only very slight. There was little she could do except sit with him. Conversation tired him. Sometimes she read to him, but he didn't seem to be able to concentrate for long. Thus it wasn't surprising that an unexpected letter from her niece was opened immediately.

> Avon View,
> Clifton Gardens,
> Bristol.
> June
> 1915.

Dear Aunt Sarah,

> I'm writing because I must tell you my news. My training with the Red Cross is nearly finished and I've been asked if I'll nurse some of the soldiers sent home from the battlefields. I've been told that it won't be easy since they may be badly wounded. I said yes. Of course, Father wasn't very pleased as you can imagine! I'm sure that he thought that I wouldn't finish my training, but it's given a purpose to my life at long last. He keeps saying that women shouldn't see such sights and when I remind him that someone has to look after the men, he says "Yes, but not my daughter."

Sarah smiled to herself as she read these words and thought – certainly not his precious Louisa. Then looking down again she read on:

> At long last he has realized that I'm determined to put what I've learnt to good use and he said that if I must pursue this idiotic idea of mine then it'll be where he knows that I'll be safe. Anyway, I'm coming to Wales! And with his approval! The Marquess of Bute is setting up a small nursing home in a village to the north of Cardiff, near to his weekend retreat – Castell Coch (Is that right? I'm sure that that nice Mr. Parry will know). Of course father has arranged an open invitation for me at the castle. He doesn't know that I've no intention of

going. I just want to be like the other nurses and get on with my job.

Good, thought Sarah. That's less than twenty miles away. Louisa will be able to stay here when she has some time to herself. To have her company now would be marvellous. Let's see what else she has written. Oh! Not much by the look of it.

I've no more news of myself but what of uncle? I do so hope that he has improved – if only a little. Give him my love. I also send it to you my dear Aunt Sarah.

Louisa.

I must write back today to get more information, thought Sarah. Perhaps I'd better write to my sister for she'll know the details. Louisa is far too excited to be bothered with them.

Placing the letter on the table in front of her, Sarah finished her breakfast. Then getting up from her chair, she walked out of the room and made her way to the staircase to go up to tell her husband her news. Changing her mind at the foot of the stairs, she turned and went into the drawing room. There she sat down at her desk and taking out some paper began her letter to her sister in Bristol.

Events developed at a pace. It seemed that no sooner had the Marquess of Bute agreed to establish the hospital than it was ready. The furniture was stripped out of the rooms of the old house and replaced with iron bedsteads. A team of nurses was gathered together by the Red Cross and a local doctor was persuaded to lend as much time to the hospital as he was able to. No special facilities were installed, as it was to be a place for rest and recuperation rather than a nursing home for the badly injured.

Louisa's next letter to Sarah was written soon after she arrived in Cardiff and was full of praise for how much had been achieved in such a short time.

> *Bron Rhyw Hospital,*
> *Cardiff.*
>
> *Dear Aunt Sarah,*
>
> *We've been here nearly a week now and we're expecting our first wounded at any time. We've been very busy – we've scrubbed, washed and polished everything! Matron keeps saying that the greatest enemy of disease is cleanliness. We have four senior staff that are very experienced, but the rest are just like me – straight out of training. You should see our uniforms!*

That's Louisa, thought Sarah. Always thinking about clothes.

> *We wear long grey dresses with stiff white collars and white cuffs that we put on over the sleeves of the frocks. They almost reach the elbows. Then on top we have a huge white pinafore. We've got funny caps for our heads too. At least they're not as severe as the long triangular head dresses of the four sisters!*

Sarah couldn't help laughing out loud. I'll take this letter upstairs and read it to him. He might show some interest. Perhaps it'll even bring a smile to his face, she thought hopefully, but first let's see what else Louisa has to say.

> *We're living in the gatehouse. It's quite small but things will get better when we're really nursing for some of us will always be on duty so we won't be so crowded all the time. Matron and the sisters are using the servants' quarters in the house.*

Louisa living in such a small place! She complains that the rooms here are tiny. And scrubbing floors! What will her father say? She seems happy enough though – far happier than I am. My life lacked excitement before his illness, but now!
Sarah stared into space as she thought of what could have been and although she dutifully attended to her husband and didn't like seeing him so weak, she now knew that she did not love him and probably never had.

"Don't lose your freedom yet, Louisa," she whispered. "If you are true to yourself then you'll only marry the man you love."

As Sarah read her letter, the first of the wounded were arriving at Cardiff General Station. For many the journey had been horrific. A few could remember the stripped out carriages, the layers of stretchers and the handful of nurses who had done their best to see to their needs on the journey through France. Some, like Dafydd, had joined the train from a hospital and their wounds had already been treated. Others had been brought straight off the battlefield, caked in mud and dried blood. To even clean the wounds had been a nightmare for the nurses. There was only one small primus stove to heat all the water required on the train. The nursing staff had worked ceaselessly throughout the long journey to the port. The train had waited for hours at signals and in sidings for it was not given priority over other traffic. Some men died who could have been saved if they had reached the ships and medical help sooner. The emphasis was on getting soldiers and supplies to the front, not on returning the wounded.

Once on this side of the channel, they were at last given priority and were dispatched as quickly as possible to their home areas. At Cardiff, ambulances waited to meet the train. People stared in horror as the men were brought off. From the station the wounded were taken to a local school where they were assessed by medical staff and allocated to different destinations. A few of the less badly wounded were sent to the new Bron Rhyw Red Cross Hospital. Pretty young nurses waited to greet them but nothing stirred in the loins of these battle weary men. Even the walking wounded were too far away from recovery to pay even the slightest attention to what was happening around them. Most just slumped on their beds without even attempting to take off boots or clothing.

"I'm going to see the M.P.," said Carrie after the postman had passed yet again. "I can't stick this waiting any longer. I want to know one way or the other. Watts Morgan M.P. was responsible for getting Dafydd to enlist and he ought to know what's happened to him."

"Ssh now, Carrie, that'll be no good. He'll be in London now, at Parliament."

"But, Mam, we can't go on like this."

"Yes we can. We mustn't give up hope."

"I don't know if Dafydd is alive or dead. Is he injured or still fighting? Sometimes I think that he'd be better off dead.

At least then I'd know that he'd be in Heaven and singing with the angels. George, the butler says that life in the trenches is terrible. They haven't even got clean water to drink, let alone make a nice cup of tea."

"I know, love. I know. But don't you go believing everything that that butler says."

Carrie didn't seem to hear what Granny Price had just said and carried on talking about the water.

"Contaminated by oil. Strike a match and you can set fire to it. Oh, Dafydd, where are you?" And on yet another day the tears rolled down her cheeks.

This time it was Emlyn's turn to comfort her for he had been standing in the passage listening to the two women.

What will she do when the news does come?

Knowing more about the progress of the war than the women, deep inside him Emlyn felt that his son must be dead.

"Collect the bowls, nurse," said the sister. "We've breakfast to serve and then we've to tidy the ward before the doctor makes his rounds. Matron will expect everything in its place."

Louisa pushed the big wooden trolley, stopping at each bed to collect the enamel basins. She carefully tipped the dirty water into one of two bowls she had placed on the top shelf and then stacked the empty ones on the bottom.

"You haven't washed, have you," she said gently as she looked at the clear water in the basin on the small table by the side of one of the beds. "Shall I help you or will you do it for me now and I'll come back for your bowl after I've collected the others?"

Blank eyes stared back at her.

You poor man, she thought. What horror have you lived through?

Encouragingly, she smiled at the soldier and as he looked back at her some sign of recognition seemed to rest for a second on his face. It was as if something had stirred in the deep recesses of his mind but he was not quick enough to catch it. The young nurse watched as he turned to the bowl and started to go through the motions of washing his face and hands. Another day in Bron Rhwy Red Cross Hospital had begun.

The weather was kind in that early part of the summer and in the afternoons the men were encouraged to sit outside in the grounds. Some were already responding to the treatment. Not so much to the medical attention but to the rest and the tranquillity of their surroundings. The horrors of war receded and they began to think of other things. Physical wounds were obviously healing. Scars didn't seem to matter so much and even lost limbs were not a total disaster as bodies adjusted and compensated a little. They formed friendship groups and sat talking together in the afternoon sun. They spoke of going home and picking up the threads of their lives, but one young soldier sat alone. With encouragement, the rest sometimes got him to sit on the edge of a group. But other times he was lost in the dark tunnels of his mind.

On one such afternoon, when the men were reminiscing, the talk turned to that first Christmas in the trenches when the opposing sides had tried to out sing each other.

"Of course we could make more noise than the Huns," said one of the patients. "Hadn't been singing in the choir for years for nothing. We sang our lungs out."

"Aye, that was a night," remarked another. "Remember when we burst into Welsh and ended up singing My Hen Wlad Fe Nhadau. That foxed them all right."

With that one of the group began to sing softly. The talking tapered off as one by one they joined in. They went from one song to another, from the songs of the war to the hymns of the chapel and finally, as a feeling of hiraeth overcame them, to the haunting melodies of traditional Welsh ballads.

> *"By her image I am haunted*
> *Through the watches of the night*
> *Better to declare my passion,*
> *Than in silent anguish pine.*
> *Beam upon me, a star of beauty*
> *Promise quickly to be mine."*

Sang a solitary tenor voice.

"It's Jack! Well I never. He's not dumb. What a voice!" One of the men got up and limped over to the young soldier.

"That was great, boy. Where did you learn to sing like that?"

But the veil had descended as quickly as it had lifted. There was no answer and the singer stared into the distance with his unseeing eyes.

This miracle, for to the patients it was little short of one, was the main topic of conversation for the rest of the day.

"You should have heard him, nurse. Beautiful it was."

"At least we know that he is able to speak. All we've got to do now is to encourage him to sing more," she replied. "We'll soon have him talking then."

"Why don't you sing to him? I bet that you have a lovely voice."

"You never know, I might just do that," laughed Louisa as she moved on to the next bed.

The thought of getting Jack to sing intrigued her and by the next morning she was determined to give it a try.

"Good morning, how are you feeling today?" she said as she put the bowl on the table by the side of the bed. "You have a wash and I'll tidy the bed."

As she folded blankets and sheets she began to hum and this naturally turned into singing. Her clear soprano voice filled the ward. The young man stopped and listened. Then he too began to sing. The others listened appreciatively as the two sang in perfect harmony.

Louisa's mind was working all the time she sang.

I know that voice, she thought, but from where? And then it all came back to her – Ebenezer chapel, the singing festival, the soloist on the balcony. She searched his face for familiar features. Was it him? The voice was the same but this one is so thin, everything pinched, the lines around his eyes… How can I be sure? I don't know his name. I must find out.

The song came to an end and as the nurse moved on to the next bed, there was silence as the young man lapsed back into his inner hell.

That evening, Louisa wrote to her Aunt Sarah for she felt that someone in Morganton must know the name of her patient.

"Mr. Parry," announced George as he ushered the visitor into the drawing room.

"I'm so glad that you could come," said Sarah as she rose to greet the choirmaster.

"I gathered that it was rather urgent so I came as quickly as I could. What can I do? It's not about Mr. Lewis is it?"

"No, there's no change. He doesn't seem to improve, just lies there." Then after a few seconds she carried on, "I received this letter from my niece, Louisa, this morning. She is a Red Cross nurse at a hospital for the wounded near Cardiff. It has some news in it that I would like you to read."
Puzzled, John Parry took the sheet of paper and read:

> ... We have a patient who is very badly shell shocked and, because of some mix up in France, we don't really know who he is. He doesn't speak and is either unable to, or unwilling, to tell us his name. Yesterday, some of the less ill soldiers were sitting outside in the sunshine and he, as usual, sat some distance away - a solitary figure staring into nothingness. The men started singing to pass away the time and to everyone's surprise, the young man joined in as they sang a haunting ballad called The Maid of Sker.

At this, John Parry's pulse quickened. The song, his favourite, could it be?

> This morning, I sang as I helped him wash and made his bed. Again he joined in and, Aunt Sarah, I think that I recognized his voice. Remember the Singing Festival, the man who sang the solo, but he doesn't look the same person to me. His face is so thin and drawn.

The choirmaster looked up excitedly and said, "Can it be Dafydd Price? Oh, Sarah, let's hope it is."

This is the first time he's called me by my Christian name and he hasn't noticed, she thought as he read on to the end. "John," she said gently as he finished. "Can you go to see if it is him? Cook has told me how worried Carrie Price is about her son. I don't want to build up her hopes and then have them dashed because Louisa has made a mistake."

"Of course, I'll go tomorrow. I agree we must keep this news to ourselves. I sat with Emlyn in the vestry the other day and I think that he has given up hope. Oh please, God, let it be the boy."

They spent a few more minutes talking about the letter and then, lapsing back into formality, John Parry enquired about her husband's health.

"No, I'm afraid that he doesn't seem to improve. Dr. Williams says that he must have bed rest and that we are to encourage him to eat. But whatever the cook prepares for him doesn't seem to tempt him."

"And the colliery? Who is running it now?"

"We have a manager. The coal is being dug out and then sent to Cardiff docks for the navy, but for how long we're going to have the contract I don't know. We are under strict instructions not to bother Mr. Lewis with any problems. I'm sure though that the pit is on his mind all the time."

"Yes indeed, it must be a worry to you all," replied the choirmaster as he prepared to take his leave. "I'll find out the nearest station to the hospital and catch an early train. As soon as I'm back I'll come straight here. If the patient is Dafydd then we can break the news to his family. If not then we keep it to ourselves and we haven't raised their hopes. Until tomorrow, Mrs. Lewis."

It had been raining when John Parry left Morganton but once the train had passed out of the valleys the clouds had dispersed and the weather had cleared up. The railway station was about a mile and a half from the hospital and walking that distance in the wet would not have been very pleasant as John noticed that there were only a few cottages along the route and nowhere really to take shelter.

That's it, he thought as he turned the bend, Castell Coch. It's like something out of a fairy tale with its round towers and their pointed roofs. There must be a tremendous view from those windows, perched as it is on the side of that hill. It would be nice to see it close to, but perhaps another day. I've more important things to do today. The hospital can't be far now.

Within a few minutes he was turning into the gate. Walking up the drive he noticed well-tended lawns and flowerbeds.

There can't be any sheep here, he thought wryly, or they wouldn't last. No wonder the colliers don't do anything with their gardens except keep chickens in them. Sheep eat everything. They can jump back walls when they have a mind to and it's impossible to confine them to the mountains.
John Parry had never quite got over the scene that met him, when he first came to the valleys, of sheep walking in the street.

Once inside the old house he was ushered into matron's room. He used all his charm as he explained his mission

"We would indeed be very pleased to know who he is, Mr. Parry. Undoubtedly the regiment will identify him in due course but if we knew for certain then news of his family, or perhaps a visit, may put him on the road to recovery."

"Yes indeed, I agree with you. That's why I've come this morning. Would it be possible for me to see him?"

"Of course, I'm sure that you will handle this sensibly. Come I'll take you to the ward."

With trepidation, John Parry followed her up the stairs and into a large room with a row of half a dozen beds – only one of which was occupied as the other patients were gathered round a table at the far end, chatting, playing cards and generally passing the day away. Without hesitation, the matron marched up to the man who sat on his bed staring at a spot on the opposite wall. The choirmaster followed and looked down at the soldier.

At first, he thought it's not him. I've come here for nothing.
He had expected to see the Dafydd that he knew – strong arms, wide shoulders smiling eyes…Gradually realization dawned on him. This drawn and emaciated form was Emlyn's son!

"Dafydd," he whispered. Then more loudly "Dafydd, Dafydd Price."
 But there was no response.

"It's him," he said turning towards the matron. "But how did he come to be like this?"

"We don't know what horrors he's been through. If only we could reach him. The only thing he seems to respond to is music and then not always."

I know what I'll try, John Parry thought. Startling matron, he announced "Now men we'll have The Maid of Sker. Dafydd Price will sing the first verse." He raised his arms as if conducting Ebenezer choir. "One, two, three" and as he indicated for the tenor to come in, the young soldier began to sing his favourite ballad. The choirmaster could feel the tears running down his own cheeks as he thought, thank God we've found him, but are we too late?

At the end of the first verse the young man stopped singing. He looked as if he was listening and John Parry prayed that the voices of the choir filled his mind. Then the soldier's eyes lost their life, his body became still and he concentrated yet again on that spot on the wall. Matron gently touched John Parry on the arm and together they quietly left the ward.

Once back in her office, she said, "You are certain, Mr. Parry, about who he is?"

"Without a doubt. There is only one person I know that has such a fine tenor voice. He's Dafydd Price all right. He's from Morganton. Joined the Welsh Regiment last winter and has been in France since. His family hasn't heard from him for some time. I know that they are very worried."

" Now that we know his name, I'll make sure that all the records are put straight but can I leave it to you to tell his relatives?" asked the matron.

"Of course, I'll see them as soon as I can. They'll probably insist on coming to visit him. Perhaps the sight of them will have some effect." Then looking at his pocket watch, he stood up. "I've a train to catch. I must be on my way soon. Before I go can I see the young nurse? I want to thank her for being so observant."

"Yes, I'll send for her. But there is one other thing – who is Jack? It's the only spoken word we have had out of him and he responds to it as if it's his name."

"His best friend, Jack Davies, a married man with a young child. Do you know anything about what's happened to him?

"I'm sorry, we know no more than the name."

Morganton at last, thought John Parry as the train pulled into the station. He'd already let out the leather strap to open the window and as the carriage came to a stop he turned the outside door handle. He pushed the door outwards and stepped onto the platform. Walking quickly to the gate, he thrust his ticket into the stationmaster's hand. Then he hurried up to the main road where he barely acknowledged the greetings of the townsfolk.

I've got no time to talk. I must tell Sarah and then work out what we are going to say to the Prices, he said to himself as he turned up the hill on his right and walked as quickly as his lungs would allow him to Rock House.

"Is Mrs. Lewis in, George?" He asked, knowing full well that she was as he could hear her playing the piano.

"Yes, if you'll come this way, Mr. Parry."

Sarah stopped playing when she heard the door opening and on seeing John she stood and went over to him.

"Is it?" she asked.

Not wanting to reveal any information that might lead to gossip. He simply nodded.

"Thank you, George, that will be all."

"Yes, madam," and the butler left the room, closing the door behind him.

"Oh, John, thank goodness!" she exclaimed as she walked towards him with her arms stretched out in front of her.

Clasping her hands and with his voice full of emotion, he said "Louisa's got sharp eyes. I didn't recognize him at first. He's so drawn and thin. What he's been through, I don't know."

"The important thing, John, is that we've found him. He's lucky in a sense; he's coming home to his family. Lots are not. Is he badly wounded?"

"No, his wounds are healing but his mind…"

"There then, that's less to deal with. Think if he had lost a leg. How would the family manage?"

"His parents, we must tell them and put them out of their misery."

"I think that you had better go to see them on your own. They'll be more at ease then. They can't have the grand Mrs. Lewis descending on them, can they?"

John responded to the lightness in her voice with a smile and said, "You are right, we must concentrate on the positive side. I'll go straight to Edmund Street and tell them the good news."

Yet he was reluctant to take his leave of her, as he was ever conscious of holding her hands.

"Come, John, it's only right that they are told immediately. Have tea with me tomorrow and tell me about your reception at the Prices then."

Reluctantly, he let go of her hands and turned to leave the room.

"Hello, Mr. Parry," said Emlyn in surprise when he opened the door. "Have you news of the choir? Will you come in?"

"I will, Emlyn, but it's not about the choir that I've called. It's something more important than that. Is Mrs. Price in?"

"Which one? They're both in the front room sewing. There are garments everywhere in there. No room for us to sit down. Come into the middle kitchen, though what Carrie will say taking visitors in there I don't know."

The two men walked down the short passage and into the door on the right.

"Please sit down, Mr. Parry."

"Thank you, can you get the two ladies in here because they need to listen to what I have to say."

Puzzled, Emlyn went to fetch them. The choirmaster looked around as he sat on the high-backed wooden armchair in front of the now empty grate. His eyes admired the large rosewood chest of drawers standing against the far wall.

What a lovely piece, he thought, and so strange to see it in a miner's cottage amongst this ordinary pine furniture. He could hear the sound of Emlyn's voice in the next room.

"Carrie, Mam, John Parry B.A. is here. He wants to see the three of us. He's in the other room. Put down your sewing quickly."

"Why did you take him in there? What does he want?" Puzzled, Carrie looked at her mother-in-law. "Oh, Mam, it's not about Dafydd, is it?"

"Now, now, Carrie, how could he know anything about our boy? It'll be about the choir. He'll ask us to make some fancy clothes for them. Come on we'd better see what he wants," said Granny Price lightly but deep down she thought that her daughter-in-law could well be right and she didn't expect good news.

John rose as the ladies entered.

"Please don't get up, Mr. Parry. Mam you sit on the other side of the fireplace. Emlyn, have you got a chair? Yes, good then I'll sit here. Now what can we do for you?"

"I've a story to tell you all. This morning I visited a hospital near Cardiff..."

And so he proceeded to tell the family about finding Dafydd.

"He's safe, he's safe!" Carrie repeated as the tears streamed down her cheeks.

Emlyn went over to her and drew her to him as he thanked God for the news he had never expected to hear.

The ever practical, but non the less grateful, Granny Price asked, "How bad is he?"

"Physically, he's recovering. It's his mind. He doesn't speak but we know that he can for he's just started to sing again. With rest and his family to look after him, I'm sure that he'll get well."

"I'm going to fetch him, Emlyn, tomorrow."

"Sh, Carrie, we know that he is safe, Mr. Parry will find out for us when Dafydd can come home. It sounds as if he's not well enough yet. Perhaps we can go and visit him. How's that?"

"I'll see what I can arrange, Mrs. Price. He's still ill but now that they know who he is, I'm sure that the doctors and nurses will make him well again. Mrs. Lewis's niece Louisa has promised to take special care of him and since she knows Morganton, I've no doubt that she'll get him interested in life again." Then, rising from his chair, he continued, "I'm glad that I've been able to give you such good news. I've been out since early this morning and its time I went home."

"Oh, Mr. Parry, I haven't offered you a cup of tea!"

"It's all right, Mrs. Price. You have much more important things to think about."

"Good morning, Dafydd. How are you feeling today?" asked the nurse brightly as she put the bowl on the cupboard. "I'm Louisa. I've seen you before in Morganton. Do you remember?"

The young man looked at her.

"Louisa," he repeated slowly as he stared at her for the first time with seeing eyes and then the tears began to flow down his face. "Oh Jack, oh Jack," he whispered as he cried.

She put her arms around him and comforted him as best she could, knowing that the healing process had begun.

Chapter Sixteen

That afternoon, John Parry once again made his way up the hill to Rock House but this time at a much more leisurely pace. By now the whole village knew of Dafydd's safe return from the war and everyone he met wanted to know if there was any more news. One of these was Nellie Evans, May's mother.

"Isn't it good news, Mr. Parry, but what about Jack?"

"I don't know any more, Mrs. Evans. The only one I've seen is Dafydd and he is in no fit state to tell us anything."

"It's such a worry. May doting on that baby and not a word about his father."

"Don't give up hope. I know that Emlyn nearly did – but look what's happened."

"I suppose you are right, but no news, no letter, and they say that the newspapers are full of lists of soldiers who have been killed. I don't know, I've got this bad feeling..."

John Parry could do nothing more than try to reassure her again but it was a half-hearted attempt since he remembered the matron's words – he cries out in his dreams, the same two words Jack, Jack.

As John turned into the grounds of Rock House, George, the butler, was hurrying towards him.

"It's Mr. Lewis, he's taken a turn for the worse. I'm going for Doctor Williams."

John Parry walked quickly up to the front door and waited impatiently until one of the young maids answered his knock.

"Madam's upstairs, Mr. Parry Will you go up or wait in the drawing room?"

"Down here. Don't disturb your mistress. She has enough to do at the moment. I'll stay until Doctor Williams has been in case I can be of any help."

"This way then, if you please, " she replied ushering him through the hall and into the empty drawing room.

He stood for some time in the large bay window watching the drams carrying the spoil up the mountain to the tip at the top.

At what cost, he thought? Men losing their lives underground or to the dust. Young widows forced to take any job to maintain their families and thus destined for an early grave. Now even the colliery owner himself succumbing to coal's deathly grip.

His reverie was disturbed by a commotion in the hall.

"I'll go straight up," a man's voice said.

Then he heard footsteps on the staircase and the sound of feet walking across the landing. Unable to restrain his curiosity, he opened the drawing room door and stood in the doorway listening. He thought he heard the sound of a woman crying. Then George came down the stairs and when he saw the choirmaster shook his head.

"He's gone, another heart attack," the butler said softly as he walked towards the kitchen.

John didn't know whether to go or stay but he couldn't allow Sarah to be on her own at such a time. Then he heard sounds from the landing and he recognized Dr. Williams' voice.

"There was little we could do, Mrs. Lewis. Your husband's heart was very weak. Even if he had lived, he would have been an invalid. He certainly couldn't have run the colliery again."

"Yes that pit," came the bitter reply. "Without it what would he have done?" And with that she started to cry again.
The choirmaster had to force himself to stay where he was for his instinct was to run up the stairs, take her in his arms and comfort her. He remained there for some minutes, straining to hear what was being said upstairs but the two had retreated into the bedroom. At last, he again heard the sound of footsteps walking along the landing. The doctor's arm supported Sarah as the two came slowly down the stairs.

Noticing the visitor, Doctor Williams said, "Ah, Mr. Parry, just the person. I suppose you have heard the sad news. Unfortunately, I must be off. I've other patients to attend to. But with you here, I won't worry so much about Mrs. Lewis." Then turning towards her he added, "Come, my dear, sit in here with John Parry. I'm sure he'll do his best to look after you for me."
And with that Doctor Williams hurried to the front door.

"John, he's dead!" Her voice trailed away in disbelief.

"Come, Sarah, sit on the sofa. I'll ring for George and get you a cup of tea."
Some minutes later, sipping slowly, she regained some of her composure.

"What am I to do?" she asked. "I must contact my brother-in-law, he will know."
Just then there was a loud knock on the front door and a few seconds later the Reverend Evans was announced.

"My deepest sympathy, Mrs. Lewis. I came as soon as I heard. The Doctor called in on the way to the surgery. There's much to be arranged – but first I must go and pay my respects," he said. Then he hurried out of the room and up the stairs.

Seeing that Sarah was badly affected by this loud intrusion, John went over to her and put his arm around her shoulder. She cried softly for a few minutes but eventually, taking comfort from his presence, composed herself in time to hear heavy footsteps descending the stairs. She sat upright waiting for the next onslaught.

As he entered the drawing room The Reverend Evans began speaking excitedly, "A funeral fit for a man of Mr. Lewis' status. We must have a service at Ebenezer, the choir singing at the graveside. Yes, yes – the miners must be given time off. Leave it all to me, leave it to me. I'll call in on the undertaker on my way home. My condolences again, my dear lady." And without waiting for their comments, he left.
The two looked after him in disbelief.

"I'm so sorry, Sarah, he means well I suppose."

"Don't worry, in his own way, he's only trying to do the best for my husband. They were very much alike you know. Both were very intense. They would spend hours arguing over some obscure biblical point. I think the minister feels a loss too – but of course the formidable Reverend Evans cannot show it."

How can she be so charitable at a time like this, thought John Parry. Then he said, "You don't have to have such a funeral. It could be smaller. A service here at Rock House, and then a small gathering at the graveside."

"No, John, the minister is right. My husband was the most important man in Morganton and he'll be buried in a fitting manner," she said firmly as her eyes filled with tears once more.

Again he went over to her and put his arm around her shoulder. As the tears ran down her cheeks she began to wipe then away with her delicate handkerchief.

"Here, Sarah, use this," he said as he held out his.

"I must tell my sister and her husband, and Louisa of course."

Getting up she went over to her desk and wrote quickly. When she had finished she summoned the butler.

"See that these telegrams are sent, George."

"At once, madam. If you'll excuse me, but the staff were wondering if there was anything else we could do?"

She shook her head as she managed to half smile her thanks as her eyes filled again.

John Parry followed the butler to the drawing room door and said quietly, "Check that the undertaker knows and get him to come here tomorrow, not today. Tell the cook to make sure that Mrs. Lewis has something to eat this evening too."

"Leave it to us," the butler replied softly. "Don't worry we'll look after her until the family arrives."

"Do you want me to do anything, Sarah? " asked John as George left.

"There's nothing now that anyone can do. I think that I would like to be on my own. Its not that I'm sending you away but…"

"It is all right, I understand. If there's anything, anything at all, then send for me. You stay there. I'll leave you now," he said as taking one last look at her tearful eyes he left the room and went in search of the cook. He found Mrs. Lloyd in the kitchen.

"I'm sorry to intrude on your domain but…"

"Mr. Parry, isn't it dreadful news, such a shock. But don't you worry about Mrs. Lewis; we'll take good care of her. She'll need some time to herself and then I'll see if I can get her to eat a little. You go. She'll be all right."

The funeral was indeed fit for a colliery owner. Everyone of note in Morganton and the neighbouring valleys made sure that they were seen to play their part in the proceedings. Mr. Lewis' rich relations travelled from all parts of South Wales and Sarah's family came from Bristol. By right, since her husband had no near relations, Sarah Lewis' brother-in-law was in charge of the proceedings. The Reverend Evans, however, had other ideas. As the carriages arrived outside Ebenezer, both were seen directing the mourners and, since neither took any notice of the other, their contradictory instructions caused chaos on the road outside the chapel. Inside the minister reigned supreme. He somehow managed to extol the virtues of his recently departed friend to the overflowing congregation whilst at the same time preaching them a hell and damnation sermon. In deference to the visitors he spoke in English but, as the excitement mounted within him, he lapsed more and more into his native tongue. The local community thought nothing odd of this for often their every day language was a mixture of Welsh and English. Sarah's brother-in-law, having to suffer being preached at in a strange language by a man who he had made up his mind was an idiot, couldn't hide his indignation.

I don't want to know what he's thinking, thought Sarah as she hid a smile behind her veil.

At last, the long service was over. The ladies were taken back to Rock House whilst the hearse, followed by a procession of carriages, drove slowly through the village and up the long steep road to the hillside cemetery. The main road was full of people waiting to pay their last respects. Many wore black armbands and the men took off their hats as the coffin passed them. At the wind swept graveside the choir waited.

The horses pulled the hearse in through the gates of the packed hillside cemetery. They stopped at an unfinished brick vault at the front of one area of open ground. In the days following the funeral, the old stone mason would clad the sides and the top of the grave with polished black granite and then, to give the colliery owner as much importance in death as in life, carve a tall black obelisk large enough to be seen by every visitor. The Reverend Evans conducted the ceremony as if he was burying the most important person on earth and in a sense he was because without the colliery owner what did the future hold for that community? But it wasn't until the choir sang the Twenty Third Psalm that tears came to the mourners' eyes as the sense of loss overcame them. He had not been a bad employer, or a good one. He had simply been a businessman. He had recognized that the success of the mine meant a future for Morganton and its inhabitants. But who would come next? The new owner could be far worse.

The service over, the body was interred and the crowds dispersed. The mourners returned to their carriages and were driven directly to Rock House. The dining table, though large and fully extended, could not accommodate all in one sitting. John Parry, realizing this and intent on making Sarah's day as trouble free as possible, alighted quickly from a carriage at the end of the line and hurried up the gravel drive. He caught up with the minister just before the front door.

"Reverend Evans, I wonder if you could do Mrs. Lewis a favour?" asked John.

"Of course, Mr. Parry, what is it?" he replied visibly extending with importance.

"As you know, some of the people here have travelled long distances and in a couple of hours they will have to catch trains home. But others are from the locality and can stay longer. For this reason there will be two sittings at the table. Mrs. Lewis of course will be at the first but she needs someone to take charge of the second. She was wondering if you would oblige?"

"Tell her not to worry, I will be there," and with even more importance he marched in through the front door and down the hall to the drawing room.

That's a relief, thought John Parry. Sarah will be more at ease when she sees that her brother-in-law and the minister are not eating at the same table.

The kitchen at Rock House had been a hive of activity since early morning. All the servants were involved in the preparations for the funeral meal. As soon as the cook heard the ladies returning from the chapel she gave instructions for the maids to transfer the food into the dining room.

"Take in the pickles, sliced beetroot, the red cabbage, that pie, the cold meats... That's right, everything on this side of the kitchen. Mary, it's up to you to make sure that they are all laid out properly. I don't want any complaints from Mrs. Lewis on today of all days."

"It's all right, Mrs. Lloyd, we know what to do," said Mary patiently. "And before you ask, George has enough china and cutlery. Why don't you sit down for a bit? You've been on the go since first thing. There's nothing more for you to do until the gentlemen return."

Just then, the scullery door opened and Carrie walked in.

"I've come to help with the washing up, as I promised," she said. "You should have been down the main road. There were people on both sides. What a procession! You could have heard a pin drop when the hearse passed. The police sergeant and the two constables stood to attention and saluted. All the men took off their hats and nearly everyone had a black arm band."

"Morris the Draper must have made a tidy profit out of black ribbon," remarked Mrs. Lloyd, the cook.

"No, Mam put a stop to that," replied Carrie. "She still remembers some of the old tricks she learnt in Aberystwyth. She mixed a measure of gin with some honey and soft soap. Then used this to wash the bits of old ribbon and satin that people gave her. When they were dry she had me press them with a very hot iron. They came up like new!"

The men ate heartedly of the food that the cook had prepared. They piled their plates with cold meats, slices of pies, pickles and chutneys... .The maids walked to the kitchen and came back with more bread and butter, or baked ham, or another game pie. The conversation around the table inevitably rested on the future of the pit.

Who was going to run it? It obviously had to be sold. They looked at each other furtively as they tried to estimate a price.

Who could afford to buy it?
All were very attentive of Sarah's brother-in-law for who else was she going to turn to for advice at this terrible time?

When the last of the mourners had departed, there was only a small party left at Rock House – Sarah, her sister and brother-in-law, and Louisa.

"Yes, a good send off," said the man thoughtfully.

"Come now, Father, you could barely put up with the minister," said Louisa.

"Too full of his own importance and his sermon! How anyone understood it, I shall never know. All things considered, I suppose it went off well enough.

"How are you now, Sarah?" asked her sister considerately.

"Tired, glad that the funeral is over. It's strange but I feel empty."

"You need a good night's rest. Why don't you go to bed? I'll arrange for a hot drink to be brought up to you and I'm sure that Louisa will look in on you in a little while. She needs an early night. Tomorrow she returns to the hospital."

Chapter Seventeen

"Have I got everything now, Emlyn?" asked Carrie early the next day.

"I should think so. You've repacked your bag at least twice that I know of."

"I don't want to forget anything. I think I'll go now. I mustn't keep Miss Louisa waiting."

"The train isn't due for another half an hour and it is only a five minute walk to the station. You'll be far too early."

"Let her go, Emlyn. Both you and I would be the same if we were going to see Dafydd."

"You're right, Mam. How I wish we could have all gone."

"Don't fret now, Carrie will be enough this first time and if she can find a way for us to get from the station to the hospital more easily then we can all go the next time. Let's see her off now and remember to thank God that Dafydd will be coming home to us."

"Good morning, Mrs. Price, a big day for you," said the stationmaster as Carrie arrived at the station."

Yes indeed. I never thought that it would come. Has Miss Louisa arrived yet?"

"No, I've not seen anyone from the Big House. It's a bit early for the train yet," he said consulting his pocket watch. Then looking over Carrie's shoulder, he continued, "Wait a minute, is that George pulling into the yard? Yes, I can see the trap. You and Mrs. Lewis' niece travelling together then?"

Carrie didn't think that it was strange that the stationmaster, like everyone else in the village, should know where she was going for this was typical in the valley communities. The inhabitants took an interest in each other, pulled together in adversity, and celebrated everyone's good fortune. They lived close together in their terraced houses and this, with the interdependence of the miners underground, fostered a community spirit that softened their hard lives.

"There you are, Carrie," said Louisa when she entered the station. "Come with me to the booking office."

"Two first class tickets to Cardiff please," she said to the clerk.

"First class! I've never travelled like that before. Come to think of it I haven't had many rides on a train."

"Good, it's a treat for you then, Carrie. And that's how it should be on a day like this."

They waited for a few minutes on the platform until the train pulled in. Then the station master held open the door of a first class compartment and beamed at Carrie as she got in after Louisa. George saw to the young lady's case, the door was closed, the whistle blew and the train was flagged on its way.

Louisa watched as Carrie looked around. The large comfortable seats, the arm rests, the mirrors and the photographs were all duly noted so that their description could be relayed to her husband and mother-in-law when she got back home.

"Are you comfortable?"

"Yes, thank you, Miss Louisa."

"Good"

"If you don't mind me asking, but how is Mrs. Lewis today? Yesterday must have been an awful strain for her."

"Indeed it was, but she is coping quite well. I was sorry that I couldn't stay longer but I must get back to the hospital. My parents will remain for a few more days. Father will see to business matters and my mother will look after Aunt Sarah. Thank you for asking, Carrie, and I know that you were a great help in the kitchen yesterday."

"That's good of you to say so, Miss Louisa."

The pair lapsed into silence for a while as both thought about what lay ahead of them.

After a while Louisa said, "Now that we are on our own, I want to talk to you about Dafydd."

A look of alarm appeared on Carrie's face.

Seeing this, the young lady said, "Don't upset yourself. He's no worse, if anything a little better. But you do understand how ill he is? His wounds are healing nicely, but he's very thin, eats very little and hardly speaks. It's as if he's reliving his worse nightmare time and time again."

The older woman nodded slowly as she thought of her son.

Lightening her voice, Louisa continued, "I'm sure that your visit is going to make a huge difference. I'm only sorry that Mr. Price couldn't come with us, but it is a long walk from the station."

Carrie nodded her understanding, but she didn't mind how far it was for at the end of it was her son.

Dafydd, as usual, was sitting on his bed and staring at the opposite wall when his mother entered the ward. Louisa gently took her arm and led her to the young soldier.

Carrie stood there looking at him and then said softly, "Dafydd, my son."

He turned towards the sound, looked, his eyes focused on her face and the tears fell as he cried out "Mam, Oh Mam!"

Carrie took him in her arms and together they wept as Louisa withdrew quietly.

After a few minutes the lad pulled away from his mother's shoulder and, with some alarm in his voice, said, "Where's Dad and Granny Price?"

"It's all right. They're fine. It's just too far for them to walk from the station to here."

"Thank God for that. I couldn't bear it if something had happened to them, not after Jack"

"Dafydd, what happened to him? You know that he has a son?"

But the young man had lapsed into silence again.

At first Carrie was at a loss to know how to deal with this change in her son but drawing on the collective wisdom of the mining community, she opened her bag and said brightly, "I've brought you some things. There's some sweets from your father, socks from your Granny and John Parry B.A. has sent you a new song to learn."

Thus she recaptured his interest as they opened the parcels together.

At the end of an hour, Louisa, now dressed in her uniform, came towards them.

"I'm sorry, Carrie, but Dafydd needs to rest now. You've given him things to think about and they may open other doors in his mind."

Reluctantly the mother rose from the chair by her son's bedside.

"I've got to go now," she said. I'll tell Dad and your granny that you are getting better. Don't worry, we'll soon have you home."

She hugged him one last time and picking up her bag, she made her way out of the ward. The soldier's eyes followed his mother until she disappeared through the door.

After Carrie had left, Louisa went back to see Dafydd. She found him looking at the music that the choirmaster had sent him.

"Is that a new piece for the choir?" she asked.

"Yes."

"Is it something you know?"

"No."

"Try singing the notes," she said encouragingly.

Quietly he sang the tonic sol-fa, at first bar by bar and then line-by-line, as if he was in the vestry learning a new tune with the rest of the men. Louisa smiled to herself as she walked softly away. At last he had something else to think about and she felt certain that his recovery had began.

Carrie's homecoming in Morganton was marred by the news that had spread through the village almost before it had been received. The telegraph boy on his red bicycle had been seen stopping outside Nellie Evan's door. It could only mean one thing said the knowing neighbours as soon as they saw him. The boy handed the telegram to May. She opened it, read the first few words – we regret to have to inform you – and then she folded it up again quickly, clutching it in her hand.

"No answer," she managed to say as she turned and stumbled down the passage as the tears flowed from her eyes. Nellie, coming out of the back kitchen, took her daughter in her arms and held her tight as she sobbed.

Thank God for the baby. At least May has him, she thought as she led her daughter to the old rocking chair. "Let's see the telegram," she said softly as she took the piece of paper from May's hand… *missing in action, believed dead*, she read.

"Why him, Mam, why Jack?" And then again, "Dafydd has come home, why not Jack?"

"Sh, love. Sh," was the only reply Nellie could make.

The recently widowed Sarah Lewis was also thinking of her husband. She was, of course, sorry that he had died but she could not deny that she felt a sense of freedom. Over the last few months she had come to realize that her marriage was a mistake. Her attitude to life had changed. Louisa was right; the world was becoming a different place. Women didn't have to marry for position and wealth anymore. They could make their own way in society, even earn enough to support themselves.

Look how many are now involved in the war effort and having once tasted independence, they'll not go backwards when the fighting is over, she thought.

She had even witnessed her brother-in-law say proudly to others at the funeral that of course his family was doing what it could. His own daughter was nursing the wounded in a hospital in Cardiff. And this said by a father who previously wouldn't let his precious Louisa out of his sight!

What am I to do? Sarah thought. Sell the pit and go back to Bristol as my sister wants? Put a manager in and go back, or stay here? I don't know. I've got to make up my mind over the next few weeks. She looked around at the drawing room. Everything was so familiar. Would she want another family living here with someone else as mistress of Rock House? It was then that she realized that no, she didn't. This was her house – decorated and furnished to her satisfaction.

Life in Bristol is much livelier, she told herself. But so much shallower, she countered. Wives mistresses of their own large houses but not always of their husbands. Married couples met at breakfast and again possibly at dinner. They paraded their togetherness at parties and balls, and then slept in their separate beds. She'd even heard it said that in some of the grander houses the wife was not allowed to even enter her husband's bedroom in case he was entertaining! She shuddered - no, not another loveless marriage. At least here, there are real things to do. On times she had ached when she had seen the plight of young widows and their children. Now perhaps she could do something to help. Perhaps she could build a small cottage hospital in memory of her husband. She might even learn something about the running of the colliery. Yes, why not? There was plenty to do here in Morganton.

"Well, Sarah, have you made up your mind?" asked her sister at breakfast the next morning. "Are you returning with us to Bristol?"

"I don't think so, not just yet anyway. I want to make sure that the burial vault is completed properly first."

"Of course," said her brother-in-law. "That is right and proper. It must be a monument to his life."

"But afterwards, Sarah?" urged her sister.

"I don't know. I need some time to myself. I've no worries about the pit since the manager has run it for the last few months and I know if there are any difficulties then I can always call on you," she said as she looked directly at her brother-in-law. "Don't worry about me. If I do get lonely and need some company then I'll come to stay for a while; but at the moment I can't bring myself to sell what my husband put so much effort into. Perhaps in a little while, I just don't know."

"Well if that's what you want. You may change your mind in a few weeks, once everything has settled. You can come to us then."

Morganton was as busy as on any other weekday morning. Women were shopping and of course they were gossiping – for there was much to talk about.

"The telegram was to be expected after all this time with no news," said one of a small group of women standing on the pavement outside the Co-op.

"Yes," said another as she nodded her head. "And what about the death of the colliery owner? It has been a bad week for the village."

"Ill for such a long time, couldn't have been any coming for him; but he had a lovely send off. I was standing just here and I saw it all," remarked a third. "It was the longest procession I've ever seen."

The women stood silently for a few moments as they recalled the funeral. But there were other things to report and it wasn't long before one of them had the chance to impart her news.

"Did you know that Carrie Price has seen her son?"

"No" replied the others in unison.

"She's seen Dafydd. He's very weak they say and he doesn't talk much but I'm sure that he'll be all right when they get him home."

John Parry heard snippets of conversation as he walked up the main road but he didn't find out what he wanted to know. Since the funeral, he had stayed away from Rock House. He couldn't call on Sarah uninvited with her family there. He desperately wanted to know when they were going back to Bristol but who could he ask? Surely someone in this hive of information must know the answer. Then the thought struck him, Carrie Price.

She does the washing for Rock House and must be aware of the comings and goings – if only in the terms of the dirty laundry waiting for her. I'll walk down to Edmund Street to inquire after Dafydd. Carrie's bound to say something about what is going on in Rock House. Minutes later he was saved a journey as he saw Carrie Price walking on the other side of the street. He went over to ask how things were at the hospital.

"Good morning, Mrs. Price. I hear you've been to visit your son."

"Oh yes, Mr. Parry, had a shock when I first saw him but nothing that good food and being home won't put right."

"I'm glad to hear that. Did he say anything about what happened to him?"

"No, but it's something terrible and it is playing on his mind. His father says that if he could only talk about it then he would get better much more quickly. At the moment our Dafydd says very little about anything."

"Patience, Mrs. Price, patience. We don't know what horrors he's been through. Just remember that he's safe now."

"You are right, Mr. Parry but I won't be satisfied until I have him home. Not like poor May. Have you heard that she's had a telegram? Jack is never coming back. I'm going there next to sympathize with her. Nelly says thank goodness there's the baby. It must be awful, married such a short time and worst of all no body to bury."

They both paused for a minute as they thought of the young soldier lost on some battlefield in northern France.

"There's going to be a lot more," said John Parry, shaking his head. "The papers are full of the fighting and lists of our men dead or missing. We must thank God that we've got one of them back."

Seeing that Carrie's eyes were filling with tears he managed to both divert her thoughts and ask the question that was uppermost in his mind.

"How are things at Rock House?"

"Better than expected, but Mrs. Lewis was never one to show her feelings. She will find a big difference though when her family goes back to Bristol. Going tomorrow I understand. Cook has warned me because there'll be a lot of washing. I'll have to be there early to get it all done."

"Make sure that you don't work too hard now, Mrs. Price, for you must save your energy to look after my best singer. When he comes home, you tell him that I want him back in the choir."

"We won't be able to keep him away when he's better," she replied with a smile.

And on that happier note the two went their separate ways.

Chapter Eighteen

There's no time like the present, thought Sarah, as she returned to the drawing room after the departure of her sister and brother-in-law for Bristol. She went over to her writing desk, sat down and pulled out a sheet of paper from the drawer.

Rock House,
Morganton,
July 1915.

Dear Mr. Davies,
I know how busy you are managing the colliery but please come to see me here, at Rock House, tomorrow morning at ten o' clock as I would like to discuss the future of the pit. If this time is inconvenient please let me know and we can arrange another appointment in the very near future.
Yours sincerely,
Sarah Lewis

Sealing the envelope, she rang for her butler.
"Can you deliver this by hand please, George?"
"Certainly, Mrs. Lewis," he replied looking at the address. "I'll go straight away."
Now what else, thought Sarah. The stone mason; when George comes back he can take me in the trap to the cemetery and then this afternoon I'll start going through the

papers in the study. Perhaps I'll learn something before Mr. Davies comes.

She found the old stonemason carefully assembling the black granite slabs that made up the sides and top of the vault.

"Good morning, Mrs. Lewis," he said when he saw her. "A lovely piece of stone, just as you ordered."

"Yes I see that it is coming along nicely."

"There's just one thing, Mrs. Lewis, the lettering on the obelisk – gold I presume."

"That's right and you've got my inscription."
He nodded in reply.

"Good, when will this be finished?"

"The letters take the longest, another few days, a week perhaps."

Sarah was well satisfied. The monument to her husband would be in place far sooner than she expected. The Reverend Evans had been right. A vault was much more fitting than a grave and since no time was needed for the ground to settle, her husband's monument would soon look over the valley to the pit that had been his life.

At the hospital, Dafydd's progress was slow but sure. He regained some of his appetite for life, but he still wouldn't talk about Jack – not even to Louisa. His feelings for her had grown back strongly, but although she spent time with him – encouraging him to eat or to pass the day with the others - he felt that she did no more for him than anyone else in her care. He didn't realize that she was taking a special interest in him.

Only for Aunt Sarah's sake, she told herself in an attempt to deny her increasing emotional involvement with him. He was the first person her eyes sought as she entered the ward in the morning and the last she looked at when she went off duty.

"Good news, soldier," said the doctor one morning. "You can go home in a couple of weeks. I'll talk to matron about it."

Dafydd met this news with mixed emotions. Home meant an end to the war as far as he was concerned. He would be back with his family but there would be no Louisa, and he didn't want that. Not that he had a chance with her. Perhaps he'd be able to forget her then. Yes, that would be the best. But his resolve was always temporary for as soon as he saw her, he knew that she was the one he wanted.

Louisa too found herself strangely disappointed when she heard.

"Going home, that'll be nice," she managed to say to Dafydd. "You must have been looking forward to it for weeks."

"Yes, I suppose so. Mam and Granny Price will be pleased."

"Of course they will. They'll fuss over you and give you every thing you want. You'll be able to go back to the choir. What's the name of that song you're always singing?"

"The Maid of Sker."

"Where's Sker?" she asked.

"Don't know, must be in Wales somewhere."

Impulsively Louisa said, "I'll find out and if it's not too far away I'll take you there on my day off – if matron will allow it."

That evening, she asked the other nurses if they knew of a place called Sker. One remembered reading Blackmore's The Maid of Sker.

"I read it after Lorna Doone but it wasn't as exciting. If I remember it was a story about a little girl found drifting in a boat near Sker point. But I don't know where that is or if it really exists."

Bron Rhyw Hospital,
Cardiff.
August 1915.

Dear Aunt Sarah,

    How are you? I hope that you are not too sad.

    I'm writing to ask if you know anything about the Maid of Sker. Let me explain, Dafydd Price is to be discharged from here soon and I've said that I would take him to Sker. The problem is that I don't know where it is. He keeps singing a song called The Maid of Sker. I'm sure that Mr. Parry will know something. Can you ask him?

    I must dash now,

        Love,

        Louisa.

"Hello, John," said Sarah as she rose from her chair to greet him. "It's good of you to come."

"My pleasure but what's so urgent? Is something wrong?"

"No," she replied quickly. "I hope I didn't worry you but it's Louisa. You know how she gets carried away with things. Well she's promised to take Dafydd Price to Sker. There's only one problem, she doesn't know where it is! I felt sure that you would know. Do you?"

"That's an easy one to solve. Sker Point is just to the west of Porthcawl. You know, the seaside town."

"Yes," she replied hesitantly. "I've heard of that place but I've never been there."

"If Louisa wants to take Dafydd for an outing," continued John Parry, "then they can go by train from Cardiff and when they arrive in Porthcawl I'm sure that they'll find someone to take them to Sker Point. But what they hope to see there apart from rocks, sand and sea I don't know."

"I think that sometimes she takes her nursing duties too seriously but I suppose she is only trying to heal his mind. In her letters, she often writes of him singing the ballad The Maid of Sker."

"That sounds like him," said the choirmaster. "He loves that sad song. Its funny how all the miners seem to be imbibed with a sense of melancholia. The song is about a rich farmer's daughter who wasn't allowed to marry her true love – a poor harpist. He persuaded a friend to write the ballad and he used to sing it to her. Her father locked her up until she agreed to marry the man he'd chosen for her."

"That's awful, John."

"I know, but she never forgot her first love and strangely the harpist didn't marry until he was fifty, and that was long after she had died."

"What a sad tale," said Sarah and then more quietly added, as if to herself, "Things haven't changed much after all these years."

John, pretending that he hadn't heard the last remark, continued, "He wed a young girl and went on to have eleven children with her. I'm sure that his new wife must have reminded him of his first love. He had remained faithful to the

Maid of Sker for so long, there must have been a resemblance."

"Thank you for telling me, John. I'll have lots to tell Louisa when I write back to her. She'll be able to arrange the outing. It won't be too far so I'm sure that Matron will allow it. Dafydd Price must be much improved. He'll be back in Morganton before long and I expect that you'll be glad to see him at choir practice."

"Yes, him and anyone else. More and more of the young men are enlisting. There seems to be no end to the war in sight. What a waste of young lives."

They both paused for a minute as their thoughts turned to the people that they would see no more.

"Oh, Sarah, I'm so sorry. I didn't mean to remind you of..."

"It is all right, John, I'm not going to be distressed. He was my husband and I miss his presence but I don't think that I really loved him. I suppose that in some ways I sympathize with the Maid of Sker." Then realizing what she had admitted, to cover up she said, "I'm a poor hostess, I haven't even offered you a cup of tea. You see, I'm learning to be a lady of the valleys."

Matron gladly gave her permission for the day out in Sker.

"Now you're sure that you're strong enough?" fussed Louisa as they sat in the train before it departed from Cardiff.

"Don't I look it?" teased her patient.

She pretended to examine him more closely. "I suppose so," she admitted grudgingly. Then as their eyes met they both burst out laughing. Their attitudes to each other had changed as soon as they had left the hospital grounds. Strangely she became unsure of her position and he regained some of the confidence he had left behind on the battlefield. He was no longer Dafydd Price coal miner, but a man who had fought for his country and the equal of anyone. She, for the first time, found herself in a situation where she was more interested in the man than she thought that he was in her. For once the supremely confident Louisa was not so sure of herself.

They chattered amicably throughout the journey. They sat opposite each other and when the conversation faltered there was always something to be seen through the window and then remarked upon. After what seemed to them a very short time, the train pulled in to Porthcawl station. Louisa, seeing herself once more as being in charge, immediately busied herself in finding someone to take her and Dafydd out to Sker Point.

"They don't usually come here for Sker," said the ticket collector. "You need to go over Nottage way. Now I wonder who'll be going there." He looked around the station yard and then turning to Louisa said, "See that cart over by the wall? He's going that way, go and ask old Sam for a lift."

Louisa hurried over and explained her problem to the weather beaten man sitting on top of the cart.

"I'll take you to the top of the lane that leads down to Sker House but you'll have to walk the rest of the way."
The pair quickly squeezed on the bench besides Sam. Dafydd had never been so close to Louisa. It felt so natural. But then the doubts fingered into his mind. She'd never have him. Look where he came from. He watched her as she talked to Sam. The old man answered her questions easily. Dafydd vowed that for this one day he would try to forget the difference in their situation. They were just a man and a woman on an outing to the seaside.

They left the town behind and headed towards the old village of Nottage. They trotted past the smithy, the church and the houses and were soon going westward again towards the sea. A couple of miles further on, Sam pulled on the reins.

"Down that track, that's the way. But after the house you'll have to walk over the fields to the point. When you come back, walk the way we've come. Someone passing will pick you up."

After thanking the old farmer, Dafydd and Louisa jumped down from the cart and started down the track. The going was rough and it was only natural for the soldier to take the arm of the young woman and help her over the uneven ground. At the bottom, the land opened out and in front of them was the imposing edifice of the vast lonely house of Sker.

Louisa shuddered and Dafydd automatically tightened his arm around her.

"It looks so uninviting," she whispered. "And that poor Maid of Sker locked up in it. No wonder she gave in to her father and didn't marry the harpist."

Dafydd laughed softly. "You've read too much into that old tale. It is only a song and the house is someone's home. This is a lonely spot and the house is in need of some repair but that's all," he said reassuringly.

As if to emphasize what he had just said, a black and white dog and a young boy came round the side of the house.

The lad saw the couple and shouted, "Mam, we've got visitors."

Soon a middle-aged lady appeared in the doorway. "Hello, what can I do for you? We don't get many strangers down here. It's nice to see people."

The appearance of these ordinary folk broke the spell cast by the first sight of the house, and recovering quickly,

Louisa said, "We didn't mean to intrude but is this Sker House?"

"Yes, this is the farmhouse,"

"We've come because of the ballad."

"I thought as much. We get the odd one or two who come looking because of that old story. But there's nothing special about us down here. You'll soon find that out. Come on in, have a cup of tea. It's a long walk down that lane."

The farmer's wife fussed over them in the large kitchen at the back of the house. She didn't often have visitors and made the most of them when she did. She was very welcoming but talked non-stop.

"The school outings are my favourite," she said as they drank their tea. "A few weeks ago they came from Connelly school. The local farmers brought the children here in carts and we had food laid out for them in the barn across the yard. The boys and girls had a lovely time playing on the beach."

"That's where we want to go, to Sker Point," said Louisa. "Is it much further?"

"No, just across the fields. It won't take long to get there."

The farmer's wife was reluctant to let them go but she had work to do. Pushing her chair away from the table, she said, "The boy and the dog will show you the way. Take care and mind you call in on the way back."

The young couple sat on the grass overlooking the beach and the point.

"That must have been where all the boats were shipwrecked," said Louisa, remembering what the woman had told her.

"Mm," murmured Dafydd in assent as he looked across the channel to the other coast. He could feel his whole body relaxing as the gentle sound of the waves soothed his mind. He looked at Louisa and he couldn't delude himself any longer. They weren't just friends on an outing. He loved her and didn't know how he was going to conceal his true feelings from her.

Jack's voice came back to him, "Not your class, lad, stick to your own."
But Dafydd believed that, like the harpist in the legend, he would never really love anyone else.

"Dafydd, are you all right? You haven't said anything for a while."

"Haven't I? I was just looking at the view. You can see for miles and look how the sun shines on the water. It's so peaceful and there's no one else around."

"Are you glad you came?" asked Louisa.

"Of course I am. I feel free just as I did when I used to walk the mountains on a Sunday after working down the pit all week." And then, because he couldn't help himself, he continued, "Only today I've a beautiful woman sitting besides me."

Louisa's eyes lit up. "For that you deserve a reward," she said lightly as she moved towards him and kissed him on his cheek.

Surprising himself, he gathered her face in his hands and kissed her lips. She didn't pull away; she just stayed still and waited until he kissed her again. This time, he allowed some of his passion for her to show itself. Again he looked at her and saw her smile at him.

"That was nice, Dafydd Price," she said softly as she looked into his eyes. "Kiss me again," she murmured.

He held her close and for a few minutes he forgot the barrier that lay between them. But his doubts came back.

We are just friends, thrown together by the war. There cannot be anything more. He released her gently and said, "It's time we were getting back or we'll miss the evening train."
Realizing that the moment had passed, Louisa reluctantly got to her feet and the pair walked back to the farmhouse.

Chapter Nineteen

Morganton station was busier than usual. The platform thronged with people waiting for the train from Cardiff. Dafydd was at last coming home.

"I do hope that you don't mind me being here," said Mary. "But I can't wait to see him."

"Of course not, it's nice that he has so many friends," replied Carrie. "I'm sure that he'll be pleased to see you. That hospital was all right but I'm certain that he'll be glad to be home."

"Yes and now you can look after him properly. I'll pop in to see him most days, if that's all right?"

"Of course it is, girl. A bit of company is just what he needs. It'll bring him out of himself. Listen, is that the train?"

"No, by the noise of it, only empty trucks for the colliery. But the train shouldn't be long now."

At last the engine steamed into the station. Carrie peered anxiously into each carriage as it passed, searching for her son.

"There he is," shouted Mary as she waved madly. Then grabbing Carrie's hand she pulled her over to where a young soldier was getting out of a compartment.

"Dafydd," cried his mother as she embraced the man. Then stepping back, she looked him up and down. "You're better than when I saw you in that hospital but you could still do with fattening up."

"Welcome home, Dafydd," said Mary excitedly as she hugged him too.

Taken by surprise, Dafydd automatically returned the embrace.

"It is so good to have you back," she said softly as she looked into his eyes.

Carrie watched the pair with some satisfaction. He's home for good now, she thought.

"Where's Dad?" Dafydd asked with some concern in his voice.

"Don't worry about him. He can't get his breath today and that trip up from the station is far too steep for him."

Satisfied with her answer, Dafydd turned to acknowledge some of his old mates who had come to meet the train. Automatically, he looked for a familiar face until he was hit by the thought that sadly he would never see his pal Jack again. The moment passed as Will Jones patted him on the shoulder and shook his hand.

"Good to have you back," he said.

Mary managed to stay by Dafydd's side and at times even held on to his arm. Soon the people of Morganton were satisfied that they had welcomed their hero home and they began to disperse.

Dafydd noticed that there were fewer people about and said to his mother, "It's time to go home to Dad and Gran."

"Are you coming too, Mary?" asked Carrie.

"I'd love to but I can't. Cook let me slip out and I've got to get back now." Then turning to Dafydd, she proprietarily planted a kiss on his cheek and whispered, "See you soon."

The soldier, still a little bemused by what was going on, failed to see the significance of her actions but Carrie's mind was racing towards a wedding. Reluctantly, Mary let go of

Dafydd's arm and walked quickly back up the hills to Rock House where she met her mistress.

"You look flushed, Mary. Have you been hurrying?"

"I went to meet the train, Mrs. Lewis. Cook said that I could go. Dafydd is back."

"Oh good, and how is he?"

"A bit thin but otherwise he seems all right. Carrie says that I must call in to see him when I have time off. She's sure that he'll be pleased to see me."

Sarah smiled and thought, he'll not be the only one – you'll be equally as pleased to see him.

"There were a lot of people at the station," chattered Mary as she tidied the grate. "I didn't see Mr. Parry there though," she continued as she took a sly look at her mistress' face. But to her disappointment not a flicker of interest showed on it. Sarah was far too astute to allow her feelings to be seen by a gossip such as Mary.

Dafydd spent the rest of the day and the evening in the arms of his family. In turn, his brothers and their families called in to see him. By the time they lit the lamps, Emlyn could see that his son was exhausted.

"You could do with a good night's sleep. Now no arguing, off to bed with you."

The young man was indeed glad to climb the stairs and to get into his own bed. Although he was tired, he slept only fitfully but at least his nightmares had changed to dreams. Now he thought of that day at Sker - the sea, the peace and Louisa's kiss. Did she care for him? Sometimes he dreamt that yes she did but more often he found himself as one of many suitors begging for Louisa's hand - a hand that he never quite managed to clasp.

True to her word, Mary spent every spare minute she could at the Prices. She gossiped away ignoring Dafydd's lack of response. "Effects of the war," she would say to others in way of an explanation of his silence. "He'll get over it in time." But one thing she said did make him take notice.

"I saw May on my way home yesterday. She had the baby in a shawl. He looks just like his father."

I must tell her about Jack, I must, he thought as he half listened to Mary's tales.

The following morning he surprised his family by announcing that he was going out.

"Shall I come with you? Are you strong enough?" was his mother's immediate response."

"No, I'm only going to see May."

Carrie and Emlyn exchanged worried glances as he walked out of the house.

Dafydd paused in front of the brown door. Eventually he lifted his arm and banged on the knocker.

"Come in," a voice shouted from somewhere inside.

Like every other house in the village, the door was not locked and with a twist of the knob it opened. Hesitantly, Dafydd went to push it but at that very moment the door was pulled from behind and Nellie Evans stood there in front of him.

"Well I never, Dafydd Price." Then turning, she shouted, "May, there's someone here to see you. Come on in, lad; come on in. Go through to the middle kitchen. They're in there."

"Hello, May."

"How are you, Dafydd?"

"Is that the baby?"

"Yes, come and sit here and hold him."

"But I don't…"

"Of course you do," she replied as she placed the baby in his arms.

As May bent towards him, the scent of lavender water made Dafydd look up into her lovely eyes and for a moment he wanted to embrace her.

"What's his name?" he managed to ask as he stiffly held on to the infant.

"I've called him John after his father, and John he is to stay. No calling him Jack," she managed to say as the tears welled up in her eyes. Then almost immediately she voiced the thought that had been uppermost in her mind for so long, "How did he die?"

As May sat and waited for an answer, Dafydd struggled with himself. At last he began his tale. At first he stumbled over it but then as he recalled the terrible events his narrative picked up speed.

"It was all right until the bombardment. The props began to shake and dirt started to fall, but we had been in worse so we just kept on digging. Then there was an almighty bang. The whole place shook. I shouted to Jack as I thought we had better get out of there. Then, as I watched, some of the props fell to the floor. They went down like dominoes, one after the other. Then everything went black."

The pair sat in that small room, each with their own thoughts but united by the tears that rolled silently down their cheeks. The quiet was broken by the sound of the baby crying.

May stirred and looking over to John she said, "Give him to me. He's nearly falling off your lap. You're not much good with babies. Ssh, Ssh," she whispered as she took young John in her arms and gently rocked him until he fell back to sleep.

"I'm sorry, May, but that's all I know. They pulled me out but Jack was further in, where the fall was deeper and the Hun was still bombing us. They couldn't keep on digging or every one of them would have been killed. He couldn't have been alive. All the earth caved in. Jack died then in that fall."

"Thank you for telling me. At least now I know that he wasn't badly wounded on some battlefield and left to die in agony. The thought of that has haunted me for weeks." Then looking down at the baby, she continued, "At least I've got John and he'll always remind me of his father."

Nellie had been standing quietly in the doorway. Yes, she thought, thank God for the baby. He gives her a purpose. She has to take care of him whether she feels like it or not. Now that May's greatest fear had disappeared, her life can start again.

Chapter Twenty

Dyffryn House,
September 1915.

Dear Mrs. Lewis,

I am writing this to express my deepest sympathy on the death of your husband. I remember him as a highly principled man who always put a great deal of effort into all his undertakings. I deeply regret that I was unable to attend my cousin's funeral but I was touring some of the country's great houses collecting ideas for further improvements to the gardens here at Dyffryn. We have only recently returned and the sad news has come as a shock to both Mrs. Cory and myself.

I remember how much you enjoyed our winter walk in the grounds but there was little to see then. With this warm autumn weather, there are still roses in bloom and many of the beds are full of colour. I write therefore to extend an invitation to you to visit Dyffryn in the next few weeks. Mrs. Cory believes that the peace and tranquillity here is a great healer and I look forward to showing you the gardens.

Yours sincerely,

Reginald Cory.

A smile lit Sarah's face as she read the letter. A short visit to Dyffryn would provide a welcome diversion. Perhaps in the quiet of the gardens she would be able to think through some of her problems. Yes, she would go and the sooner the better.

Sarah walked from the eastern end of the terrace of the great Victorian house, along the gravel path and then into the panel garden. The morning air had not yet acquired an autumnal chill so she could enjoy her stroll to the full. Her hosts had shown genuine pleasure on her arrival and had endeavoured to make her feel at home. It was as if they instinctively knew that the peace of the gardens would allow her to think more clearly about her future. In the panel garden itself, the Irish yews were somehow reassuring in their formality and the statues provided just the right amount of interest to lift her spirits.

Did she want to stay in Morganton? It wasn't many weeks ago that she had decided yes, but now she didn't know. It was the loneliness more than anything. At least when her husband was alive there was someone sitting opposite her at breakfast and again in the evenings. Now there was no one. Then there had been dinner guests too, but, being so recently widowed, how could she invite people? Who was there anyway? The Reverend Evans of course but he was her husband's friend not hers. The doctor and possibly one or two others, but again they were really only acquaintances. Then there was John – schoolmaster, conductor and the aim of every spinster in the village. Her eyes smiled as she thought of all the unmarried chapel ladies attending to his every whim. But what did Mary tell her a few days ago? It was about Miss

Williams, the doctor's daughter, who now taught the younger children in the school.

"Sweet on him, if you ask me," she had said. "A bit young for him, but he's so handsome in a mature sort of way. It's about time he got married and if the school teacher plays her cards right she could catch him."

Sarah knew, or thought that she knew, that John's feelings didn't lie in that direction but she was well aware how a pretty face could turn a man's head – especially if the two spent a lot of time together. Teaching in the same school, going to him for advice, making him feel indispensable, and being so obviously available. Was there something in what Mary said? What had she, Sarah Lewis, done for John Parry over the last few months? Nothing, she thought. I've not even invited him to dinner recently. But how can I on my own? What would people say with me so recently widowed?

Sighing audibly, she retraced her path to the terrace and then walked to the west side of the house. Once there, she went down the steps and through an arch into the large walled kitchen garden. The trees were full of fruit and standing by one of them was Reginald Cory. She watched as he lifted an apple gently in his hand and then turned it. With a snap its stalk came away from the branch.

"Yes, just as I thought, they're ready for picking," he said to no one in particular.

"You have a good crop," called Sarah.

Reginald turned, saw his guest and smiled.

"Come and see the rest. I'll show you what can be grown with a mild climate and the proper protection from frosts," he said enthusiastically.

Sarah couldn't help but respond to his interest and they were soon absorbed in the trees and vegetables of the garden.

"How are you, Mr. Parry?" asked Mrs. Williams as she walked down the hall towards him. "Thank you, Jane, I'll see to things now. Come on in, we've a nice fire in the sitting room. These September evenings can be chilly. Elizabeth won't be long. She is so pleased that you are able to come to supper."

"It's my pleasure, Mrs. Williams," said the ever- polite schoolmaster. "I don't get invited out to dine very often these days."

"Don't you? I would have thought that some of the unmarried ladies in the chapel would have had you round. But there again, so many of them have their old mothers to look after."

"Never fear, Mrs. Williams, some one is always dropping in something for me to eat – pies, tarts, jams. I'm not neglected in that respect by any means."

"Look at me talking away and I haven't offered you a chair yet. Take that one by the fire."

"Thank you, is the doctor at home?"

"No, but he won't be long. Evening surgery should be just about finished." Then hearing some movement behind her, the doctor's wife turned towards the door. "There you are, Elizabeth. Mr. Parry has been waiting for you."

That's not strictly true, thought John. But he had to admit to himself that the pretty young lady standing before him seemed far removed from his junior teacher. Not bad, not bad at all. Elizabeth is a pretty young lady. Then Sarah's image came into his mind, but it was not as sharp as it usually was. Why had she gone off like that without even writing a note to say where? The schoolmaster looked again at Elizabeth and returned her smile.

Supper was far less formal than the dinners at Rock House. The oval dining table was not as imposing and the four sat easily around it. Jane brought in large platters and tureens of steaming food. The diners helped themselves to the plain but well cooked dishes.

"More potatoes, Mr. Parry? What about some carrots?"

"Leave John alone, my dear," said the doctor. "He'll take what he wants. As I was saying, I went to see Jimmy Wilde fight. I've never seen anything like it. He ducked and weaved and won against a much heavier opponent. Best prospect I've seen in these valleys for years. I'm convinced that he'll get a Lonsdale Belt and who knows he may get a crack at the world title."

"Mr. Parry, you'll have to forgive my father but he's so keen on boxing that he thinks that everyone else is too."

John smiled as the doctor ignored his daughter's remarks and continued with his favourite subject. His enthusiasm made him an interesting person to listen to for he had the knack of interspersing his narrative with little known tit-bits.

"Wilde's not encouraged by his wife, you know. She positively hates the sport. Makes him train in a small back room with the furniture pushed up against the walls."

And so the doctor went on, but the conversation was by no means confined to boxing. The family displayed interest and knowledge in many things. The schoolmaster hadn't enjoyed himself so much for a while. It was no surprise that they were on first name terms long before the end of the evening and it was with reluctance that John Parry departed for home.

Sarah's few days at Dyffryn were at an end. The tranquillity of the gardens and the attentiveness of her hosts had restored some of her equanimity. She had been able to think about her future and had come to some conclusions. She was now convinced that she should try to build a new life for herself in Morganton. She would insist on an involvement in the running of the colliery.

Whatever misgivings Mr. Davies, the manager, may have, I own it, she thought. And I will know more about it.
Then digressing a little, she made a mental note to arrange for coal to be sent to Dyffryn in the winter as she remembered Reginald saying that since the war started it was difficult to get enough fuel to heat the greenhouses and that in the frosts of February he had lost some of his precious plants. He reckoned that there would be a greater shortage in the coming months for there was no sign of the war coming to an end. Then her thoughts went back to the village. She wanted to build a memorial to her husband but at the same time help the people of Morganton. She decided that building a cottage hospital in her husband's memory was the best option open to her.

Yes, a small infirmary where treatment will be free. Louisa will help me to set it up. She must know some people who can assess Morganton's needs and thus advise me on establishing it.
But it was inevitable that no sooner had her thoughts turned to the Valleys than John Parry came into her mind.

Why had she avoided him these last few weeks, she asked herself? And could give no satisfactory answer.

She had tried to explore her feelings for him but had been unsuccessful. Prejudices formed in earlier years coloured her judgment. She was now a wealthy widow and by Morganton's standards very rich indeed. She thought that John was comfortably off. She had heard rumours of a private income. After all he wouldn't have been sent away to school and then to university without money in the family. But he wasn't... Stop, her mind scolded. This is 1915. Women are doing men's work all over the country. They decide things for themselves – including whom they marry. Do you love him, Sarah Lewis? If you do, tell him. But she knew that it wasn't as simple as that. Louisa would be able to do it, but could she?

The thought of John had set up a longing inside Sarah that made her impatient to return home. She had not forgotten Mary's gossip. Elizabeth Williams, schoolteacher, was a very different person from the young girl that had gone away to college just two years previously. She could imagine her hanging on to her mentor's every word, catching his eye across the hall as he took morning prayers and then staying behind after school on some pretext or other just to time her departure to his so that they walked home together. Sarah knew deep down that if she wanted to be part of John's life then she had to do something about it.

George was waiting at Morganton station when his mistress arrived on the Cardiff train.

"There you are, Mrs. Lewis," he said as he moved towards the first class compartment and helped her down the step and onto the platform. Expertly he gathered her luggage together and they were soon in the trap and trotting through the village. Morris the draper was in his shop doorway as they passed.

Once back inside, he said to his wife "I see that Mrs. Lewis has returned then. I wonder if it is because of John Parry B.A.?"

"What do you mean?" asked Mrs. Morris?

"Well Dr. William's wife was in here yesterday and talked non-stop about her Elizabeth and the schoolmaster.

Been round to supper and they are all going to a concert in Cardiff."

"So that pretty young thing has caught him, has she?"

"Mrs. Williams thinks so, but the rich widow may have other ideas."

"You don't mean that she's after the schoolmaster?"

"That's what George reckons and he ought to know."

But, as soon as Morris said that, he knew that he had made a mistake and sure enough his wife picked it up

"Where did you see George the butler? He never comes in here."

Now the draper had to think on his feet if his wife wasn't to find out about the true nature of his Saturday nights out. George and the barmaid at the Morganton Hotel were brother and sister. The butler often went there late on a Saturday evening after he had finished work for the day. The unlikely pair would chat about this and that as Morris waited for his lady friend – the butler's sister.

"Met him outside when I was cleaning the window yesterday. I asked after Mrs. Lewis and he mentioned something about the comings and goings at Rock House. That's all."

"Why didn't you tell me about this before?" demanded Mrs. Morris.

Luckily he didn't have to answer as just then the shop bell rang and a customer came in through the door.

Chapter Twenty-one

Bron Rhyw Hospital,
October 1915.

Dear Aunt Sarah,
I have a few days off starting on Saturday. It is not worth going to Bristol so can I come to stay with you please?
I'll be arriving at about eleven o'clock. Send George to meet me. There's no need to reply, unless it is inconvenient.
Love,
Louisa.

Sarah smiled as she read the short note. Louisa coming – just what she needed. I'll invite John to dinner on Saturday, she thought. Surely no one can object if my niece is here too. Finishing her breakfast quickly, she went into the drawing room and, sitting at her writing desk, penned a short note to him.

... Do say that you can come. It'll be good to see you again.

And I've missed you, she thought as she signed her name. After addressing the envelope she rang the bell for George.

Louisa brought life into the house again. She was full of tales of the hospital and wanted to know everything that had happened since she was last in Morganton.

After lunch, she announced, "I'm going to call on my patient."

For a moment, Sarah didn't know whom she meant and then it came to her – of course, Dafydd Price.

"Do you think that you ought to go there unannounced?" she asked.

"Why not, Aunt Sarah? I got to know Dafydd quite well when he was in the hospital. I'm sure that he'll be pleased to see me."

"It's not that. You know that the Prices live in a small terraced house."

"What has that got to do with it? I've learnt over the last few months that it is the person who is important and not how much money he has or who he's connected too."

"I know that you are right," said Sarah. "But you may cause some embarrassment on their part."

"Don't worry, I won't turn up like some Lady Bountiful. I'll walk there and simply enquire after Dafydd. I'm sure that Carrie will be pleased to see me."

True to her word, that afternoon Louisa walked through the village to Edmund Street, whilst Sarah made the final preparations for that evening's dinner party.

"Miss Louisa," exclaimed Carrie when she opened the door. "I was wondering who was knocking. Most people round here just open the door and walk in. Come in, come in." She ushered her guest into the front room where Granny Price, as usual, was busy sewing.

"This is my mother-in-law, Mrs. Price. Mam, this is Dafydd's nurse from the hospital. You know, Mrs. Lewis' niece."

"Hello, Mrs. Price, it's good to meet you. Dafydd talked a lot about his family the last week or so he was with us."

"Let me clear a chair for you," said Carrie as she moved the sewing.

"How is your son?" asked Louisa. "Is he home?"

"He's in the middle kitchen with his father. I'll go and fetch him."

The young man entered the parlour with a mixture of delight and trepidation. He never thought that he would see her again – except possibly from afar when she visited her aunt. And now she was here, in front of him, in his home. But had things changed between them? The hospital was an unreal world. Young ladies from privileged backgrounds looking after the likes of him. Once outside it, things must revert to the established order.

"Hello, Dafydd, and how's my patient?" said Louisa as soon as he came in through the door.

"I'm all right, thank you."

"Well you certainly look better than when I saw you last. No doubt it is due to your mother's cooking."

Dafydd nodded in agreement but made no move to come further into the room.

Granny Price noticed the awkwardness between them and said, "Talking about food, haven't you got some broth simmering on the range, Carrie? You had better go and give it a stir. I'm sure that Miss Louisa would like a nice cup of tea. I'll come and give you a hand."

Putting down the sewing, the old lady rose from her chair and her daughter-in-law had no option but to follow her.

When the two ladies had gone, Louisa said, "Well aren't you going to sit down? Tell me what's happened since you've been back home."

Dafydd went to perch on his grandmother's chair but as they talked, he relaxed and sat more comfortably in it. He was soon laughing at some of her anecdotes about the hospital and she in turn listened with interest to his tales of Morganton. Louisa was particularly pleased to hear that Dafydd had been to see May and that he was able to tell her about Jack's death. At last, she thought, he is putting the War behind him.

They were so engrossed in themselves that neither noticed that the cup of tea didn't materialize. Eventually, Louisa realized that she had stayed longer than she had meant to and that she would have to make her way back to Rock House if she was to be ready in time for dinner. Reluctantly, she said," I'm sorry, Dafydd, but I must go. Aunt Sarah has invited John Parry to eat with us tonight. I think that this is the first time that she has had a dinner guest since my uncle died. But before I go, will you do something for me? Come for a walk with me tomorrow morning and show me the view of the valley that you described so vividly in the hospital."

"Well, tell me what she had to say. Wasn't it good of her to come to see you," said Carrie after Louisa had departed. "Called in to see if you were getting better, I suppose."

"Yes, Mam."

"Did she say how long she was staying?"

"A few days, I think."

"That will be nice for Mrs. Lewis. She must be lonely in that big house. Mary was telling me that there is to be a dinner party this evening in Miss Louisa's honour. Only a small one, but John Parry B.A. has been invited."

"So Mary's working tonight then."

"Yes, that's what she said. It's a pity because she won't be down to see you. Why don't you go to the Royal Oak?"

"No thanks, Mam. I'll go for a walk tomorrow morning instead. It'll do me more good."

Carrie appeared to be satisfied with this as she thought that he didn't want to go out without Mary. But, Granny Price had sensed the chemistry between her grandson and the young lady. She knew where his true feelings lay and it went through her mind that perhaps he wasn't going for a Sunday walk on his own.

Sarah looked at herself in the mirror and sighed as she acknowledged that black wasn't her best colour. Still, her waist was trim, her bust full and the low neckline of her dress was barely disguised by the lace inserted into the front. Would it be enough to provoke John's admiration or had the pretty Elizabeth Williams caught his fancy?

She had heard that John had gone with the doctor and his family to a concert in Cardiff and she had no doubt that it had been carefully arranged by Mrs. Williams that her daughter had sat next to the schoolmaster. She could imagine how he would have been appealed to for explanations of some of the finer points of the music and how Elizabeth would have hung on to his every word. How could any man ignore her? Yes, Sarah was jealous and in her situation – recently widowed – there was little she could do about it, unless she was prepared to flout every convention. Her counter-attack had to be subtle. She had carefully arranged the dining table so that the three places had been set close together at one end. She and Louisa would sit on the one side and John directly opposite. She had also had the carver chair removed from the head of the table so that, for the next few hours, she would not feel the presence of her late husband.

Louisa returned from her visit full of her ex-patient's progress.

"We're going for a walk in the morning to see the valley from the top of the mountain." And before her aunt could reply, she had disappeared through the door again calling out, "I'm dressing for dinner."

Sarah shook her head as she thought, yet again, that her niece took her nursing duties far too seriously.

As usual, John Parry arrived at the appointed time. Sarah heard him talking to George as he took off his hat and coat. The sound of the choirmaster's melodious voice sent a flutter through her and she found it difficult to even remain outwardly composed.

"Mr. Parry, madam," announced the butler as he opened the door to the drawing room.

"Thank you, George."

The manservant hesitated long enough to see the welcome his mistress gave to her visitor and then, with a look of satisfaction on his face, he went out and closed the door behind him.

John's greeting to Sarah was far less effusive. He hadn't quite forgiven her for disappearing to who knows where, without saying anything to him. In contrast, he greeted Louisa with obvious delight and the two were soon engrossed in conversation about the hospital in general and about matron in particular, for that formidable woman had made a lasting impression on the choirmaster.

Over dinner, however, his attitude towards Sarah softened. How could it not, being seated opposite such a beautiful woman? He thought that the black dress quite became her and she in turn knew that the low neckline, barely disguised by the fine lace was having the desired effect. She talked about Dyffryn, the Corys' welcome, the gardens and how much better it had all made her feel. She admitted that she had gone away on a whim but it had been the right medicine.

"Whilst there, I made some plans about the future."

"What are you going to do? Are you going back to Bristol?" asked Louisa.

John found himself holding his breath as he waited for Sarah's reply.

"No, I'm not. I've decided to stay here in Morganton."

A sense of relief flooded through the choirmaster as he listened to her answer. He felt sure that the others must have seen his reaction but, if they had, they gave no sign of it.

"I want to do something for the community and I've decided what that is. I'm going to set up a small hospital where the miners and their families can get free treatment," Sarah continued.

"Oh, Aunt Sarah, that would be a very generous thing to do and such an asset for everyone."

Not surprisingly, for the rest of the meal, nothing else was talked about. Louisa was enthusiastic and John grateful. A cottage hospital would indeed benefit the community that he had come to love and reduce the suffering of that tough but compassionate group of men - the valley miners.

George was late getting to the Morganton Hotel that evening. There was hardly anyone left drinking in the bar and there was no sign of his sister.

"Gone upstairs with you know who," he was told. "Are you having a pint while you wait?"

"Yes, give me one," replied George as he fished in his pocket for the money. "I'll go and join those few over there while I'm waiting for her."

Upstairs, the barmaid looked round her bedroom with some satisfaction and thought, best thing I did, carrying on with a draper. Fancy curtains, cushions for the bed and of course all those clothes in the wardrobe. I'm never short of a bob or two now either. He's easy to tap up for money and come to that it doesn't take much to satisfy him. Once a week that's all. He'd come more often though if he thought that he could get away with it. I wouldn't like to be him if his wife finds out.

And with that thought a small laugh escaped from her lips.

"Did you say anything?" asked Morris as he straightened up after untying his shoelaces.

"No, I was just thinking that's all."

"About what?"

"That you're taking a long time to get your boots off and I'm waiting here for you."

To hurry him up, she sat up and allowed the quilt to fall off the top half of her body. The sight of her large breasts put Morris the draper in a tizzy. He became all fingers and thumbs as he tried to undo his trousers. He yanked his shirt over his head and then he saw them - his combinations.

That wife of mine made me put them on. I had to do it for peace, he thought as he heard her voice ringing in his ears. "It's cold in the nights now, so put them on before you go to that hotel. Why you have to go out at this time of night, I don't know. There wont be many others there. It's much too late. "

Now Morris had yet another set of buttons to struggle with! At last he pulled his arms out of the tight sleeves and then he sat on the edge of the bed to peel off the rest of the awkward garment. Finally he could slip in under the quilt and move thankfully towards those big breasts.

Chapter Twenty-two

Dafydd walked along the street but instead of going down the track that led to the stepping- stones as he usually did on a Sunday morning he turned up and made his way to the main road. Not many people were out and about. The shops were shut and it was too early for chapel. He was able to walk quickly and soon came to the hill that led to Rock House. He turned the corner and strode up it. His thoughts were focused on Louisa. He couldn't imagine why she wanted to go for a walk with him! Call on him – yes perhaps. He had been her patient and she his nurse. They had talked a lot those last couple of weeks he was in the hospital and then there was that trip to Sker. He'd kissed her, but that was different, they had been carried away by the war. This was Morganton. This was real. No, there was far too big a gap between them for anything to come of it. Mam was right, settle down and marry Mary. But, as he thought this, he knew that he couldn't. Why had Louisa come back into his life?

At the same time, Louisa was walking down the hill towards him.

"Good morning isn't it a lovely day for our walk," she called as soon as she saw him. "Which way are we going?"

Pulling himself together, he managed to reply, "If we cross over just before your aunt's house we can go through the gap and onto the path. I didn't think that you would come down to meet me. Did you tell Mrs. Lewis where you were going?"

"You needn't worry, I told her yesterday, when I got back that I had arranged for you to show me some of the sights of Morganton this morning. I don't think that she took much notice though. She was far too engrossed in her preparations for John's visit," she replied as they turned onto the path.

Once they started to climb, she held out her hand and it was the most natural thing in the world for him to take it. Some of the magic they had felt at Sker reasserted itself and the barriers between them faded into the background. They talked easily as they walked. Louisa told Dafydd about the plans for the hospital and how she was going to be involved in setting it up.

"So you are going to see more of me not less. Are you pleased?" she asked looking directly at him.

She watched the struggle in his eyes and didn't press for an answer. She thought that she knew what was going through his mind. She herself had spent many a sleepless night, since he had left the hospital, worrying about her feelings for him. Her parents wouldn't approve. A good match was her mother's only ambition for her. What would she say if she found out that her daughter was in love with a collier? And her father – he'd order her home at once. There must be a solution, but what?

They climbed on in silence and eventually reached the old quarry where another generation had taken the stone to build the terraces that stretched out before them.

"There's Rock House," she said excitedly. "And below that the big building must be the Welfare Hall. Look, there's the river right down in the bottom of the valley. And up on top, on the other side, there's a farmhouse. Are those white dots the sheep?"

Dafydd laughed at her excitement. "I told you that you could see for miles up here. If you walk up to the top of this ridge and then up the next, at one place you can follow the valley all the way down to the sea."

"Let's do it," she enthused.

"Wait a minute. It's a long climb and they would be sending a search party out for you. We've been long enough. It's time I was getting you back before your aunt begins to wonder where I've taken you to."

Louisa nodded her head in acquiescence but to herself she said, "One day, Dafydd Price, one day we'll walk up to the top together."

That evening, Carrie was surprised when Dafydd said that he would go with them to chapel for he hadn't been to Ebenezer since he had returned home.

"He must be getting better," she said to Emlyn. "He's almost like his old self."

"Well we could do with his voice. So many of them have joined up, that there's only women and old men in the congregation."

"You're not old," retorted Carrie.

"That may be but I feel it. Especially with the winter coming on."

"Stay in and not go climbing those hills. You'll be a lot better then." But Carrie knew that however little he did, sadly his days were numbered.

The Prices sat in their usual pew as they waited for the service to begin. One or two people were still coming in, when Mrs. Lewis and her niece arrived. They walked quickly down the aisle to their seat in the front. Granny Price watched her grandson as the two women went past. Her observations of yesterday were confirmed.

You've got over one tragedy, she thought, and now you are letting yourself in for more heartache. Dafydd, why couldn't you have fallen for someone like Mary?
Within minutes, The Reverend Evans followed by the elders processed out of the minister's vestry. He climbed into the pulpit, looked around at his congregation and announced the first hymn. No one could have failed to hear the tenor whose voice soared above the rest. He sang for one person only that Sunday evening, and she didn't fail to receive his message.

Chapter Twenty-three

Sarah sat at her desk reading some of the documents that Mr. Davies, the colliery manager, had prepared for her. She couldn't deny that they were difficult to understand but she was determined to make sense of them. His parting words to her had been, "A decision, Mrs. Lewis, we must have a decision!"

But how was she to decide between keeping the steam driven winding engine or replacing it at a large cost with a new electric winding plant – the first of its size in South Wales?

Now let me go through these figures again, she thought. The existing engine raises two drams of coal per wind. The new electric one could raise one thousand four hundred tons up the shaft in seven hours and each wind only takes forty five seconds. But how much coal does a dram hold? How long does it take the old steam engine to lift the coal up the shaft? Where can I find this information?

She read through the papers yet again and was then as certain as she could be that the answers to her questions were not in them. Her mind was made up. There was only one thing to do. She would have to go to the colliery offices and if the manager couldn't spare the time to explain things to her then there must be some one in the building who could.

The colliery manager's other question about extending the watering system of the main haulage roads for keeping the coal dust damp was for Sarah a far easier one to answer. Even she knew how inflammable the dust could be and anything to reduce the danger of an explosion and save men's lives was, to her mind, the right thing to do.

So that's one decision, she thought as she put the papers together. I'll go down to the offices now whilst I have some idea of the other problem.

She was right; Mr. Davies wasn't available but the young under-manager, Alban Thomas, who endeavoured to explain things to her, was very enthusiastic.

"So you see, Mrs. Lewis, we could get the coal to the top more quickly."

"What you are telling me is that this electric winding engine plant is worth building."

"Well look at it this way," said the young man as he took up a pen, dipped in an uncapped bottle of ink and began to write some figures on a piece of paper. He spoke as he wrote. "Each dram carries one and a half tons of coal. Under the present system we bring up two per wind. A wind takes…" And so he went on.

Sarah didn't follow everything that he said but she understood enough to see the economic sense of the new electric winding plant.

Right, she thought, that's another decision made.

As she left the building, she saw a queue of men starting to form outside a large window. Curious, she asked Alban Thomas why the miners were lining up.

"It's pay day, Mrs. Lewis. They get their wages through that window there."

"Do they stand out here whatever the weather?"

"Yes"

"But what if it's raining or snowing in the winter?"

The under-manager looked surprised.

"They queue just the same."

"Why can't they be paid in the office and line up in the corridor?" asked Sarah.

"They're straight off their shift. Look how dirty they are. It wouldn't be practical."

Yes, I see that now, she thought. But surely some sort of shelter can be built for them to wait under. When I see Mr. Davies about my decisions, I'll bring this up too. A glass canopy wouldn't take the light from the offices and would keep the rain off the waiting men.

Back at Rock House, Sarah Lewis felt a sense of achievement. At last she was involved in the running of the colliery. Now she could set the wheels in motion for building the new hospital. She was sensible enough to know that she needed the help of others, but whom? For the second time that day, she sat at her desk and began to write out a list of suitable names.

Dafydd opened the vestry door and looked in. "I thought that I was too early for practice," he said out loud as he saw the empty hall.

He was just about to go back out when a voice from within said, "Whoever it is, don't go. Come and help me sort out these music sheets."
On hearing this, Dafydd peered into the gloom.

"I'm at the back by the big cupboard," the voice said.
Dafydd made his way between the old benches and, on seeing the choirmaster, asked what he could do to help.

"Sort these into piles," said John Parry B.A. "They've got all mixed up. It's a job I've been meaning to do for some time."
The two chatted as they worked.

"Had my discharge papers this morning. Don't know whether to be glad or sorry," Dafydd said.

"What do you mean? You don't want to go back to the trenches after all you've been through."

"No, but I've got to find a job now and that means the pit."

The choirmaster had heard from Louisa how the young soldier had been buried alive on the battlefield. He could imagine the mental agony Dafydd would suffer if he went back underground.

"Couldn't you get a job on top pit?"

"I might be able to. I'll have to go to the offices and ask. I know that they want men to work on the face. They've dug some cross measure drivages and been able to open a new yard seam below the two foot six one. That can't be bad to work. The tunnel must be nearly five feet high. Almost room to stand upright in." Then after a few seconds he continued, "I'd still rather work on top, even if the money is less."

Seeing the young man's despondency, John Parry changed the subject. "You sang well in chapel last Sunday. I hope that you are in the same good voice for tonight's practice."

Dafydd smiled in acknowledgement.

"Have you thought of going further with your singing?"

"I sing in the choir, solo too. What else is there?"

"You've a good voice, Dafydd Price. No, a great voice! Some training, the right contacts and I think that you could make a living out of singing."

The young man laughed as he thought to himself, you earn your money by digging coal, laying roads or working in a shop, not through singing!

But John Parry persisted and eventually, Dafydd agreed to allow the choirmaster to ask Madame Clara in Cardiff to take the young tenor as a pupil.

"It's very good of you to come," said Sarah Lewis, colliery owner and soon to be benefactress of the new hospital, as she greeted yet another of her guests. The drawing room at Rock House was filling up with some of the more influential men of the area. They had all been invited to dinner and no doubt, most were wondering why. Only the schoolmaster, John Parry B.A., knew the reason for this gathering. He listened politely to comments and managed to give the impression that he too wasn't aware of the purpose of the meeting, without actually saying so.

I wonder how she is going to handle this, he thought as he watched Sarah move from one group to another playing out her role of the perfect hostess.

Occasionally, as she stopped to talk, he felt a pang of jealousy as he noticed one or two admiring glances. He knew only too well that some of the pillars of the community were not as upright as they liked to be thought of. But the lady was too intent on her task to notice their interest in her.

In the kitchen, Mrs. Lloyd grumbled as she rushed about. "For weeks we've had nothing to do and now two dinner parties in a few days."

"The last one was only a small affair," said Mary trying to placate her.

"You're right, that wasn't too much trouble I suppose. But this one! All those men have huge appetites especially when there is a free meal. I hope I've cooked enough for them."

"Plenty by the look of it and good plain food too," said Mary as she looked at the two large legs of lamb resting on their racks. "Not like the fancy dishes Mrs. Lewis likes to serve when she has special guests – particularly you know who."

"Stop it girl. She's only been widowed a short time. You watch what you're saying."

Luckily, just then George came into the kitchen to say that all the guests had arrived and that the mistress wanted dinner served. Mary was forced to keep to herself the latest gossip about John Parry B.A. and the two women that were after his affection.

Over dinner, Sarah broached the subject of the hospital. Dr. Williams immediately whole-heartedly welcomed her proposal.

"An infirmary is just what the community needs. A male ward, a female ward, a surgery for the miners to come to have their wounds dressed, a small operating theatre, a..."

"Wait, wait," cried Sarah smiling at his enthusiasm. "I said a small cottage hospital."

Reluctantly, the doctor scaled down some of his ideas but she could still see how pleased he was.

"What do you think of the idea, Mr. Roberts?" asked John Parry of the manager of the Welfare Hall. "Do you think that the miners want a hospital?"

"Of course they want one and need one but will they be able to afford the cost of the treatment? You know how it is, Dr. Williams, they only call you out as a last resort because they can't afford to pay."

"I understand that," said Sarah softly. "That's why I propose to subsidize the medical costs from the profits of the colliery."

There was a moment of stunned silence as the men digested what she had just said. They couldn't believe her generosity. Then they all started speaking at once. But, the lady was pleased because she knew that she had their backing for her plan and that more importantly when it came to fruition it would be of benefit to the whole community. As the men talked she looked across the table towards John and as she saw the admiration in his eyes she felt the colour rising in her cheeks. He smiled at her, but was it simply in approval for her scheme and the way she had handled the meeting or did it mean more than that? How she wished that she knew.

By the end of the evening, a small sub-committee had been formed consisting of Dr. Williams, Mr. Roberts, Thomas Thomas the builder and The Reverend Evans – who couldn't be left out of anything. Thomas Thomas undertook to find a suitable piece of land and the doctor said that he would draw up a list of medical requirements. The manager of the Welfare Hall had the important job of ensuring that the community knew about the project and that any misgivings or requirements would be passed on to the committee. The Reverend Evans of course elected himself chairman but it was important to have his full support for his opinion carried such weight in Morganton.

"Once Thomas has found the land, we can employ an architect," said one.

"Yes, then we can get started on building it," added another.

"It won't be that long before it'll be up and running, you'll see."

I wish it were as simple as that, thought Sarah as she listened to the conversation. She was certain that to see such a large project through from beginning to end would be no small task.

As the men left that evening, each expressed their appreciation of the meal and her generosity.

"The lamb was done to a turn," said the Reverend Evans as he took his leave. "The new hospital will be a fitting memorial to the late Mr. Lewis. And of course of benefit to the community."

"Very generous, Mrs. Lewis, Very generous," said the doctor. "A dream come true," he continued as he held on to her hand.

John Parry deliberately managed to be the last to leave.

"Well done, Sarah, well done," he said as he lifted her hand to his lips. One day, he thought, I'll have the courage to take you in my arms. But not yet, it is far too soon for convention to allow.

Chapter Twenty-four

One Saturday a few weeks later, John Parry B.A. and Dafydd Price waited on the station platform for the twelve thirty train to Cardiff. They were on their way to see Madame Clara. The choirmaster had written to her about the young tenor and, because John was an old acquaintance of hers, she had agreed to listen to Dafydd but without any promise of taking him on as a pupil. She had summoned them to her house at three o'clock that afternoon. Although the train journey to Cardiff was only an hour, they had to cross the city so John Parry was taking no chances and made sure that they caught an early train. He certainly didn't want to upset the great lady by being late. At last the train pulled in to the station and the two men got into an empty carriage. When they were on their way, the choirmaster asked Dafydd about his efforts in finding a job.

"There's not one on top pit. It looks as if I'll have to go back underground. Mam and Grannie Price are dead set against it but what else can I do? I can't go on depending on them. They keep saying that something will come up, but what?"

"I've heard talk that they are going to build a new winding house. Surely there'll be some work then for you."

"That's what Dad says, but when are they going to start building it? The only answer I got at the office was soon"

"What about the new hospital? Have you had a word with Thomas Thomas the builder?"

"No, he's got his own gang of men."

"Have a word just the same. He'll need more workers when the building starts."

John Parry made a mental note to speak to Sarah about Dafydd's problem. If he could get the young man taken on by Madame Clara then he certainly didn't want him working in that dust underground.

At Cardiff they had their return tickets punched as they left the platform and then the two men followed the other passengers down the long flight of steps and walked through the gate into the station forecourt.

"We don't need to catch one of those over there," said the choirmaster as he pointed to a line of trams. "It is not too far to walk."

They quickly passed the parked vehicles and made their way to St. Mary's Street. The traffic in the road surprised Dafydd. Only the trams appeared to move in any order. All types of carts vied for space on the road and the occasional new motorcar added to the confusion. He had seen some lorries and a few staff cars on the battlefield and these newer forms of traffic didn't surprise him. But here every thing moved much more quickly on the cobbled roads. How the vehicles missed each other as they weaved in and out, he didn't know.

At the bottom of St. Mary's Street they turned left, crossed over the road and walked passed Cardiff Castle. They stopped for a few minutes to admire it.

"How old do you think it is?" asked John Parry B.A.

"Must be ancient," replied Dafydd.

"Not really. Most of it has been rebuilt. See those big stones at the bottom of the wall over there to the left? They're some of the original ones."

"Yes, they're different from those above them."

"Money made from coal was used to rebuild the castle. The Marquess of Bute and his family live here now." As he said this, the choirmaster took out his pocket watch. "We'd better walk on. I wouldn't want us to be late."

When they came to the end of the castle walls, John Parry stopped and said, "That's the street – Cathedral Road. The house is not far from the corner."
Dafydd followed his mentor into a street of grand houses.

As they walked, the young man wondered why families needed so much space to live in. Many of the houses had three storeys and some were double fronted with bay windows on either side of a front door that was embellished with brass. He noticed too how the nails in the soles of his boots clicked noisily on the paving stones.

It's about time that we had a proper pavement in Edmund Street, he thought. No wet feet and mucky boots then.

Just then, John Parry said, "See that house across the road? The one with the big brass plaque. That's the one."
Dafydd nodded to indicate that he had seen it and together they walked over to it. He read out what was written on the plate.

Madame Clara Novello-Davies
Teacher of Music and Singing

John Parry rang the bell and they waited for the door to open.

A few seconds later they heard a maid's voice ask quite sharply – "Yes?"

"We've an appointment with Madame Clara Novello-Davies," replied the choirmaster.

John Parry took some out of his small leather case, placed the sheets on the piano and asked, "Shall I accompany him?"

"Yes, that's a good idea. I'll sit here and I'll be able to give Dafydd Price my full attention."

John beckoned Dafydd over to the piano, where the two quietly discussed the music. Then he went to sit on the stool whilst the singer took off his white muffler and put it and the cap, which he had unconsciously twisted in his hands since he had entered the room, on one of the chairs. Standing nervously besides the piano, Dafydd was ready to begin. The intelligent choirmaster knew how to put Dafydd at ease – soon the whole room was filled with the haunting melody of the Maid of Sker. Lost in the pleasure of his singing, Dafydd effortlessly progressed from one piece to the next. Each had been carefully chosen to show off the range and depth of his fine voice. At the end, even Madame Clara Novello-Davies, a lady of exacting standards, expressed her appreciation.

"Bravo, well done," she enthused, then turning to the choirmaster she continued, "You were right, John, he is an exceptionally fine singer."

"I thought perhaps that Dafydd would make a tenore d'agilita, if he had the right training of course."

"I can see why you say that. He has such extraordinary rapidity and accuracy through the coloratura runs and top notes. Hm, he would be a challenge to train but what a tenor he would make. He already sings from his chest. It's not as if there are many bad habits to break."

On the train home that evening, John Parry tried to explain to Dafydd what the future could hold for him. Not only had the great lady offered to teach him but she had proposed to include him in her Christmas Concert at the Park

The woman looked the two up and down. The older gentleman she could accept but the younger one with the flat cap, white muffler and boots was another matter. Didn't he belong around the back? It was a bit early for the miners though and he wasn't covered in coal dust. What was it going to be - the house or the marquee in the garden? Looking at them once more, she made up her mind.

"If you'll come this way," she said as she stepped aside and indicated that they should enter the room on her right.

The two walked into the music room. It was dominated by a grand piano, the likes of which Dafydd had never seen before. He looked around the room wide eyed. The large bay window draped with velvet curtains, the marble fireplace with its insert of pretty tiles, the thick carpet with its border of polished wood, the ruby-red sofa and its matching chairs... all beyond his experience. The choirmaster watched Dafydd and hoped that he would not be overawed.

Perhaps the marquee in the garden, where the miners come for their singing lessons not to dirty the house, would have been more suitable, he thought. No, he contradicted himself, if Dafydd Price is to be a great singer then he has to get used to all of this.

Just then the door was flung open and in walked the famous lady herself.

"John, how are you?" she exclaimed as she advanced towards him. "It's been a long time!"

He kissed her hand and said, "This is Dafydd Price, the tenor I wrote to you about."

Madame Clara looked the young man up and down.

"I understand that I'm to listen to you singing. Have you brought any music?"

Hall. Her internationally renowned choir of Welsh girl singers would of course top the bill but as she said, "There were items where the young man could sing with them." John laughed as he remembered the condescension in her voice, but he hadn't been fooled. She must have thought that she had found a very special voice to offer to include Dafydd in one of her concerts. It was November now and only a few weeks before the big night so there was no time to lose. Dafydd must be encouraged to take up the offer.

"No one denies that you have a fine voice, Dafydd, but a few lessons with Madame Clara and then rehearsals with the choir and people will say that you have a tremendous one," said John with enthusiasm.

But Dafydd didn't seem to be convinced and answered with a very subdued yes.

"Don't you see, lad, this could be the making of you. You could end up singing all over Europe and being paid – well paid – for what you enjoy doing more than anything else."

Dafydd still didn't respond. The choirmaster was referring to another world, which wasn't for the likes of him. Besides, where would the money come from? He had to find a job now that he had finished with the army. Then there were the train fares to Cardiff, the cost of the singing lessons and where was he going to find the time if he was working?

John Parry couldn't understand the lack of response. What opportunities, surely the lad wasn't thinking of turning them down? Then the penny dropped. The cost – how were the Prices going to be able to afford the singing lessons and then there were the travelling expenses? Dafydd's not going to miss this chance. I'll pay, thought the choirmaster, but he knew that it would be very difficult to get a proud family like the Prices to accept what they would see as charity.

"I know that it'll mean sacrifices, lad," he said at last. "But it'll be worth it. I promise that I will do all I can to get you a job on top pit. Then you'll have money coming in. I'm sure that your lessons can be fitted into your shift pattern and most of the choir rehearsals are on the weekend. If you are still short of money then I'll lend you enough to cover your lessons."

John stopped for he saw the startled look on Dafydd's face.

"A loan I said, so don't turn me down out of hand. It's something that I want to do and when you are rich and famous you can pay me back – agreed?"

"I don't know."

"Well think about it. Don't let your pride make a fool out of you. Imagine how proud Emlyn would be to see you singing in a great concert hall packed with people."

John Parry let it rest there to allow Dafydd time to dwell on what he had said. He felt sure that there would be a positive outcome because he knew the mother and grandmother. They certainly wouldn't pass up such an opportunity. His parting words to his protégé were "Don't forget to tell your family all that has happened today."

Chapter Twenty-five

Dafydd had no option because his family was eagerly waiting for his return. As soon as he opened the front door he heard his mother's voice shouting, "Is that you, Dafydd?"
The three were sitting round the fire in the middle kitchen.

"Come and sit here," said Carrie as he entered the room. "It must have been cold walking up from the station. Here give me your cap and muffler." She fussed over her son until he was settled in a chair in front of the fire and then inevitably she asked, "What about something to eat and a nice cup of tea?"
Carrie put dishes on the table, cut thick slices of bread, and made tea in the old brown teapot with the water from the kettle boiling on the hob. Dafydd went to sit at the table and was surprised to see a pig's trotter on his plate.

"Thought that you would like it," said his mother. "I bought it in the Co-op this morning as a treat for when you came home. There's some rice pudding in the oven too."

"And when you've finished all that son," said Emlyn. "You can tell us about this Madame Clara."
So Dafydd ate his supper and then turning to face the three he related his tale.

"You mean that you are going to sing in Cardiff!"

"It's not as simple as that, Mam. I've got to have lessons. Go to rehearsals. All this is going to cost money and there's me without a job. John Parry B.A. says that he will put a word in for me with Mrs. Lewis and I'm not to worry about work. But even with money coming in I don't know if we can afford it."

"We'll manage somehow," said Emlyn.

"I can do more washing," said Carrie.

"No, Mam! No more sacrifices. If, and it's only if, I have these lessons then I'll borrow what money I need from the choirmaster. He's offered and I think that's the only thing to do."

Just then, Granny Price, who until now had been unusually silent, got up from her chair and walked across to her rosewood chest of drawers. Bending stiffly, she pulled open the bottom drawer. From the back, underneath a pile of clothes, she took out a black leather purse. She then walked over to her grandson and handed it to him.

"There's no need to borrow. There's money enough in there. Use what you want." Looking at her astonished family she said, "I've been putting bits away for years. It's to bury me but I have no intention of going for a long time yet. When Dafydd is rich and famous he can pay for my funeral. Then looking at him she said, "Nothing but the best mind!"

The other three began talking at once.

"I can't take this," protested Dafydd.

"Mam, that's yours," said Emlyn.

Carrie simply remarked, "That's settled then. Singing lessons it is. But mind you go after that job on top pit Dafydd Price."

The following morning, John Parry made his way up to Rock House and, as he was about to ring the bell, the door opened. Out walked a young man.

"I've just had Alban Thomas here, you know Thomas Thomas the builder's son," said Sarah when they were alone

in the drawing room. "He's under-manager at the colliery and he has been very helpful. I've arranged for him to come here once a week to help me understand how the pit is run. He has more patience with me than Mr. Davies, the manager. I can follow Alban's explanations much more easily."
John was surprised by the animosity that he felt towards the innocent young man.

He's got no right to come here, he found himself thinking. Calm down, calm down, he told himself. Alban Thomas is only doing his job. Probably been instructed to keep Sarah away from the pit as much as possible.

"It's good to see you, John, but it's not like you to make an unexpected visit. Is anything wrong?"
John Parry hastily pushed his thoughts to the back of his mind and began to explain his purpose.

"It's about a job," he said.

Sarah laughed. "You are not telling me that you want to work down the pit!" she teased.

"No, I'd better start from the beginning. Yesterday I took Dafydd Price to see Madame Clara Novello-Davies in Cardiff hoping that she would accept him as a pupil. She's agreed to take him on but singing lessons cost money. So you see, Sarah, Dafydd needs a job but not underground. I don't want his voice ruined by the coal dust."

"I'll ask Alban Thomas. I'm sure that he'll find something for the young man. Especially if he knows that he'll be doing me a favour," she said mischievously.
For such an intelligent man, John Parry B.A. fell for this immediately.

"No, I think it would be better to approach the manager directly."

"Why, John, what have you got against poor Alban?" asked Sarah, purposely omitting to state the young engineer's surname. But when she saw the discomfort on her visitor's face, she couldn't continue to tease him. "Mr. Davies it is then," she said. "Now tell me all about your trip to Cardiff. What is Madame Clara really like? Was her famous son at home?"

It wasn't long before the whole village knew that Dafydd was going to Cardiff for singing lessons.

"You'll be too big to come here to do the washing before long," teased the cook when Carrie walked through the scullery door a few days latter.

"Oh get on with you. Our Dafydd is only going for a few singing lessons. Why I don't know. Everyone says that he has a lovely voice, but I suppose that John Parry B.A. knows best."

"You'll be walking out with a celebrity before long, Mary," said Mrs. Lloyd addressing the maid.

Mary blushed but didn't reply. Courting, she thought, a few walks and the odd kiss. Nothing to write home about. Gallivanting to Cardiff, goodness knows whom he'll meet. Especially if what people say is right and he's going to sing with that girls' choir.

"You want to nail him now, before he gets too famous," went on the cook. "Aren't I right, Carrie?"

"All I know, Mrs. Lloyd, is that I wish he would settle down like his brothers. Lovely grandchildren I've got," she said looking straight at Mary.

At home that evening, Carrie repeated this conversation to her mother-in-law. "By now, Mam, he ought to be married and Mary will make him a good wife."

"Don't be too hasty, Carrie. Let the lad be. Perhaps he wants more time to himself after all he's been through." And he doesn't want Mary, thought the old woman.

Madame Clara was no easy taskmaster. She thought that she had found the singer who could take over from her own dear Ivor whose singing voice had been as clear as a bell. People had flocked to hear him sing at Magdalen College. Then came the greatest tragedy in Madame Clara's life – her son's voice broke and never returned. Since then she had been searching for a sound that she held in her mind. As soon as Dafydd started to sing, she knew that she had found it. She was determined that the young collier would be the singer that her otherwise talented son could never be.

For Dafydd, the first lesson was nerve wracking since there was no John Parry to guide him. He didn't understand why his voice had to be trained. Singing was something that came naturally to him. Scales – what were they for? Luckily his nervousness prevented him from voicing his thoughts and his army training ensured that he responded quickly and accurately to the great lady's instructions. He didn't know which was worse – the lessons or the rehearsals with the choir! He pitied the girls for they were forced to repeat and repeat until the verse, phrase or even the note was exactly as Madame Clara wanted. Luckily, he was unaware of the choir's international reputation. If he had known then he would have questioned his own appearance in the concert even more. After a number of rehearsals, Dafydd still didn't realize that in the pieces he sang the choir was there to support him and not the other way about.

Chapter Twenty-six

Rock House,
November 1915.

Dear Louisa,

I am writing to tell you some news that I'm sure that you will be pleased to hear. Your old patient, Dafydd Price, is having singing lessons with the famous Madame Clara Novello-Davies! Apparently he's to sing with her famous choir at the Christmas Concert at the Park Hall. John has arranged the lessons. I wish I could go to the concert but as a widow without a suitable escort it is impossible. John of course will be there.

At this point, Sarah stopped writing and sighed as she wished that she could go with him and flout convention but she knew that she just didn't have the courage. Besides, if she was to do anything worthwhile in Morganton she needed to preserve her reputation. Sighing with resignation, she returned to her letter.

You will be pleased to know that we have found the land for the new hospital. Thomas Thomas the builder is drawing up the plans for the building and...

Bron Rhyw Hospital,
December 1915.

Dear Aunt Sarah,

  I was very interested to hear about Dafydd Price. He has such a good voice. It is good to know that he is getting some recognition for it. It's a great pity that you can't go to see him sing. Perhaps you could have a concert in Morganton or invite him to sing at a dinner party. Put my name down on the guest list but make sure that you give me sufficient notice to get leave.

  We are receiving more and more injured here at the hospital. We are making room for extra beds but there are so many wounded coming in that we do not always have space for them. The sisters now share one bedroom in the main house and if we have to take any more men then matron is going to sleep in her office and give up her room too.

  The soldiers' stories are heartbreaking. One has told me how he put an overcoat over his friend on the battlefield and placed a bottle with some rum in it in his hand. Then he had to leave him to continue the assault. He knew that by the time the stretcher bearers got to his mate it would be too late. Others speak of equally dreadful incidents. I don't know how even some survive it all!

  I must end now and go back to the ward. I'm glad to hear that the plans for the hospital are progressing. Think about a concert or a dinner party.

      With love from
        Louisa.

"I don't know how he is doing it all, Mam," said Carrie. "Two weeks to go to that concert and he's working every day on that site for the new engine house."

"Don't fret, it's only for a short time now, he'll manage. But before the big night we've got a job to do. Have you thought of what he's going to wear?"

"Why his suit I suppose."

"Not to a place like that and on the stage on his own too," retorted Granny Price. "He'll need a black worsted and a waistcoat with a nice watch and chain. A white shirt and a bow tie." Yes that should do it, she thought as she remembered how the gentlemen dressed all those years ago in Aberystwyth.

"Well he's got the last two but not a black worsted suit and where will we get a pocket watch and chain from?"

"Never mind about that, it's the suit that's important. I'm off to Morris the draper to see what cloth he's got. Are you coming?"

The two women wrapped up well for it was cold that December morning and then set out for the main road. There were icy patches where the water in the ruts had frozen and Carrie helped the old lady as they negotiated their way along the street. The hill was criss-crossed by shiny ribbons where the children had been sliding. The two women could do nothing but edge their way up very slowly. At last they reached the main road and were able to walk on the new pavements. They made straight for Morris' shop. Opening the door, they were glad to feel the warmth of the paraffin stoves. Without hesitation, Granny Price walked straight to the counter at the back where the bales of cloth were kept.

"I want to see some of your best material," said Granny Price to the draper.

"Making a suit for Dr. Williams or for the Reverend Evans, are you?"

"No. I want a black worsted."

"For Thomas Thomas the builder then?"

"No, nor for the landlord of the Morganton Hotel," replied Granny Price with a meaningful look over towards Mrs. Morris who was talking to Carrie.

The shopkeeper hastily turned to the shelves and pulled out a bale of black worsted. The tailoress felt the cloth between her finger and thumb.

"Not bad," she muttered. Then looking at the shelves, she asked "What about that one over there?"

"Dearer but better quality. I'll get it down for you."

Granny Price knew which material she wanted but was determined to give no more for it than she had to.

Raising her voice she said, "I met George the butler yesterday. Asked him about his sister. You know the barmaid at the Morganton Hotel."

Morris kept looking over to his wife during this unfortunate part of the conversation. He felt his stomach churn when he saw her look towards them on hearing the words Morganton Hotel.

Hastily he said to the old lady, "As you are such a good customer, I can let you have this at a special price. Let me see now."

Granny Price left the shop well satisfied. She had obtained Morris the draper's best-worsted cloth at her price. Now there was one more thing to do.

"Shoe shop next, Carrie."

"What for, Mam? No one needs new boots."

"Dafydd cannot sing in Cardiff in his boots. He must have black shoes."

The shopkeeper was quite used to selling men's shoes to women. He seldom saw any men in his shop. The miners were always in work and so the wives bought their boots as well as every other item of clothing for them.

"Black shoes, not boots, size sevens, Arthur, please," said Granny Price.

"Shoes! That's posh, who they're for?"

"Our Dafydd," replied Carrie and then she couldn't resist adding, "He's singing in the Park Hall in Cardiff."

"Yes, I've heard. It's a step up for him. I'll see what shoes we've got in his size," said Arthur as he turned and looked along the shoeboxes stacked behind him. "What about these? They're made of a nice leather and will always polish up."

The two ladies carefully inspected the shoes.

"You're right, Arthur, there's good leather in these. Have you any others?" asked the old lady.

"I could show you a few other pairs but these are the best."

"If you say so. We'll take them."

A few minutes later, the two ladies were outside the shop. Carrie carried the large brown paper parcel containing the cloth and her mother-in-law carried the shoes.

"We'll have to be even more careful going back down that hill. I wish the boys wouldn't make slides when it's icy. Shall I carry the shoes as well, Mam? Easier for you to walk. Can't have you falling now because, as you said, we've a busy week ahead of us."

A few days later the postman delivered a small package to the Price's house.

"A parcel!" exclaimed Carrie as she took it from him. "Who's sent us this?"

Emlyn looked at the address and said, "It's not for us."

"I thought it must have been a mistake," said his wife.

"No, no mistake, it's for our Dafydd."

"Dafydd, who would send him a parcel?"

"Don't know, we'll have to wait until he comes home to find out. Put it on top of the chest of drawers and give it to him when he comes in."

For the rest of the day, whenever Carrie had a spare minute she looked at the small brown paper parcel and wondered. On a few occasions she even picked it up but whichever way she examined the package it yielded no clues as to what it contained or more importantly who sent it. It was inevitable that as soon as Dafydd's feet crossed the threshold that the parcel was pushed into his hands. He was just as surprised to receive a parcel as they had been. Who can have sent me this? He wondered as he stared at it.

"I can't open it now, Mam. Look at me, I'm filthy. Let me wash first."

And Carrie had to wait yet again before her curiosity was satisfied. At last Dafydd came into the middle room after washing away the day's grim. Slowly his fingers untied the string and then he carefully unfolded the brown paper to reveal a black box with the words H. T. Jenkins, Watch Maker and Jeweller written on the top.

"What is it, Dafydd?" Carrie asked impatiently.

"Give me a chance, Mam," he answered as he opened the lid of the box.

Nestling inside was a silver watch and chain.

Dafydd looked at it in amazement. His first thought was that it was a mistake. Somehow it had been delivered to the wrong address. Then he saw the edge of a card protruding from under the watch. Taking this out he read silently:

> *Sorry I can't be at the concert. Hope this will bring you luck.*
>
> *Louisa.*

His face changed colour.

"What does it say?" asked his mother.

Dafydd gulped and managed to reply, "It's from Louisa, to wear at the concert."

"Oh, that's kind of her. Mrs. Lewis must have mentioned about you singing when she wrote to her niece. Who'd have thought that Miss Louisa would have done such a thing? Your granny was only saying the other day that a watch and chain was what was needed to set off your new suit."

And so Carrie went on about kindness and thoughtfulness and how smart her son would look but her words were lost on the young man as he concentrated on stopping his hands from shaking and his heart from pounding as he gently handled his new silver pocket watch and chain.

Chapter Twenty-seven

At last, the day of Madame Clara's concert arrived. Dafydd and John Parry B.A. were to travel together to Cardiff. The choirmaster was determined to give his protégé as much moral support as possible. The two men met on the platform and John was astonished by the change in Dafydd's appearance for he looked every inch a gentleman.

Dressed like that and with his voice he can't fail, thought John Parry. Then out loud he said, "I see that your grandmother has been busy. You really look the part, lad."

"New suit and shoes as well. They've fussed over me for days," said Dafydd as he stood a little taller.

"Well it was worth it. That silver chain sets off that waistcoat. Was it your grandfather's?"

"No, it's a present, " replied Dafydd awkwardly. "To bring me luck."

Sensing some embarrassment, the choirmaster didn't pursue the matter any further. Obviously from an admirer, he thought. Perhaps someone he's met at Madame Clara's. Louisa's name simply didn't enter his mind.

Walking through Cardiff they saw posters advertising the concert.

CHRISTMAS CONCERT

AT THE PARK HALL
FEATURING

MADAME CLARA'S FAMOUS GIRLS CHOIR
AND
TENOR DAVID PRICE.

"Look, Dafydd, that's you on those posters," exclaimed the choirmaster.

"David Price, that's not me."

"Of course it is. It's the English for Dafydd."

"But I'm Welsh and why change my name? I'm going to complain. I'm not singing under that name!"

"Calm down. Now don't ruin things. It's only what they call a stage name. You'll still be Dafydd to the people who matter. David is easier for some people to say, especially when you'll sing in England. Think, this is only the beginning. Now don't spoil your chances." John Parry sensed the unease in the young man's mind. He knew that Madame Clara was right for by anglicising his name she made Dafydd instantly more acceptable in musical circles. "Take my advice lad, if you are introduced to people as David Price then just accept it."

But Dafydd wasn't very happy about it and everything else that was to come that day. His singing had always been in familiar surroundings and in front of his own kind. The thought of singing in the Park Hall in Cardiff made his stomach churn.

Why I agreed to have lessons in the first place, I don't know, he thought. Madame Clara has made me alter the way I sing and now she has seen fit to change my name! The wording on the poster had emphasised to Dafydd that he was on the threshold of a new life and he didn't know if he wanted to leave his old one behind. He couldn't help remembering that his first attempt at leaving the valleys had ended in tragedy. Where was this path going to take him? Yet he recognized that it was his big chance to get away from the pit. And that was so important to him.

The two men walked on in silence until they reached the Park Hall. There was still an hour before the concert but people were already arriving. Although the dearer seats were numbered, the others were not and the early arrivals wanted the better places. The two men walked around the building and in through a door that opened on to the back stage area.

"There you are at last!" exclaimed Madame Clara as she saw them. "Come over here. Let me see you." She looked Dafydd up and down from his carefully greased hair to his shinny new shoes. At last she nodded with approval. "You'll do," she muttered and then added quietly, "Yes, you'll do very nicely."

Almost immediately she was back to giving last minute instructions to her girls and now to Dafydd as well. John smiled as he saw the command she had over her singers. They wouldn't dare to sing a wrong note on this or any other evening. He noticed that some of the girls had made room for Dafydd to stand next to them.

Yes, he's fitting in nicely, John Parry thought as he turned and made his way out of the back stage area, around the great building and in through the main entrance.

For a few minutes the choirmaster stood in a corner of the foyer and took in the scene. The night was obviously an occasion. Some of the ladies were resplendent in their furs and their male partners in evening dress. Even the poorest of the concertgoers were dressed in their Sunday best. He caught snippets of conversation:

"I did so enjoy last year's concert, I hope that this one will be as good."

"What a sound the choir makes."

"Who is this David Price?"

"Oh didn't you know? He's Madame Clara's latest discovery. My maid said that he is quite handsome too, or so she's heard. You know how servants gossip."

"I only hope that he can sing," remarked her male companion.

John smiled as the group drifted away from him.

He can sing all right, he thought. Just wait 'till you hear him.

Back stage, the choir was getting nervous. They had performed on so many occasions and each time had acquitted themselves well, but it was the same every concert or competition – as the minutes ticked by so each singer felt a little more of the pressure. Dafydd was no exception. This was his first performance at such a venue and he had plenty of time to think about what could go wrong since his first item wasn't until just before the interval. So much depended on this concert. If he sang well and the audience liked him, then John Parry said that he would be asked to sing in others. Each time he would get paid for singing! He still couldn't quite believe that it was possible to make a living from singing, whatever the choirmaster told him. But if he could, then he wouldn't have to go down the pit again. No more winter days of darkness with sunlight only on a Sunday.

At last, the girls were on stage. Dafydd stood listening to them. He knew every word and note they sang but then the thought struck him – what were his? He started to go over them in his mind but the more he tried, the less he remembered. This was stupid. He'd sung the carol so many times before. He'd never had trouble with the words.

I'll make a fool of myself. I can't go on, he panicked.
But Dafydd knew that he had to. The expectations this time came from his family and friends, not from King and Country. As his mind raced his fingers played with the silver chain that crossed his waistcoat.

I can't walk out of here, he thought. There's Granny Price's money, the suit, the shoes and Louisa's watch. I have to sing and sing well.
Suddenly, he realized that Madame Clara was speaking to the audience and his mind registered her last few words.

"… will be sung by David Price."
Dafydd didn't move. All those people were waiting for him.

"Go on, lad," said a voice behind him. "That's you."

As if in a daze Dafydd walked on to the stage but the hours of practice and drilling came to his rescue. He automatically positioned himself correctly and waited for the music. As he heard the familiar notes, he started to sing the carol Silent Night. There wasn't a sound or movement as the audience came under his spell. At the end, the tremendous contrast between the peacefulness generated by Dafydd's rendition of this well-loved carol and the swelling sound of the applause could not fail to make an impression on the sternest critic in the hall – Dafydd himself. Madame Clara, of course, had known exactly what she was doing when she put her programme together and offered her audience a taste of the young tenor at the end of the first half of the concert. Inevitably, in the interval, he was the main topic of conversation.

"His voice, what a tenor and so good looking," said one lady.

John Parry smiled as he heard her. Dafydd had made an impression on the concertgoers and he had only sung one carol.

By the end of the second half, there was no doubting Dafydd's success. The applause for the choir was loud but for him it was deafening! And for the first time, he started to believe that yes perhaps John Parry B.A. was right and he needn't go down the pit again. As he came off stage after the last curtain call, Madame Clara insisted that he followed her to meet some of the important people in the audience. Very much in a daze he was introduced to one person after another.

"This of course is my tenor, David Price."

Time and time again the young man shook hands, barely registering the change in his own name. The people and their praise seemed unreal - until he saw a familiar face.

"Well done, lad, well done. You're the talk of the Park Hall. The first rung Dafydd, the first rung!" exclaimed an excited John Parry.

It was a long time before the last of the admirers departed. Eventually, the two men were able to take their leave of Madame Clara and say goodnight to the young ladies of the choir. As they walked hurriedly through the city to catch the last train back to Morganton, the young man's hand kept returning to his trouser pocket to feel the coins in the bottom. His fee of five guineas was a fortune, and all for standing on a stage and singing. He still couldn't believe it. He could pay his Granny Price back and if John Parry B.A. was right there would be more in the future! He even allowed himself to think of Louisa. Perhaps she was not so unattainable after all.

Chapter Twenty-eight

Mrs. Williams could barely restrain herself. In the Co-op she had heard that Mrs. Lewis was spending Christmas with her sister in Bristol. There would be no Yuletide dinner at Rock House this year. But she was the Doctor's wife and the second lady of Morganton. It was surely her duty to invite people to Christmas dinner. Mrs. Williams' mind raced. How many to invite? Who should she ask? Was it going to be a turkey or goose? There was certainly a lot to do.

"I'd better get home quickly and talk to Elizabeth," she said to no one in particular as she hurried back along the way she had come and abandoned all thoughts of visiting her friend Mrs. Morris the draper.

The first thing she did when she arrived home was to walk into the dining room and stand before the table.

"Hm, with the leaves put in the middle this will seat ten, perhaps twelve at a push. There's the three of us and of course John. Then the Reverend Evans, the colliery manager and his wife, Mr. and Mrs. Morris the Draper – that'll be nine. What about the undertaker or Thomas Thomas…?"

"I thought I heard you come in," said Elizabeth as she came into the dining room. "But who were you talking to?"

Ignoring the last remark, Mrs. Williams said, "Have you heard the news? Mrs. Lewis is off to Bristol."

"That'll be nice for her. She'll be less lonely being with her family over Christmas."

"Don't you see, Elizabeth," said her mother impatiently. "We'll have to entertain on her behalf."

"What do you mean? Has she asked you to represent her at some function?"

"No, of course not but there'll be no Christmas dinner at Rock House. We'll have to invite people instead. Now how many do you think that we can seat around this table?"

Trying to keep a sober face and managing to suppress her laughter, Elizabeth gave her mother her undivided attention. She knew that any such grandiose scheme had to be reined in or her father would throw a fit when he heard. Gradually, and with some ingenuity, she persuaded her mother to curtail the party to the three of them plus of course John and Mr. and Mrs. Morris.

"You know how father likes to eat at about one o'clock and not in the evening. That'll be too early for the minister since he'll not long have finished taking the Christmas service. I'm sure that there are ladies in his congregation who'd love to invite him to dinner and he must accept sometimes. Besides he does so dominate the conversation at the dining table and you know how agitated father gets when that happens."

Mrs. Williams knew that what her daughter said made sense. As for inviting the others, well, perhaps not. They were acquaintances, not friends and they probably had other plans anyway. Yes an intimate Yuletide dinner party – as Elizabeth had put it – would be the best. After all she could always say that in Mrs. Lewis' absence they were inviting people on Christmas day and leave it at that.

At Rock House, Carrie and Mrs. Lloyd were drinking their mid morning cup of tea.

"I hear that you're to have an easy Christmas," said Carrie.

"Yes, that's right. With Mrs. Lewis away, there'll be no fancy dinner to prepare. We'll have ours in here. I've a couple of geese in the larder. George is bringing his sister, the barmaid, and I've told Mary to ask your Dafydd but she says that she hasn't seen him lately."

"It's that concert. He did very well by all accounts but what with the practice and working he's had no time to himself. Perhaps things will settle after Christmas so tell Mary not to worry."

"Is he going to sing again? It would be nice if it was nearer then we could all go to see him on the stage."

"I don't know. He says that John Parry B.A. keeps telling him that he could earn his living from singing. I ask you!"

"Yes, for the likes of us money only comes through hard work and talking about that, Carrie, we'd better get on."

"Not so much washing today though. Thankfully, in this weather because the clothes won't dry out of doors. I'll have to hang them in the scullery." Carrie pushed her chair away from the table and went to fill the bucket with more water for the big copper.

Christmas morning – so much has happened in the last year, thought Dafydd as he lay in bed in his tiny room. Twelve months ago I was singing carols in the trenches and just last week on the stage in the Park Hall. He smiled as he remembered the audience's applause and how he had been introduced to people as "My new tenor." He acknowledged to himself that he admired the great lady. Madame Clara knew what she wanted and wasn't satisfied until her singers produced it. She'd been hard on him making him repeat and repeat, but even after these few weeks he knew that he was a better singer. Then his mind turned to a more pressing problem – Louisa and the watch. How was he going to thank her? He remembered that his mother had told him that Mrs. Lewis was going to Bristol for Christmas because her niece was working at the hospital. That's it. The trains are running tomorrow afternoon. I'll go to the hospital and say that I've come to visit some of my mates. I'm bound to see her.

Satisfied, the young man got out of bed, dressed quickly in the cold bedroom and went downstairs for breakfast before the rest of the family arrived.

As usual on Christmas day, the Price's house was filled with Carrie and Emlyn's children and grandchildren. Granny Price had made sure that each child had something new to wear, the best tablecloth had been brought out and the smell of the capon roasting in the oven pervaded the house.

"Have you bought anything from the cheap jack, Mam?" asked one of Carrie's daughters-in-law. "He had a stall on Queen's Square last week."

"No, I didn't want any thing this time but I've heard that he's been up to new tricks. He's painted over the flaws in the china. Nellie Evans bought some cups and saucers from him and when she went to wash them some of the flowers disappeared and there were cracks instead!"

"Didn't she take them back and give him a piece of her mind?"

"By the time she'd found out, he'd gone. You know how sly he is."

"Yes, he's a sharp one all right. I always check what I buy in front of him. You can't be too careful where he is concerned."

After dinner, Dafydd sat with his father and brothers in the front room whilst the women washed up and acted as arbitrators for the now squabbling children until the youngsters were persuaded to go out the street to play cattie and doggie. Inevitably Dafydd was asked about his singing.

"Yes, I'm still having lessons."

"No, I don't know when there'll be another concert."

"Yes, Madame Clara is Ivor Novello's mother."

"No, I've not met him. He's in the Royal Naval Air Service."

"Yes, it's true that Ivor was in a terrible plane crash. One of the girls in the choir told me. That's why he works in the war ministry in London now. But according to his mother he's spending more and more time writing songs for the Gaiety Theatre."

"He'll be writing one for you before long, Dafydd," teased his eldest brother.

When the good-humoured laughter subsided, the conversation turned to other things and Dafydd was able to sit back and let it flow around him as he planned his visit to Bron Rhyw Hospital.

Mrs. Williams' Christmas dinner was a success. Everyone praised the food and it had to be said that the turkey was particularly good – very tender indeed. Elizabeth and John talked happily together throughout the meal and, since there was little in Morganton that escaped the doctor or the draper, they were never at a loss for conversation around the table. Afterwards in the drawing room, the party naturally split up into three groups. The two older ladies gossiped together as they sat in front of the fire. Mrs. Morris couldn't wait to tell her friend the latest news about the Reverend Evans.

"Didn't you know, he's been offered the Mount Stuart Square Chapel in Cardiff? It's a big step up for him. He's sure to take it."

"But who will we have for Ebenezer?" asked Mrs. Williams.

"Apparently there's a student from the college in Bala interested. He's particularly keen on doing things for the young people. Impressed by our Sunday school though. There were two hundred there last Sunday when he came to visit."

"A student, you say. But he won't have any experience!"

"The deacons know that but you should have heard him preach that night. Put the fear of God into me. Impressive – everyone said so."

Mrs. Williams nodded her head as if in agreement though she had not heard the young preacher. Her friend encouraged by this continued.

"He has some idea about starting up a ramblers' club for the young people. Catch the train to a different station every week and then walk from the station to whatever is interesting in the area. You know, a castle or something like that."

"That sounds good. I'm sure that Elizabeth would be interested and of course the young minister would always have John's support. So much experience to call on – him being headmaster and choirmaster."

Mrs. Williams looked over to her daughter and John Parry B.A.

Her friend followed her gaze and remarked, "They seem to be getting on very well."

"Yes, they always have a lot to talk about. The same interests – the school and music."

"They make a nice couple. Are they walking out together?"

"No, not yet. But I've hopes. Elizabeth talks a lot about him. It's John this and John that."

"You won't have long to wait I'm sure," said Mrs. Morris as she looked at the pair and nodded her head knowingly.

But if the ladies had been able to hear the conversation of the two teachers they would have been very disappointed. There was nothing personal about it, nothing to raise the hopes of Mrs. Williams.

Elizabeth would indeed have liked to change the subject and get away from discussing the village school and its problems; but how and to what?

Why can't we talk about ourselves? What can I say? Little did she know that John Parry was trying to control the conversation in order to remain fair to Sarah. He didn't like it that she had gone to Bristol for Christmas. He could understand why but he had hoped that they could have spent some time together. Even, if for convention's sake, it had to be in the company of others. And now here he was sitting by the side of a very pretty young lady trying not to succumb to temptation. But, after the Doctor's port, losing the battle. The affects of the wine made him agree to play a duet with Elizabeth. There was nothing for it but to follow her to the piano.

"Look everyone, we're having some entertainment," said Mrs. Williams.

The ladies shuffled their chairs around as Elizabeth chose some music. Then fingers sped expertly over the keys.

The piece was lively and at the end John exclaimed, "Well played!"

Elizabeth's eyes sparkled and, as her cheeks flushed in response to his praise, the last of his resolve melted away. Sitting closer together, they began to play again.   Mrs. Williams smiled happily as she watched the two pianists.

"You won't have long to wait before there's wedding bells," whispered Mrs. Morris. "You mark my words."

While all this was going on, the two older men had been sitting at the far end of the room savouring the doctor's vintage port. They got on well enough but more because of their wives' friendship than any mutual liking of each other. Both, however, could think of far worse ways of spending a Christmas afternoon and were content to allow the conversation to ebb and flow as the mood took them. Naturally, the doctor's thoughts were concentrated on the new hospital though the draper's were not so focused. Earlier he had conversed happily about his shop and the state of business in the town, but on seeing the two at the piano his mind strayed to the Morganton Hotel and that big feather bed. He wondered if he could persuade Mrs. Morris to let him go there for an hour after they got home. Perhaps the ginger wine would make her sleepy and she wouldn't know that he had gone.

If I could only get her to drink a glass of this port, he thought as he looked over to where the two women sat. He noticed that their glasses were empty. Seizing his chance, he picked up the bottle of port and said, "The ladies will think that we're neglecting them. Shall I fill their glasses?"
The doctor, still thinking about the new hospital, only half heard the question and grunted a reply. Morris, taking this to mean yes, went over to the two and poured each a glass of port wine – making sure that his wife had a very generous measure indeed.

Mr. and Mrs. Morris were the first to take their leave that evening.

"I don't know why I'm feeling so sleepy. I suppose it serves me right for sitting in front of the fire. It has been a lovely day. I really enjoyed my dinner and we've had such a nice chat together."

"Come on, my dear," said her husband impatiently. "Let Mrs. Williams get back to the others," and he took his wife's arm to guide her down the path.

They hadn't gone many yards, when Mrs. Morris said, "I feel quite strange. My legs are weak."

"They'll be all right. I expect it's the cold air after being in that warm room. Hold on to my arm and we'll soon be home. Perhaps an early night is called for. You've had a busy day."

Dafydd stared at the castle clinging to the hillside. That's the Marquess of Bute's, he thought, and where Louisa belongs. Not with the likes of me. He remembered her telling him, as they walked the hospital grounds last summer, that she had been invited to spend the weekend there on a few occasions but had been far too busy to accept. She's bound to stay there sooner or later and then she'll meet someone of her own kind, fall in love with him and that'll be that. Already the confidence he had gained from his triumph at the concert was ebbing away.

A few minutes later he turned into the hospital drive. His quiet knock on matron's door was answered by a loud "enter". Her eyes lifted from a large ledger as he walked in.

"Dafydd Price, or should I say David?" she exclaimed as she recognized him. "Come in, take a seat. I was at the Park Hall. Everyone said how well you sang. Of course I told them that you had been one of my patients. Wounded in battle and quite a hero."

The young man felt the colour rising up his cheeks as she continued in the same vein for a few minutes.

Then getting up, she said, "I must tell Louisa that you are here. You were a particular favourite of hers. Sit on that chair. I won't be long."

Overwhelmed by his reception, Dafydd sat and waited.

It wasn't long before the matron returned with Louisa. Matron, oblivious of the two young people in the room, talked on about the concert, Madame Clara and, of course, her new tenor. Louisa, sensing Dafydd's discomfort, went over to congratulate him.

"I'm sorry that I wasn't there but I've heard tremendous things about your performance. Congratulations, I'm sure that your family is very proud of you."

"Yes", was all that he could think to say in reply.

Taking charge of the situation, Louisa said, "You haven't come all this way just to see us nurses. Let's go and see some of the men."

"Yes indeed," said the matron. "You take him along to the ward. I've these accounts to finish. But bring him back here for tea."

In the corridor, Louisa's face broke into a huge grin for she could hardly keep herself from laughing.

"Oh, Dafydd, what a welcome! You're an important person now. You've performed on the stage at the Park Hall in front of all those dignitaries."

"It was only a concert. I've sung in plenty in the valleys."

Recognizing his embarrassment, she smiled encouragingly at him and said, "Shall we go into the ward?"

"Wait a minute. There's something I want to say to you. The pocket watch and chain – I've never owned anything as grand. Granny Price said it was just what was needed on my new suit. I came to say thank you."

Looking down at her upturned face, it seemed the most natural thing in the world to kiss her lips. But as soon as he did it, he thought – what have I done? Looking in her eyes, he saw no hint of rejection. Yet, however much he wanted to, he couldn't bring himself to kiss her again.

Too soon to go further, she thought. He'll run away if I'm not careful. Then to him she said, "I'm glad that you liked it. Wear it for me at your next concert for I'm sure that there will be another one very soon. Come on, let's go and cheer up some of the patients."

Going home on the train that evening, Dafydd reflected on the day. He'd been able to bring some comfort to the wounded since seeing him fully recovered from the horrors of war gave them hope. Everyone seemed to have heard of the concert and two of the older men trapped him into singing for them. He'd ended with "Keep the home fires burning" and wondered how many knew that Ivor Novello had originally called it "Till the Boys come Home." - a particularly apt title in their situation. Madame Clara, in one of her more expansive moods, had talked about her son Ivor and for him that was the melody that unlocked the door of fame and fortune. Then had come tea with matron and as many of the nurses that could be spared. He remembered Louisa sipping her tea and smiling as she enjoyed the attention he was given. She had walked with him through the hospital grounds to the gate and before he left he had thanked her once again for the silver pocket watch

"Wear it and think of me," she had said and then reaching up kissed him gently on his lips before they had parted.

Christmas at her sister's had been pleasant enough. Sarah was certainly grateful for the company. Renewing friendships and acquaintances, she saw a much-changed Bristol society. The war of course affected everyone and they did their bit as a matter of course. All knew someone who was away fighting and many young ladies were involved in the war effort through the Red Cross or other charitable organizations. Her brother-in-law was proud to tell everyone that not only was his daughter nursing the wounded and that he'd funded a motor ambulance, but also he was thinking about becoming a special constable. However, the changed conditions of the war years affected young women more than most. They, like Louisa, had become much more independent. This Sarah could applaud for wasn't she striding in the same direction.

Her thoughts were interrupted by a knock on the bedroom door.

"Come in."

"Madam sent me, Mrs. Lewis, to see if you needed any help with your hair."

"No, I think that it's all right, Ruth," Sarah replied as she looked in the dressing table mirror. "But there's my necklace to fasten."

The maid walked over to her and secured the jet beads around her neck. Then looked appraisingly into the mirror at Sarah.

"Perhaps if I pinned your hair a little higher, Mrs. Lewis, and allowed some of the curls to brush your face?"

"Very well, Ruth, I'll leave the finishing touches to you," laughed Sarah.

Looking in the mirror as the maid worked, she saw the reflection of her bedroom.

Changed since I was last here, she thought. But I do like that pretty William Morris design wallpaper and the matching curtains. There's so much more choice in the shops in Bristol. I'm definitely going to buy one of those cherry pattern fire screens to take back with me, and a pair of those pretty enamelled vases like those on the mantelpiece.

"How's this, Mrs. Lewis?"

"You're right, there is a difference!"

Sarah stood up and walked over to the long oval mirror to see the overall effect. The image of a very elegant lady smiled back at her.

Still in black though, she thought with a sigh. It's still too soon for anything else

"Have you seen the new Poiret designs, Mrs. Lewis?" asked the maid. "They're very oriental, all flowing and such magnificent turbans. Pretty colours too."

"No, I haven't, Ruth."

"My friend's mistress had one of his designs sent from London. A pretty patterned silk robe and the headdress was quite something." The maid sensing Sarah's interest continued, "I told Madam about it and I think that she is going to order an outfit. As I said to her, we wouldn't have to worry about lacing up her stays then."

Smiling, Sarah started to move towards the door as the maid said, "Not that that would be of importance to you, Mrs. Lewis, you have such a small waist."

Downstairs, the dinner guests were already gathering in the drawing room. Sarah still hadn't got used to the brightness of the room. If they can have electricity at the colliery then I can have electric light in my sitting room, she thought. The oil lamps and the overhead gasolier give such a poor light compared with this. Yes, when I get back to Morganton there'll be many changes at Rock House.

Inevitably, her sister had seated Sarah next to an eligible gentleman. She had made it clear that it was time for Sarah Lewis to look to the future.

"You can make a very advantageous second marriage, she had said. "What with the money you now have and that colliery. Sell it or at least leave the running of it to the manager. A nice town house here in Bristol would suit you. It would be so good to have you near again, especially with Louisa away because of the war."

But Sarah had other ideas. Despite her sister's best effort, none of the proposed suitors interested her. She was determined not to make a second loveless match for the sake of a position in society. As had been pointed out to her, she was financially independent and very rich indeed by Morganton standards.

The after-dinner gossip amongst the ladies served to strengthen her resolve. It was obvious from the innuendoes that some of them had taken lovers and there was open talk of husbands and their mistresses – even about her so seemingly upright brother-in-law!

"Doesn't bother me now, we meet at breakfast and again at dinner. If he goes out in the evenings I don't ask where and he doesn't enquire too closely about my afternoons."

Sarah could hardly believe it. Not only did he have a mistress but also it sounded as though her sister had taken a lover! And then it struck her – if they see no wrong in what they are doing, then what's to prevent me seeing John? But she knew that it would be at least the summer before the people of Morganton would sanction any new man in her life and strangely she cared very much indeed about their good opinion of her. Pretending to listen to the gossip, she concentrated on thinking up a scheme to bring her and the choirmaster closer together. At last she decided on a musical soirée.

Dafydd Price, invite him to sing at Rock House. I can ask Louisa, she'll be my chaperone. Keep the party small though and only invite a few others. Yes, her mind was made up. She'd organize the evening as soon as she was back home in Morganton.

Chapter Twenty-nine

After Christmas, the people of Morganton fell back into their old routine. The day started with the sound of the first hooter and the men walked into the colliery as the second went off. Dafydd's life followed the same pattern but on top of this, twice a week after work he caught the train to Cardiff for his singing lessons. John Parry B.A. returned to school and he took more and more notice of his attractive young teacher. He was never at a loss for an invitation to supper and spent many an evening listening to the doctor whilst admiring his daughter. He even found himself contemplating giving up his bachelor status. There were changes, however, at the chapel. The Reverend Evans departed for Mount Stuart Square and William Hughes was ordained in Ebenezer on the last Sunday in January.

The service was packed. Everyone wanted to see the new minister. Young and charismatic, he was bound to make an impression and not least on Elizabeth Williams. Like many others in the congregation, she could not take her eyes off him as he preached. For the first time in many months John Parry faded into the background.

"What a preacher," said Carrie as the Prices walked home from chapel. "So much energy, but easy to understand."

"Yes," replied Emlyn. "He puts things in our language. Did you know that he's going to set up a band of hope? I overheard the doctor's daughter offering to help with the children."

"Did she indeed," said his wife. "The talk is about her and John Parry B.A. But I wonder now. The new minister is much nearer her own age. He'd be far better for her."

Emlyn smiled to himself for Carrie was always matchmaking, but recently she seemed to have left Dafydd in peace. Not so long ago it was Mary this and Mary that. Perhaps she realizes at last that he has no interest in the girl. No time either with his singing lessons and the talk of another concert coming up.

Sarah Lewis had returned to Morganton in time for the ordination service. Sitting in splendid isolation in the front pew she too was impressed with William Hughes but as she listened to him preach her eyes darted to the side seat where the doctor and his family sat for with them was John.

Not his usual pew, she thought.

Then she noticed how Mrs. Williams fussed over him.

I haven't returned too soon. It seems that I've a rival in Elizabeth. I must get things organized for the musical evening. I'll speak to John after the service.

As was customary, at the end Sarah followed the minister down the aisle to the vestibule. She welcomed him to South Wales, thanked him for the sermon and remarked on how full the chapel was. After a few more words she moved aside for him to receive the good wishes of the other members of the congregation. But, instead of departing, she waited until the choirmaster appeared.

Smiling as he saw her, he came over and said, "It's good to see you back in Morganton. I was beginning to think that we had lost you to Bristol."

"I know, I stayed longer than I meant to but my sister was most insistent and I had some shopping to do. You'd never believe how fashions are changing. I've made some purchases for the house as well as buying some new clothes."

John laughed, "I don't know a woman who could resist spending money."

"My shopping isn't what I really want to talk to you about. It's about Dafydd Price. He had such a success in Cardiff that I feel I want to encourage him. I was wondering if he would sing at a musical evening I'm planning on holding at Rock House?"

The choirmaster was delighted to think that his protégée was to receive such recognition but he was also aware that Doctor and Mrs. William's were waiting as, yet again, he was invited for supper.

"Come tomorrow evening. I'll tell you more about it then. Perhaps you can ask the young man for me," said Sarah hastily as she too noticed the impatient look on the Doctor's face.

John readily agreed and took his leave.

Yes indeed, thought Sarah Lewis, I haven't returned a moment too soon.

Rock House,
Morganton.
February 1916.

Dear Louisa,

I'm back home at last. I remained with your parents much longer than I intended. I enjoyed my visit but I'm pleased to be back in Morganton. I can tell you all about my stay and the latest gossip in Bristol when you next come to see me. When can you get some leave? I must know to set a date for a musical evening I'm holding here at Rock House. It'll be a small gathering – dinner and then I'm hoping that I can persuade Dafydd Price to sing for us. You will come, won't you?

The plans for the hospital are nearly complete and Thomas Thomas says that the building work will start in the spring. I hope that the weather improves by then for we seem to have had nothing but rain these last few days...

Bron Rhyw Hospital,
Cardiff.
February 1916.

Dear Aunt Sarah,

I received your letter yesterday and of course I will come. I worked all over Christmas so I'll be able to get some leave. I told Matron about your soirée because she has a soft spot for Dafydd ever since she saw him in the Christmas concert. He came to visit us on Boxing Day and she made such a fuss of him. I'll have to unpack an evening dress from my trunk.

I'm so glad that progress has been made on the hospital. Everyone will be pleased to see the work started. Are you going to lay a foundation stone? You must have one with Uncle's name on it. It will be a fitting remembrance.

I don't think that we've had as much rain as you but...

In the kitchen of Rock House, the servants were sat around the table eating their midday meal.

"Well, Carrie," said Mrs. Lloyd, "A musical evening with your Dafydd the star. I told you that he was going up in the world."

Carrie looked puzzled.

"Surely you don't mean that he hasn't told you? Madam's holding a dinner party with your son engaged – that was the word she used – to entertain the guests."

"Well if that's the case I'd better get his best suit out and give it a press and his shoes a polish. I wonder if he'll get paid again. He got five guineas after that concert in Cardiff and there's talk of him singing in another one soon. He says that he'll get money for that too. He might even get more!"

"He's doing all right then," says George. "But he wants to get in with that Ivor Novello. It was in the paper again this week. There's a new musical play in the Gaiety theatre in London and Ivor Novello has written most of the songs. It's a great success. If your Dafydd could get him to compose a tune for him then the money would come rolling in."

"What are you talking about," said Carrie. "London, he's not going to London. Cardiff is far enough."

Mary listened to the conversation but unusually didn't contribute anything to it.

No, give it up as a bad job, she thought. He's not for me. I haven't seen him since before Christmas and I'm fed up of moping around waiting for him to ask me out and he never does. All he thinks about is singing. I'm going to find someone else, she resolved.

But she returned to her food with little enthusiasm.

All that day Sarah Lewis fussed and instructed until the servants had had enough.

"We've had dinner parties before," said Mary to George as they laid the table. "Everything has always gone all right."

"Yes, but Mrs. Lewis has invited some important guests and she wants it to be just so."

"They're the same people we've had on other times – only the minister is new, so why the fuss?"

At last the table was set and the two stood back to admire their work. The silver shone and the glass sparkled. Mary had taken the epergne from the sideboard and placed it in the centre of the table. The cranberry glass of the delicate flutes radiated warmth and made a very pretty addition. George nodded his approval.

"You have an artistic touch," he said.

The maid smiled back at him. "There's still plenty of room for other things on the table."

"Come on, we'd better see to the drawing room next. You'll have to give me a hand with the furniture," said the butler and then unexpectedly he added, "That's if it's not too heavy for you?"

That's the first time he's shown some consideration for me, she thought as she followed him.

Mrs. Lloyd, the cook, had been busy all day. For the third time she checked the menu. The soup was simmering on the range. Yes, she had cut all the vegetables in it into thin strips as instructed and the medallions of bread were ready to put in the bottom of the soup bowls. The cod fillets had just gone in the oven but she still had to make the cream sauce. The veal cutlets were frying gently and the leg of pork resting

What else, she thought looking around. The applesauce and the orange jelly are on the cold slab. The rhubarb tart is in the warming oven. No, only the vegetables to check and the sauce to make and that's it All this fuss, I'll certainly be glad when tonight is over!

Upstairs, Sarah and Louisa were admiring each other.

"I see that you've discarded black, Aunt Sarah. That pale grey silk is very elegant."

"I bought it in Bristol. I hope that I've done the right thing. After all, it is a subdued colour but still perhaps people will think that it's too soon."

"They'll think no such thing. It's a beautiful gown. Look how the skirt flares out at the bottom."

Reassured a little, Sarah smiled and in return said "I've always liked you in that dress. The ball at Dyffryn was so long ago. So much has happened since then."

"I know, but it was only just over two years ago. I haven't worn this since. Mother insisted that I packed this gown when I came to Bron Rhyw Hospital. I think that she thought that I would be spending every other weekend at Cardiff Castle. Anyway, I'm wearing it for your soirée instead."

"I'm honoured indeed," laughed her aunt.

In a happy mood, both took one last glance in the mirror and, satisfied with what they saw, went downstairs to meet their guests.

Dafydd arrived at John Parry's home long before they needed to leave for Rock House. For some reason he felt even more nervous than when he had sung in Cardiff. It wasn't the singing so much as what was to come before. He had been invited to dinner! He already had a sinking feeling in his stomach so he really didn't want to eat very much and then there would be all those knives and forks. His mother had often complained about the amount of cutlery and the number of glasses she washed when she helped out after a dinner party.

"There were three sets at each place and different glasses to drink the red and white wines out of," she had told him after one such evening.

Wine – he'd only ever tasted it once and then he didn't like it.

"You're early, lad," said the choirmaster when Dafydd arrived. "Never mind, we can go over this evening's programme. Where's your music? Is there anything that you need to practice?"

Dafydd shook his head. "I don't think so. I've sung them all before."

But John Parry could see that Dafydd was still nervous and to encourage him said, "Good, everything will be all right as soon as you start singing, you'll see."

"But there'll be Mrs. Lewis, her niece, the colliery manager..."

"And you're worried after singing in front of all those people in the Park Hall. Look at your self in the mirror. Don't you look every inch the part? New suit, silver watch and chain, shoes – confidence, lad, that's what you need."

Sarah's guest list had had to include Dr. Williams and his family but in her seating plan she made sure that Elizabeth sat next to the new minister and that John was at the other end of the table. It was natural to place Dafydd next to Louisa for wasn't he her ex-patient.

"I'll look after him, Aunt Sarah," she had volunteered. True to her word, Louisa had unobtrusively helped him with his cutlery, prevented George from refilling his wine glass and talked to him in order to put him at his ease. Dafydd could have sat listening to her forever but eventually dinner came to an end and the party moved into the drawing room. When everyone was seated, John Parry went over to the piano, lifted the lid and looked around for Dafydd. He saw him standing in the doorway and beckoned to him.

This is silly, thought Dafydd as he walked over to the piano. I feel as nervous as I did at the Park Hall. Why? They've all heard me sing. This is Morganton not Cardiff.

As he passed Louisa, he heard her whisper, "Sing for me."

Luckily, John Parry was too busy with his music to notice the blush on Dafydd's cheeks.

The programme of traditional welsh ballads gave Dafydd ample opportunity to declare his love to Louisa. As he sang the words in The Bells of Aberdovey – "Wilt thou, love, be true to me, E'en as I am true to thee?" – their eyes met and she seemed to give a slight nod. For that moment Dafydd believed that Louisa's feelings for him were the same as his for her.

In the dining room, the servants could hear the music as they cleared the table.

"You must admit that he has a good voice," said George grudgingly.

"Yes," sighed Mary, "But I know now why he's not interested in me. Did you see him gazing at Miss Louisa? Never looked at me like that. As you said he's aiming high. You are right, he'll be too good for the likes of us soon."

"That's correct, girl. I don't want to say it but you've been wasting your time."

"I know but I've come to my senses now. There's plenty more fish in the sea," and as if to emphasize her feelings, Mary straightened her uniform and pulled her blouse tightly over her bosom. The gesture was not lost on George.

"How about you and me taking a walk when we've finished?" he asked.

For a few minutes there was no reply. Then quietly she said," We don't have to go out. Mrs. Lloyd's bound to go to bed as soon as she can after today and the likes of them won't go near the kitchen."

At last the guests had departed and John Parry and Dafydd were gathering up their music from the piano.

"The two of you were magnificent," said Sarah as she walked over. "I can't thank you enough. Come and sit back down. Surely you can stay a little longer."

Unable to refuse, the two men joined the ladies. Dafydd sat and listened whilst John Parry carried on an animated conversation with them. Louisa, noticing the young man's silence, turned to him.

"Are you tired?" she inquired.

"I suppose so."

"I was going to ask you to sing something for me, but if you are too weary…"

"No, I'd do… I mean of course I will."

"Come over to the piano. I'll play and you sing softly. We won't disturb the others. They're too engrossed in their discussions."

Louisa looked through the sheet music.

"Here it is. Remember our day out in Sker? Sing this just for me."

Her fingers gently touched the keys as Dafydd sang softly. At the end he looked at her with eyes that could not hide his love. As she smiled back at him, he wished that they were lying on the grass overlooking the beach at Sker but this time he would not stop at one kiss. She held out her hands and he took them gently. He sang quietly the first verse of the Ash Grove.

Beneath the old ash tree I sat in the gloaming,
Entranced by the ravishing voice of my love,
Who came from the meadows, where she had been roaming,
To waken the echoes that slept in the grove;
She witchingly smiled thro' the wealth of her tresses,
And rosy with blushes was soon at my side,
Where gently returning my fervid caresses,
She faithfully promised to be my own bride.

Louisa's fingers curled round Dafydd's and her eyes sought his as he sang. She wanted so much to promise to be his but the sound of movement at the other end of the room destroyed the magic. Dafydd snatched his hands away as he heard John Parry's voice.

"I'm sorry, Sarah, but it's time we went. I'm sure that the Prices will be wondering how the singing went. They won't have gone to bed. They'll want to hear from Dafydd."

"I understand, but come to tea tomorrow," said Sarah and then added hastily, "Louisa will be here and you are such a favourite of hers."

In the kitchen, George, hearing the bell, pushed Mary off his lap and straightened his clothes.

"That'll be the last of them leaving. I won't be long. Sit in that chair and drink this," he said as he held out a glass of wine. "I told you how good it was. You seem to have enjoyed the last glass. They had only the best tonight."

Laughing, Mary took the wine and snuggled further into the chair in front of the range.

"Your coat, sir."

"Thank you, George. I hope that we haven't kept you up too late," said John Parry.

"No, I've been sitting in front of the fire in the kitchen. Cook went to bed a while ago. I've only to do my rounds now."

After the two ladies had gone upstairs, the butler made a quick check of the downstairs rooms turning off the gaslights and extinguishing the lamps. Then he returned to the kitchen.

"You took your time," said Mary.

"No, it only seemed long to you because you can't wait for what's coming next."

She giggled as he came over to her and then caught her breath as he roughly pulled her to him. He kissed her fiercely and she started to pull back but then she remembered the months of disappointment and frustration.

You can keep your hoity-toity ways Dafydd Price, she thought as she responded.

George manoeuvred her over to the table, pushed her back against it and forced his leg in between hers. She didn't want him to stop but she was afraid. It was her first time but from inside her came May's voice, "If it goes right, then there's nothing better than it." Making up her mind, she reached down her skirt and pulled it up. Then she pushed down her knickers and waited.

"That's my girl," whispered George as he expertly stroked in between her legs, stopping only when he needed two hands to undo a stubborn button. His judgment was rewarded by her gasp as he pushed himself inside.

When it was over he held her tightly as the tears rolled down her cheeks.

It won't be long before you'll be back for more, he thought with some satisfaction.

Chapter Thirty

The musical soirée was to have far reaching repercussions on some of the people present – whether they were guests, musicians or servants.

For Mary, it was the end of her first love affair. A relationship that had been played out more in her mind than in reality. She had expected Dafydd to be there at the party, for after all he had been engaged by Mrs. Lewis to entertain her guests. What she hadn't realized was that he had been invited to diner too. She had nearly dropped the soup tureen when she entered the dinning room and saw him sitting at the table. It had been a real effort on her part to behave as she had been trained – positioning plates, serving vegetables, clearing away dishes – and not once during the whole meal had Dafydd looked at her. At first, she had thought that he was putting on airs and graces. Then later, she realized that he was simply oblivious of her presence. She saw that his whole being was focused on Miss Louisa. It was as if she, Mary - who he was walking out with – just didn't exist!

    It was this sense of utter rejection that had made the maid easy prey for the butler. Mary was aware that George had lusted over her for some time. When she first came to Rock House she had been a scrap of a girl. Now, a few years later, she was full bosomed and had a pretty face framed by her dark curly hair. For some time she had realized that she was attractive to most men.

"You've got to lose your virginity sometime," May had said to her.

All right I've lost it, she thought as she stood in front of the mirror in her attic bedroom and adjusted her cap in readiness for her day's work.

But her mind wasn't filled with horror. She was willing to admit that she had enjoyed the experience. She'd do it again but not against the kitchen table!

Downstairs, the servants went about their duties. George and Mary behaved as if nothing had happened, except that when they found themselves on their own, Mary made sure that she showed off her figure to its full advantage. She smiled to herself as she caught him eyeing her and then she saw him lick his lips.

Yes, she thought, you'll do for the time being.

George, the man of the world, never doubted that his charms would entice Mary sooner or later. It was always nice to bed a virgin - something to boast about to his mates at the Morganton Hotel.

But I'll not say anything yet, he thought to himself. Take her out a bit first and then see what happens.

His reluctance to share his experiences, which he had done on many other occasions, must surely mean something. Over the years he had grown quite fond of the young maid. He had watched her develop and yes he wouldn't mind if it was known in the village that he was walking out with her.

But am I? He asked himself.

All of a sudden he wasn't so sure of the extent of his influence over Mary. And didn't she say that she was slipping out to see her friend May that afternoon. It was all very well for him to boast of his conquests at the hotel but he didn't like the thought of those two women discussing him behind his back.

"Yes, Mary, you can go," said Mrs. Lloyd in answer to her request. "You worked hard enough yesterday and George said that you helped him with more of the clearing up after I had gone to bed. You're a good girl. That's saved me a lot. I don't know, I must be getting older. I'm so tired today."

"Thanks, Mrs. Lloyd, I won't be long but I've heard that young John isn't very well and I want to see how he is.

As soon as she opened the door, May knew by the look on her visitor's face that something had happened.

"I had to come. I'm itching to tell you but where's your mother? I don't want her to hear."

"It's all right, she's gone up the main road and taken John with her. But what's the matter? Come into the middle room."

Her friend listened as Mary told her tale. May had thought at first that it must be something to do with Dafydd and so she was surprised when she heard what had happened.

"Didn't I warn you about that butler. He's got a reputation that one. Always preying on women. Mind you, I've heard that he can be quite generous and not a bad lover as well."

"Don't worry, I knew what I was doing, despite the wine he gave me. Poured most of it down the sink when he went to answer the bell." Then Mary grinned, "I don't think he knows what he has done though. I'm going to string him along and see what I can get out of him. If the worse comes to the worse and I get caught – it's not a bad position being a butler's wife."

May laughed, "Do you know I think that you'll be the one to get the better of him."

After Mary had gone, May thought about what she had just heard. Dafydd and Mrs. Lewis' niece – no that wouldn't happen. Her family would never let her marry him! He needs someone of his own kind. And, without thinking, May began to smooth her arm as she remembered the feel of Dafydd's strong muscles that evening behind the co-op.

The day after the musical evening at Rock House, Elizabeth could think of nothing but the new minister. All thoughts of John Parry had flown from her mind. The Reverend William Hughes had been so interesting and considerate that she could have sat and listened to him forever. He had been very appreciative of her help with the Band of Hope and was delighted when she had said that she would be there to assist him next week. He had told her that his plans for the Ramblers' Club were well underway and the first outing was ear marked for Easter Monday. He'd asked her if that was convenient and would she be able to come on the walk. Could she come indeed! She certainly would be there. He'd even consulted her as to where they ought to go.

He'd said, "Somewhere not too far for the first outing, don't you agree? I thought that we could catch the train to Pontypridd and change there for Caerphilly. We'll visit the castle, see the leaning tower – the one that was blown up in the Civil War."

It had sounded so romantic to her that she could do nothing else but agree. She soon found that History was one of his favourite subjects. He talked about the castle and the old Roman earthworks around it with enthusiasm.

I wish I could be half as interesting, she thought. What had he said? That it was the second largest castle in Britain! He had even known the origin of its name.

"Built by Gilbert de Claire for his son hence Caerphilly – caer, the Roman word for fort and filius, the Latin for son"
He had sounded so knowledgeable!

She remembered asking him, "After exploring the castle do we come back on the train?"

"No, this is a ramble. From the castle we'll walk back into the Taff Valley and then depending on how tired we all are, we can catch a train at Treforest or further on at Pontypridd."

She knew that such an expedition would require some planning.

I can offer to help him with the details. I'll go to the library in the Welfare Hall and look for a book on castles. Caerphilly has such a big one that there must be something written about it. I can check on the times of the trains at the station too. I'm sure that he'll be pleased to have the information.

The Reverend William Hughes did indeed marry one of his congregation and the Doctor and his wife were pleased to see Elizabeth so happy.

Mrs. Williams was overheard saying to her friend Mrs. Morris the draper that "It doesn't matter that Elizabeth has to give up her post of school mistress when she marries since the minister is so important in Morganton and he'll need a wife by his side. They'll be invited every where and everyone who has heard him is agreed that he is the best preacher in the valleys."

Mrs. Morris nodded her head in agreement, "Destined for better things is the Reverend William Hughes and your Elizabeth will be with him. I've no doubt too that, before long, he'll be given a large chapel in Cardiff and a big manse to go with it."

Sarah Lewis looked back on last night's dinner party and thought it a great success. Everyone present had complimented her on the food and the music as they had left and she had no doubt that the night would be the talk of Morganton for some time to come.

John's opinion about the young singer is so right, she thought as she walked down the stairs for breakfast. Dafydd Price could well become a very famous tenor. I must give him all the help I can.

On entering the dining room she was surprised to see Louisa already seated.

"I didn't expect to see you up so early."

"I'm used to it at the hospital. I did so enjoy last night. The singing was wonderful."

"Yes, I was just thinking that we must make sure that the young tenor makes the most of his opportunities. I will certainly do what I can to encourage him."

"My feelings too, Aunt Sarah, I've promised to go to his next concert in Cardiff and I'm sure that there will be many more after that. What did John have to say about him?"

"He was very pleased but you can ask him yourself because I've invited him for tea this afternoon. I thought that you would like to see John again before you go back to Cardiff as you and he get on so well together."

Not as well as you and John, thought Louisa as she smiled at her aunt.

It was inevitable that Sarah and John Parry saw more and more of each other. There were so many things that she needed advice on – from the new hospital to the colliery. She tended to forget that she had already sounded out more professional opinions. But John Parry B.A. was not fooled. Not that he minded for he was as interested in her as she was in him.

In the spring the footings were dug for the hospital and Sarah Lewis laid a commemorative stone in the front wall in memory of her husband. For some reason laying that stone finally severed the link between the young widow and the colliery owner. At last she could start her new life. She discarded her widow's black and the gossips of Morganton predicted a summer wedding. They were not disappointed. The whole village delighted in the match and wished the couple well. Flowers were sent from Dyffryn Gardens with a simple note –

With all our best wishes for your happiness,
Reginald Cory.

Sarah's sister and brother-in-law managed to keep to themselves any misgivings that they had about the match. He certainly felt that his sister-in-law could have done better for herself. Then there was all that money. He would have had control of that if she had moved back to Bristol!

John Parry B.A. gave up the village school. In September there was another headmaster to educate the children and to turn the heads of the spinsters in the village. But the choir was another matter.

With John as conductor and Sarah as patron, Ebenezer Male Voice choir was a force to contend with in the South Wales Valleys. New members were attracted from the neighbouring villages and the choir grew to a size where it competed only with the best. Its rehearsals, however, were still held in Ebenezer chapel vestry.

No one could deny that it was the new hospital that brought the most benefit to the community. Thomas Thomas had promised a building that would last. Built of pennant sandstone with decorative brick around the doors and windows, the twelve- bed hospital opened on the first of January1917. Despite the cold, a commemorative photograph was taken outside with the bath-stone pillars of the entrance framing the background. Every one of note vied for a place in the photo. In centre front sat Mr. and Mrs. Parry flanked by Doctor Williams on one side and the new matron on the other, with councillors, mining officials and other dignitaries fanning out behind them.

Sarah Parry was indeed glad that she hadn't taken her sister's advice and instead had remained in Morganton. Not only had she married for love but also, at last here in the mining valleys, she had found a real sense of purpose.

Chapter Thirty-one

Dafydd's second Cardiff concert put him firmly on the path of a musical career. Louisa kept her promise and was there to see him sing at the concert. Afterwards, joining the enthusiastic well-wishers around David Price, she listened to their praise.

"Very well sung, I did so like the last item."

"It was such a joy to listen to you."

"When is your next concert? I must be there."

"It has been so enjoyable."

As people moved on, she found herself next in line to shake the young tenor's hand. Automatically, he held out his and it wasn't until her voice registered that he realized who she was. For a few seconds, as they looked into each other's eyes, they were oblivious of the crowd.

Breaking the spell, she said, "Some fine singing indeed Dafydd, or should I say David."

Then she was forced to move on as others clamoured for his attention and it was some time before the concertgoers disappeared.

Where is she, fretted Dafydd, as he looked for Louisa in the emptying hall? She can't have gone. Surely she will have waited.

Satisfied that she wasn't in the auditorium, he hurried into the foyer and there, just inside the main entrance were three young ladies.

"There he is," exclaimed one as she waved.

Smiling he went over to the familiar faces.

"You always liked to sing, Dafydd Price," said one of the nurses.

"We've enjoyed the evening," said another. Then turning to the third she continued, "I'm glad you persuaded us to come, Louisa."

"Yes, I told you that he'd be worth listening to. We'll come again. You'll have to write to me, Dafydd, so that we know when your next concert is. Sorry we can't stop to talk now but we've a train to catch. We'll have to hurry as it is."

"I'll walk with you," blurted out Dafydd. "You shouldn't walk through Cardiff on your own in the dark."

The three laughed. Look at the men they dealt with in the hospital. They didn't need an escort. Besides they weren't afraid. Their blossoming independence didn't allow them to think that they couldn't take care of themselves. But they compromised. Dafydd was allowed to walk along with them to the station. He saw them safely on their train and then waited for his.

If I write to Louisa she'll write back then at least we'll have some contact, he thought. But I wish she had come on her own tonight then I could have taken her back to the hospital and held her in my arms before she went inside. Why is it that we get near to each other and then she seems to slip away?

The triumph of the concert had faded into the background. On the train home, Dafydd could only think about his love for Louisa.

The arrival of Louisa's first letter caused some excitement in the Price's household. Granny Price immediately recognized the writing on the envelope.

"But why is Miss Louisa writing to our Dafydd?" asked Carrie.

"You'd better ask him," replied Granny Price.
Dafydd satisfied his mother's curiosity by telling her that the letter contained news about the men in the hospital and about a concert that Louisa had been to. Granny Price smiled to herself as she listened.

After that second Cardiff concert, Dafydd's life became even more hectic. He soon found that he was in great demand to sing at all sorts of musical events and more importantly he was paid for the engagements. It was becoming almost impossible to fit everything in – work, lessons, rehearsals and then the performance. Encouraged by John Parry and his mounting savings, he finally left the pit behind - a move that was greeted with mixed reactions from his family. His parents worried about him losing a regular wage, even though they both bore the legacy of the pit in Emlyn's ill health.

"How long will it last, Emlyn, and what if he can't get a job back in the pit?" asked Carrie when they were discussing Dafydd's future. She had no experience of life outside the mining community where people worked hard to get by and without the colliery there was nothing. Dafydd's brothers talked of him putting on airs and graces and being above his station. But his Granny Price encouraged him to grasp the opportunity with both hands. As Dafydd's reputation spread, he was asked to appear at places further afield and it wasn't always possible to return home that night. He had no option but to stay in a hotel.

Edmund Street
Morganton.
October 1916.

Dear Louisa,
I couldn't believe that you were able to make the last concert with all the wounded coming back from the Somme.

The very word made Dafydd pause as he remembered the mud of the battlefield and he shuddered as he thought of the thousands of dead and wounded - and all for what? A few hundred yards of torn-up and useless land. Shaking his head, he dipped the nib in the ink and went back to his letter.

It was so good to see you if only for a few minutes. I'm singing in Swansea in a fortnight and I'll be too late for the train so I'm staying in a hotel. The one next to the station so at least I'll be able to find it. I've never stayed in one before. I suppose it'll be like the Morganton Hotel. I don't think that we've got a case. I'll have to wrap my clothes in brown paper...

Bron Rhyw Hospital,
October 1916.

Dear Dafydd,
You'll do no such thing. Brown paper parcel indeed! Buy a small case – big enough to take your suit, shirt, shoes and nightclothes. Better still, ask your grandmother to get it. She'll know what is needed...

Nightclothes, thought Dafydd puzzled. What's wrong with my vest? I suppose I'd better see Granny Price about the case, but what a fuss!

The young man's first stay in a hotel was an ordeal. Finding it was easy. He walked out of the station and there it was in front of him – The Great Western Hotel. Carrying his new suitcase, he approached the reception desk.

"Yes, sir, what can I do for you?" asked the clerk as he peered through his small round spectacles.

"I think I'm staying here tonight."

"Your name please?"

"Dafydd Price."

"I don't seem to have a reservation for anyone of that name," said the clerk, as he looked down a list in the large book on the desk. "We are expecting a Mr. David Price."

"That's me."

The desk clerk didn't look convinced.

"It's my stage name."

"Stage name?"

"Yes, I'm here to sing."

"You're not Mr. David Price the Tenor."

"Yes, that's right."

"I didn't realize. Of course we have a reservation for you. One of the best rooms in the hotel. I hope that you will be very comfortable, sir." Then with a flourish the clerk rang the brass bell on the desk to summon the porter.

Dafydd remembered Louisa's instructions. Let the porter carry your case and show you to your room. Give him sixpence as a tip. Now all Dafydd had to do was to survive that night's dinner.

It wasn't long before staying in hotels became almost a routine. Through keen observation of the other guests he managed to use the right cutlery most of the time but it took him a while to find out which dishes he liked to eat. He found that he enjoyed most of the soups he was offered and of course it was easy to recognize a soupspoon. But one, he certainly didn't appreciate. For a start he had difficulty pronouncing the name – Mulligatawny – and it was the spiciest thing he had ever eaten! He would certainly avoid that in the future. Fortunately most of the hotels served simple roast dinners and leg of lamb and sirloin of beef were soon favourites. Very different indeed from the belly pork that his mother cooked for a Sunday treat.

The one thing that would have given away the charade was his valley speech, but Dafydd soon learnt that the so-called important people liked to hear the sound of their own voices and so to begin with he could get away with minimizing his responses. But as he himself became more important in the eyes of others then he was expected to voice opinions on the music he sang, at the very least. Fortunately, his fine ear allowed him to mimic John Parry's educated Welsh tones and his memory for words enabled him to hear and then reuse them in appropriate situations.

In some of the grander concert halls, he was expected to wear evening dress on stage. At the insistence of his grandmother, this suit was made by a Cardiff tailor and he noticed tears in her eyes when he showed it to her. She felt the cloth, checked the stitching, and fussed over specks of dust until at last she was satisfied.

"Try it on. Let your granny see you in it," said Emlyn.

"Why Granny Price couldn't have made it herself, I don't know. She's always made my clothes," muttered his son as he disappeared up the stairs with the new suit over his arm.

Evening dress completed Dafydd's transformation and no one seeing him in it could have doubted that this was David Price, the famous tenor. Soon he was getting engagements even further afield and in the spring of 1917 he sang for the first time in Bristol.

Chapter Thirty-two

At Avon View in Clifton, Louisa's mother checked the last minute arrangements for the theatre supper. As usual, her domestic staff had things well in hand - the household was used to entertaining. Re-assured, she went to dress for the evening. Stopping at the door of her daughter's room, she knocked and walked in. Seeing her mother in the dressing table mirror, Louisa turned and smiled.

"Don't worry so much," she said. "You know that everything will run smoothly. It always does."

"Yes, but I want everything to be just right. We were so lucky to have David Price accept our invitation. I know that he was asked by the Hetcott-Smythes. Didn't you say that you've met him, perhaps that's why he's coming?"

"He's sang in Cardiff on a number of occasions and I've spoken to him afterwards."

"My dear, have you really! He's the talk of Bristol. And you must have heard that he's a friend of Ivor Novello!"

"I believe that he was trained by the mother, Madame Clara Novello-Davies."

"Yes, yes that's what I said. I must go to dress. Is there anything that you need? Shall I send my maid in?"

"No, it's all right. I'm used to managing on my own now after being at the hospital all this time. You go, get ready and I'll see you downstairs in the drawing room."

The concert was a grand affair. The Prince of Wales Theatre was full to capacity. Everyone who thought that he or she was somebody was there. People felt that it was their duty to carry on especially now that the United States had officially entered the War, but surely the fighting couldn't last much longer. The young tenor delighted his audience and they in turn were reluctant to allow him to leave the stage. At last he escaped to his dressing room. He had only just collected his things together when there was a knock on the door.

The stage doorman announced, "A motor car has arrived for you, sir."

This room to myself, thought Dafydd, and now a motorcar sent for me!

But it was David Price who answered for over the months the singer had become a chameleon, slipping in and out of identities just as easily as that animal changed the colour of its skin.

"Thank you, I'll be along now."

As Dafydd stepped into the motorcar a familiar voice said, "I thought that I'd come to get you in case you were persuaded to go elsewhere."

He saw Louisa sitting inside and, as his heart raced, he said, "Yes, I did think of accepting another invitation but where else could I be in the company of such a beautiful young lady?"

Their letter writing had broken down the barriers to such an extent that now, however infrequently they met, both were immediately at ease. Each knew the feelings one had for the other but whilst Louisa at this time thought that she could give up everything for Dafydd, deep down he knew that he couldn't let her. If he became acceptable to her family, then that might be a different matter. Tonight's supper party could well provide his first indication.

"Now don't forget," she said as they walked in through the door of her home, "You are David Price the famous tenor. These people are here to see you. They want to be able to say that they've met you."

But despite all she said and how she tried to bolster his confidence, Dafydd couldn't help feeling nervous. So much depended on this evening. He saw Louisa slip off her cape and hand it to the maid and this prompted him to give his hat and gloves to the butler.

"Come, Mr. Price, let me introduce you to my parents and some of the other guests," she said heartily for the benefit of the onlookers.

Obediently, he followed her into the drawing room. For a minute there was a break in the conversation as all the guests wanted to see the famous singer. Some of the younger ladies shamelessly stared and Louisa smiled as she caught snatches of the subsequent conversation.

"Isn't he handsome. No wonder he sings so well."

"A war hero I'm told. He must have looked dashing in uniform."

"Such eyes, did you ever see such deep eyes?"

"Mother, may I introduce you to Mr. David Price."

"Mr. Price, I was so pleased that you accepted my invitation. I did so enjoy the concert. Tell me, how is Ivor Novello these days? I was only saying yesterday that we must go up to London to see his latest show. It's at the Gaiety isn't it? Come, let me show you off to some of my dear friends."

Taking his arm, Louisa's mother paraded round the room, stopping here and there to introduce Mr. David Price to the best of Bristol Society. Her daughter dutifully followed but in reality she was always ready to cover any of his mistakes. She needn't have worried for Dafydd had slipped into his other self and bowed and smiled as he was led towards the group of gentlemen standing at the entrance to the dining room.

"Louisa dear, look after Mr. Price for me. Take him over to your father and his friends."

Introductions were made and Dafydd coped with their congratulations and questions about his concerts. He even managed to deflect a reference to his war service.

"Too modest, too modest indeed young man," interrupted Louisa's father. "Seriously injured and nursed by my own daughter. We all try to do our bit. What regiment did you say it was? Do you know my cousin Major George…"

"Father, we can't get involved in who knows who because supper is about to be served and I'm sure that Mr. Price deserves his more than any of us."

"Very well, my dear, you can take him away. There will be other times I'm sure. You must come to diner, young man. Perhaps after your next Bristol concert."

Louisa placed her arm in Dafydd's and the couple walked over to the supper table.

"Well done," she whispered and then more loudly, "What can I tempt you with? Lobster salad, some veal and ham pie, mayonnaise of trout or perhaps some cold roast beef?"

Without waiting for an answer the young lady filled a plate with some of the plainest fare and handed it to him. Then they moved away from the table as the others crowded in on the food. For a few minutes they enjoyed the relative peace of a corner by the window but not for long. As soon as she was satisfied that everyone was eating, Louisa's mother came towards them, determined to make the most of her very important guest.

Later, in the privacy of his hotel room, as Dafydd took off his evening suit, he shed his other self and the doubts crept back. Would he ever be worthy of her? Look where she came from. That house, all those servants and her father – he'd not want an ex- coalminer for a son-in-law! No, however much he earned from his singing and despite how famous he might become, he couldn't see himself being accepted by her parents.

Louisa, however, had other ideas. She knew that the more well known that Dafydd became then the less her mother would look into his background. Her father, however, would not be that easy to win over.

I won't give him the choice, she thought as she sat looking at herself in the dressing table mirror. The War must end sometime and then we'll get married without telling anyone. It'll be too late for Father to do anything about it then. He'll just have to make the best of it.

But deep down she knew that it wouldn't be as simple as that for Dafydd. She was only too clearly aware that he still regarded himself as not being worthy of her. He had never really told her how much he loved her, let alone asked her to marry him. She smiled as she conjured up a picture of him asking for her hand.

No, he'd never do that. He's far too much in awe of my father. It'll have to be a fait accompli. I'm old enough and there's nothing to stop me. This is the twentieth century, I may be a woman but I am not a chattel to be married off by my parents. I have the right to choose my own husband.

Chapter Thirty-three

When Dafydd arrived home the next day, the contrast between Louisa's home and that of his own still occupied his thoughts and he was unusually quiet. Carrie wondered why he didn't talk about the Bristol concert. She loved to hear about the songs he sang and how the audience responded to them. It wasn't long before she asked, "Didn't the concert go well?"

"Yes, Mam, the audience seemed to enjoy it."

Carrie waited for him to tell her more but when nothing was forthcoming she tried again.

"What did you eat at that hotel?"

"I didn't have dinner there. I was invited to a supper party at Louisa's home."

"And you haven't told us about it! I'll get your granny from the front room. She'll want to hear all about it too."

Dafydd knew that he'd give away his true feelings for Louisa if he had to tell them about last night so he said quickly, "No, don't do that. I feel like going for a walk after sitting in trains for so long. I'll tell you all about the party this evening when Dad's here."

Dafydd intended to walk up the mountain so that he could have peace to think about what the future could hold for him and Louisa. He knew that he loved her and thought that she loved him but what if no one wanted to listen to him singing any more? How would he make a living then? Having met her father, he was certain that he'd never be accepted as a son-in-law. How could he cut her off from her family? Dafydd sighed he needed someone to talk to. He missed Jack who'd always been there to listen to his problems and to give advice. Somehow, it seemed only natural to call on May instead.

Nellie and May were watching John as he played on the floor with two tin cans.

"That's his crane. Will Jones made it for him. See how he tries to copy Will and can almost wind the cord round the bar in the bigger tin," said Nellie proudly. "Dafydd, show him how to send the small tin over the side of the table and then wind it back up."

John watched carefully as Dafydd did as Nellie asked.

"Your turn now, John," said Dafydd. "Come on, I'll help you."

The two played with the crane until the young boy tired of it and wanted something else to do.

"I'll take him out now, May," said Nellie. "You and Dafydd will have some peace then."

When they were on their own, May said, "We haven't seen you for weeks."

"No, I've been busy – concerts. I sang in Bristol last night," replied Dafydd.

"Isn't that where Mrs. Lewis' niece comes from?"

"Yes, I was invited to her home for a supper party."

"So it's true. You are soft on her," said May as she wiped a speck of dirt from her skirt.

"What do you mean? What are the gossips saying now?"

Still pretending to be concerned about the same mark on her skirt, May answered, "We all know that you get letters from her and Mary says…"

"All right, I give in. Yes, Louisa and I are friends."

"Is that all?" asked May anxiously as she looked up at his face.

"It can't be any more," said Dafydd wistfully. "You should have seen how they live. Big house – much bigger than Rock House – and servants everywhere."

"Well you are David Price, the famous tenor," she said indignantly jumping to his defence.

"I'm still the son of a collier, and besides, I felt like a fish out of water there." Dafydd sighed, "I'm only really comfortable when I come back here. Everything else still seems so unreal."

Plucking up courage May asked, "Will she have you?"

"I haven't asked her. Sometimes I want to but Louisa and I married – that's only a dream. I can't take her away from all that."

May, said carefully, "It's the war. Everything is upside down. Before it, you wouldn't even have thought of marrying the likes of her. Wait until the fighting is over and see what happens then."

"You're right, May," said Dafydd quietly. "It is better to leave things as they are."

For a time, nothing was said between them. Dafydd thought of Louisa. Could he give her up? His heart still said no but common sense told him that the gulf between them could never be permanently bridged. It might though as long as he was David Price the famous tenor – especially if he took on London engagements. Look how Ivor Novello was accepted by society. According to Madame Clara he's often invited to stay in grand houses. But Ivor had grown up in Cardiff not in Morganton. Besides it was nerve racking enough when he first stayed in a hotel. If he had to stay in a castle... No, it didn't bear thinking about.

May surprised herself with her feelings about Dafydd's relationship with Louisa. What's it to me? He and Jack were close but... and then she remembered that night in the doorway at the back of the co-op. She looked across at Dafydd.

He's still as handsome as ever and with money now, she thought. Besides it's only right that John has a father.

Then memories of Jack came flooding back and her eyes began to fill. She knew that she couldn't allow the tears to flow. To have a decent future for her and John she had to be practical. Crying over Jack might re-awaken for Dafydd some of the horrors of the war and she didn't want that. Pulling herself together, she started to talk about some of the new things that John had learnt to do. Once she had Dafydd's attention she made sure that she kept it by relating the latest village gossip.

When Nellie returned with John, she had more news.

"I've been talking to Mrs. Thomas, the builder's wife," said Nellie. "Her husband is going to build a row of six houses just off the main road. Double fronted, fancy brick round the windows and a green in front."

"They'll be nice for some people," said May.

"That's not all," continued Nellie excitedly. "There'll be three big bedrooms and a bathroom!"

"Who'll afford one of those? Not the likes of us," said May. "They'll end up calling it Gaffers' Row."

"Where did you say they're going to be built?" asked Dafydd, showing more interest in the conversation.

"You know, the empty piece of land by the turning to go up to Rock House."

I could buy one of those houses, thought Dafydd. No more hills for Dad to climb. Further away from the pit too so the house won't get as dirty. Mam won't have to spend all her time cleaning. It'll be easier all round.

He let the women gossip as he absentmindedly played with John until the boy complained of being hungry and gave Dafydd the excuse to go back home. As he handed John over to May he smelt the soft scent of lavender water. He felt the colour rise in his cheeks as memories of that night, so long ago now, at the back of the co-op came flooding back. For the first time that afternoon he noticed May's beautiful eyes and surprised himself with the thought of why can't it be you and not Louisa? Everything would then be so straightforward.

That evening, as the Price family sat around the fire in the middle room, Dafydd told Emlyn, Carrie and Granny Price about his experiences in Bristol. He spoke with pride about the applause and the congratulations he received. He told them about the ride in the motorcar and described Louisa's home in as much detail as he could remember until he seemed to satisfy their curiosity. Then, partly to prevent more awkward questions, he mentioned Thomas Thomas' new houses. He wasn't surprised when Carrie said that she knew all about them – any news travelled fast in Morganton. But his family was surprised when he told them that he intended to buy one of the new houses for them all to live in.

"We can't live there, said Carrie. They aren't for the likes of us. Besides where is the money coming from?"

"I was born in this house and I expect to die here," said Emlyn emphatically.

"Mam, never mind the money. I'll see to that. Dad, think, no more hills to climb and only a short walk to the Welfare Hall and Ebenezer. What do you say, Gran, wouldn't it be better for all of us?"

His grandmother nodded as tears rolled slowly down her cheeks. She had indeed come a long way from that tiny cottage in the hills above Aberystwyth to talk of this new house with its bathroom. Who would have thought that she would end her days like the ladies she made clothes for all those years ago?

Chapter Thirty-four

The influx of fresh, American troops into France tipped the balance of the war in favour of the allies. The German High Command knew that it had to win a decisive battle before the American soldiers were shipped to the front in huge numbers and the German offensive began in March 1918. Within weeks thousands of badly wounded men had arrived back in Britain. Beds were pushed into every available space in Bron Rhiw hospital. The nurses worked until they were exhausted. Louisa hadn't had any leave for weeks and her letters to Dafydd were short and infrequent. What was there to tell him? He'd seen terrible injuries himself. He'd been a shattered man. And besides, she was so tired. When she left the ward, all she wanted to do was sleep.

She was on duty one afternoon when a new batch of wounded arrived at the hospital. The nurses were inured to the filthy clothes, blood-soaked bandages and uncomprehending faces. Their first task was always to get rid of the grime and make the men as comfortable as possible. Louisa was working in the officers' ward – a small room containing half a dozen beds. As she gently washed a captain's face, he smiled at her and to her surprise said weakly, "I danced with you once."

"That must have been a long time ago," said Louisa. "It feels as if I haven't been out of this hospital in years."

"It was, at Dyffryn House and you are just as beautiful as I remember," he managed to murmur.

"We'll talk about it again," she said quietly. "Let me make you comfortable. You need to sleep after that long journey."

That night, too tired to get to sleep easily, Louisa thought about the Dyffryn House ball. She remembered how handsome and amusing the young men had been. She searched her memory until she found a younger and less weary version of the captain, but his name eluded her. All she remembered was the laughter as they danced.

There's been nothing here to laugh about for months and certainly nothing to dress up for since Aunt Sarah's wedding, she thought as she drifted into sleep.

The war had gone on too long and Louisa almost believed that it was never going to end. Sometimes she felt that she couldn't see any more suffering. Every day it was more difficult to smile and encourage her patients. She longed for a few days away from the hospital. Time when she could forget the horrors of war and enjoy some of the pleasures of her old life. She thought more and more of her home in Bristol and the comforts provided by her family and servants.

When Louisa went on duty the following morning, she made sure that she knew the name of the injured officer who had spoken to her the night before.

"Good morning, Captain Robinson, how are you feeling today? Better than last night I hope" she said brightly.

"Now that I've seen you," he replied with a smile. "You know who I am then."

Louisa smiled back at him. "I'm surprised that you remembered me after all this time."

"Could I forget such a pretty face?"

She had no answer to that. So the pattern was set. He flattered as she took care of him. He made light of his injuries, didn't dwell on the war and instead talked of dances and parties, of theatre outings and of having fun. In one way, it was just the medicine she needed. She regained some of her spirits but it made her long to taste some of the pleasures of her earlier carefree life in Bristol.

Captain Robinson stayed less than a fortnight at the hospital. His mother had made arrangements for him to be nursed at home as soon as the doctor would allow it. Louisa missed his cheerfulness and felt the burden of her work again. She knew that Dafydd was singing in Cardiff but she didn't go to the concert. Matron would have given her the evening off, but Louisa didn't ask. What was the point? All that ever happened was that she had a few minutes with Dafydd at the end. It wasn't worth it and besides she was too tired.

Edmund Street,
Morganton,
May 1918

Dear Louisa,

I was disappointed when I didn't see you at the concert. I know that you must be very busy and I've got no right to expect you to leave your work when there are so many that need you, but I wish that you had been there all the same...

As she read, Louisa became angry. She didn't know why she felt like this but she thought, if you wanted me to come you should have made proper arrangements. Sent someone to fetch me. Taken me out to dinner afterwards. Spent some time with me. Then she found that she could hardly read the rest of the letter because of the tears that had welled up in her eyes so she stuffed the pages into her skirt pocket, adjusted her apron and walked towards the ward.

A few days later, a motorcar drew up outside the hospital. The driver got out and opened the door for his passenger.

"It's Captain Robinson," said one of the nurses as she waved at the window. "He looks so much better."

Unable to restrain herself, Louisa went over and smiled and waved at the young man until he disappeared from view.

He must have come to see some of his men, she thought as she went back to her patient.

A few minutes latter, Captain Robinson limped into the ward. He stopped to talk to some of the patients as he passed their beds but at last he came over to Louisa.

"Hello, it's nice to see you. How are you?" she asked.

"Fine now," he said with a smile.

"The men are obviously pleased that you've come," she said.

"Yes, it seems so. Actually, that's not the only reason why I'm here. I've really come to see you, to take you out." Seeing that Louisa was about to make some objections, he added quickly, "I've seen matron. It's all right. I've brought the Ford, though the old leg won't let me drive it yet. I'm taking you for a picnic. We haven't got long. Go and get ready."

They didn't go far. They drove through the village until they came to the bottom of the hill that led up to Castell Coch. The driver went slowly up it and then parked on the grass below the castle walls. He carried the picnic hamper and rug to a spot overlooking the Taff Valley and then returned to the motorcar. Captain Robinson spread the rug on the grass and opened the basket.

"Will you be mother, or shall I?" he asked.

Smiling, Louisa sat down besides him and began to take things out of the hamper.

"Captain Robinson…" she began.

"Peter," he said quickly, "And I'm going to call you Louisa."

It was such a lovely afternoon. They sat, admired the view, and talked about inconsequential things. The hamper was full of tiny triangles of sandwiches, dainty cakes and little iced biscuits.

"No champagne I'm afraid," said Peter with a smile. "I didn't think that matron would approve of one of her nurses sampling the high life. Have some lemonade. Next best thing I'm told."

Louisa hadn't felt so relaxed for a long time. She even admitted to herself that she enjoyed being looked after for a change and she was disappointed when it was time to put the remains of the picnic back into the hamper. It wasn't until she was in bed that night that she thought of Dafydd. As she drifted off to sleep she wished that he would surprise her sometimes as Peter had that day.

As the summer progressed, Louisa saw more and more of Peter Robinson. He used every excuse to visit the hospital, especially after his leg had improved enough to allow him to drive the Ford. She was flattered by his attention. Peter always made her feel special. He was such fun to be with. Seeing him for just a short time seemed to make all the difference to her day. Before long she found herself hoping at breakfast that he would visit and she was disappointed if he didn't. Thoughts of

Dafydd were pushed back into the recesses of her mind except when it was her turn for night duty. In the quiet hours a battle raged in her head.

I do love you, Dafydd Price, she'd say to herself. We'll get married. Have a house like Aunt Sarah's in Morganton. No, we'll live in Bristol – there's my family, friends, shops, theatres… Yes, it'll have to be there.

But any plans disintegrated as soon as she thought of her father.

He can't know who David Price really is! His reaction to Aunt Sarah's marriage was bad enough. He called dear John Parry a penniless schoolmaster! I'd never get his permission to marry a miner's son. No, Dafydd will have to leave Morganton behind him and concentrate on his singing career. We can make up something about his background.

But even as she thought this, Louisa was struck by its improbability because she knew that Dafydd would never disown his roots.

Late one afternoon, Peter Robinson called at the hospital and to his surprise he found that Louisa was about to go out.

"I'm going to a concert in The Park Hall," she said. "I'm sorry but I can't stop to talk to you. David Price, the tenor, is singing. He was a patient here. Some of us go to hear him when he sings in Cardiff."

"I'll take you," said Peter. "I haven't been to a concert in years."

"But you haven't got a ticket. You might not get a seat. David Price's concerts are usually very well attended."

"If I have to, I'll wait for you outside. But I'm sure that they'll let me in," he said with a smile.

Dafydd won't mind, thought Louisa. I've nursed Peter just as I did him. Besides, how could I stop Peter from coming with me? He's so insistent. He makes up his mind and that's that.

Not only did Peter Robinson get a ticket but came back from the booking office with two of the best seats in the hall.

"Just been returned," he said. "Front row of the circle. There's the stairs over to the right."

Once settled in their seats, Peter chatted easily and Louisa relaxed. The concert hall filled up and the curtain rose. As Louisa listened to Dafydd she felt Peter's strong presence by the side of her and somehow she wasn't as moved by the singing as she had always been in the past.

At the end, after all the applause had died down, Louisa said, "I usually go back stage to see David Price. Will you wait in the foyer? I won't be long."

"Back stage, a splendid idea, I'll come with you. I'd like to congratulate him on such a performance."

The delight showed on Dafydd' face when he saw Louisa walking towards him. He held out his hands towards her but before he could say anything, she said, "Let me introduce you to Captain Robinson. He wanted to meet you after such a splendid performance."

"How do you do, Captain," said Dafydd. "I'm pleased that you enjoyed the concert."

"Indeed I did, Mr. Price. I can see why Louisa comes to your concerts as often as she can. Next time you sing in Cardiff, I promise we'll be there to hear you."

He brought her here, thought Dafydd. What has he got to do with Louisa?

From then on Dafydd didn't know how he managed to keep making polite conversation. All he could think about was that

Louisa had come to the concert with this man and he knew from the way the Captain looked at her that if now there was no more to the relationship than that between nurse and patient there could well be in the future.

Dafydd wanted so much to be on his own with Louisa, to talk to her, to walk her to the station and at the end of it to take her in his arms but now it was impossible. He didn't know what was worse – not meeting her for weeks or seeing her on the arm of another man, however innocent it might be. By the time he got to bed that night, his doubts about the future had returned. How could he compete with a person like Captain Robinson - wealthy, well schooled in all the social graces and much more acceptable to Louisa's parents?

The next morning, after he had satisfied Carrie on the success of the concert, Dafydd went out for a walk. He meant to climb the mountain to have some space and time to think, but as he neared the end of the street he saw Nellie Evans hurrying towards him.

"Oh, Dafydd, I'm glad I caught you, it's John. May insisted that I fetched you," cried Nellie.

"Why, what's wrong?" asked Dafydd quickly as all thoughts of his own problems disappeared.

"Doctor Williams is on his way. John hasn't been well for a few days - hot and grizzly. Then this morning he was very sick and now he's crying because his legs hurt." Nellie couldn't go on. She couldn't voice her worst fears.

Instinctively, Dafydd knew what she was afraid of. It's not fair, he thought. First Jack is killed and now John might not be able to walk again. Without waiting for Nellie he dashed off to see what the doctor had to say.

"Has he complained about his neck, May?" asked Doctor Williams. "Can he move it easily? It feels a bit stiff."

May clasped her hands tightly together as she watched the doctor examine John. "I don't think so," she managed to say. "He's been so hot and just crying. I've been up most of the night with him and now he complains about his legs."

"I've finished now," said Doctor Williams as he moved away from the bed. "Come and sit here by the side of John. He's not a very well young lad, I'm afraid."

There were footsteps on the stairs and Dafydd appeared in the doorway of the small bedroom.

"I came as fast as I could. What's the matter with John?" he asked anxiously.

"I was just saying," said Doctor Williams. "John is quite ill. I think that he has contracted poliomyelitis.

"No," cried May.

" I don't know how badly," continued Doctor Williams calmly. "We must hope for the best. There's nothing we can do but wait."

Dafydd went over to May and held her as the tears fell silently from her eyes.

"Keep him comfortable, cold compresses on his forehead and I'll be back after surgery. Try to remember that many patients make a full recovery and others have only a slight paralysis."

Over the next few days, May hardly left John's bedside. Dafydd called two or three times a day and made sure that Nellie understood that he would pay for any treatment that John needed. Gradually, the fever subsided and the boy only complained of aches in his left leg. It looked as if he was one of the lucky ones. Doctor Williams was sure that if there were any paralysis then it would be confined to that leg.

He wanted John to see a doctor in Cardiff for further treatment in order to minimize the effects of the disease.

"There's some new techniques now. It's important that the left leg is massaged and manipulated. We must try to prevent muscle wastage. We need to get him to Cardiff," said Doctor Williams to May and Nellie.

"How much will it cost?" asked May. "We only just about manage as it is. Where are we going to get the money for expensive treatment?"

"Don't worry yourself about that," said Nellie. "Remember I told you what Dafydd said. John is to have whatever he needs and he'll pay for it."

May looked surprised. Over the last week she had been so concerned about John that she hadn't taken in what people had said to her.

"If that's the case, I'll make the arrangements and as soon as John is fit enough you can take him to see the specialist," said Doctor Williams.

Chapter Thirty-five

Edmund Street,
Morganton,
July 1918.

Dear Louisa,

It's good news! John is recovering well. His left leg is weak but Doctor Williams is certain that with the treatment it will get much stronger. I'm so glad that I can pay for him to be treated properly, otherwise there's only that man that sells the medicines in Ponty market. Though some people in the village say that he's as good as any doctor and his way of stretching limbs seem to help some children to walk again.

As she read this piece of news Louisa was glad that at least John was getting better. Not like that poor soldier who had died in the night, she thought as her attention went back to the letter. A smile then momentarily brightened Louisa's tired eyes

May and Nellie are used to taking John to Cardiff now, but Nellie never tires of talking about their trips. I'm glad that I only had to go with them the first time because I'm very busy again. I've two big concerts to rehearse for. One of them is in Bristol on the first Saturday in August – the beginning of the bank holiday. Can you get leave for it? I've rehearsals with the choir all day Friday and Saturday morning. We could travel together on the Thursday. You could spend a few days at home. Please say that you will come. It has been so long since we have spent any time together...

*Bron Rhyw Hospital,
July 1918.*

Dear Dafydd,

I was pleased to hear that John is recovering well. It must be a comfort for you to have been able to help Jack's son. I expect that May is very grateful.

Yes, I can come to the Bristol concert, but I can only have two days leave. We are very busy. We seem to be having more wounded men every week. I'm sorry that we can't travel together. My parents have tickets for your concert and my mother is giving one of her supper parties afterwards. She's asked me to use my influence to get David Price to accept an invitation...

Oh, no! thought Dafydd as he read. Only two days leave and then having to meet all those people again – there'll be her father and he's bound to ask me about the war. He's not going to like it that I was just a soldier and not an officer.
Carrie was clearing away the breakfast dishes and he hoped that she hadn't noticed his disappointment. He glanced quickly at the rest of the letter and put the pages back into the envelope.

But Carrie had. She stopped what she was doing and asked, "How is Miss Louisa?"

"Working hard as usual," replied Dafydd. "But she's going to the Bristol concert. She's spending the weekend at home."

"That'll be nice for her," said Carrie. "She needs a rest from that hospital. Working all the time. No wonder you haven't had many letters from her recently."

But before Carrie could say anything else, Dafydd said quickly, "Mam, I'm off to see Thomas Thomas the builder. He's hoping that the house will be ready in September. We'll have moved in well before the bad weather. Have you thought about the new furniture that we'll need?"

Carrie's mind was immediately diverted from speculating about the relationship between Dafydd and Louisa. The new house and now new furniture were far more important than Granny Price's fancy about Dafydd and Miss Louisa.

"Mam, you and Granny Price need to go to the furniture department in the Co-op and if there's nothing that you want there, then we'll go to Cardiff."

Carrie couldn't believe it – not only new furniture but whatever she wanted, even from the big shops in Cardiff!

Over the next few days, Dafydd thought about the supper party. He knew that there was no way that he could get out of it. After all, he'd been invited to parties at other large houses and managed to acquit himself properly. True Louisa's father appeared to be a formidable man but so were most of the gentry he met. Why worry so much? Eventually, Dafydd realised that what he was afraid of was seeing Louisa in her own environment, for then he'd see again that, however much she said that she loved him, he was asking too much of her. Give up all that she was used to? No he couldn't expect that. May was right, the war changed things. Young men and women from different classes of society had been thrown together in emotionally charged situations. They made promises that they might not wish to keep when the world settled down again. He still loved Louisa and always would but Dafydd was beginning to recognize that the two of them could have separate and very different futures.

On the day of the Bristol concert Dafydd was getting ready in his dressing room.

"Come in", he shouted as he took one last glance in the mirror and then turned towards the door. But his smile died quickly as he saw that behind Louisa came the man she'd been with in Cardiff.

"We've come to wish you luck," said Louisa as she walked over to Dafydd and kissed him on his cheek. "You remember Peter Robinson? We travelled together. When Peter heard that I was going to another of your concerts he insisted on accompanying me. Wasn't that sweet of him."

"It's good to meet you again, Mr. Price. I trust that you are in good voice."

"Of course he is, Peter. David has a wonderful voice, as you well know."

She's changed, thought Dafydd. Calling me David – it's as if here in Bristol before her own kind she wants to disown my real self.

"Louisa's biased, she's one of my strongest supporters," Dafydd managed to say.

After a few more pleasantries Louisa said, "I'm afraid that we must go now to get settled before the start of the performance. Peter and I'll wait for you afterwards to take you back for supper."

It was with mixed feelings that David Price the famous tenor stepped onto the stage that evening, but he could never disappoint an audience. He sang as well as he had ever sung and the applause at the end was loud and long. To silence the shouts of encore, Dafydd walked onto the stage and when the noise had died down he said, "I will sing again for you but I ask for your indulgence. I'm going to sing without an accompaniment and in my native tongue. The song is called "The Maid of Sker" or in Welsh "Y Ferch O'r Scer". It's a sad tale about a young lady who was prevented by her father from marrying her true love."

As he sang, tears trickled down Louisa's cheeks for she knew that his message was for her. This is me, he seemed to say to her, Dafydd Price, the son of a miner. Is it me that you want? Someone who will never quite fit into the world that you once knew and will have again when the war is over. Then she felt a hand gently take hers and realized that Peter had noticed that she was upset. Turning to him she saw the concern on his face and managed to excuse her tears by whispering, "The song seems so sad. I remember him singing it when he was recovering in the hospital."

From the enthusiastic "Mr. Price, we're so glad that you could come" of Louisa's mother at the beginning of the evening to her effusive thank you at the end, Dafydd did not enjoy the supper party. True, Louisa was at his side throughout but Peter Robinson was never far away and Dafydd envied him his charm and easy conversation. He so obviously belonged in this environment. How was he, Dafydd Price the collier's son, going to compete with him? To marry Louisa Dafydd would have to become David Price and forget his family and background. He knew that at one time she would have had him for what he was, but then Louisa was filled with the optimism of youth. Now she was much older. Not in years or looks but in experience. The war had taken its toll. She had had enough of suffering and had no appetite for conflict. She didn't have the spirit to take on her father who, if he knew the truth, would never contemplate having Dafydd as a son-in-law. But Captain Peter Robinson, with his wealth and position in society, would be looked upon much more favourably.

There was one moment at the supper table when Dafydd knew that he had lost her. It was strange because Louisa had lapsed into her old role of looking after his welfare. As she filled a plate with the food he liked, their eyes met and hers filled with tears. To him, they seemed to say sorry and he knew then that it was all over. After that, it took all his stage experience to play out the role of David Price the singer. Never had Dafydd been so glad as to get back to a hotel room.

That night, his mind went over everything that had happened since he had come home from the war. He knew that he would never have held Louisa in his arms if he hadn't been wounded and in the hospital. At least he had loved, no still loved her and for a time she had loved him. But hers was the love of youth as his had been in the beginning when she was a pretty but unobtainable face. Then came the war and lines that were once firmly etched between the strata of society were blurred and it seemed possible to move from layer to layer. In the end, the gap between him and Louisa had proved too wide to be bridged. Dafydd couldn't pretend that his family and friends didn't exist. For Louisa the price of marrying him would be too high. She needed someone of her own kind so that when the war was over she could slip gently back into her strata of society.

Perhaps it will be Peter Robinson, thought Dafydd as he lay on his bed.

Then it struck him that, for the first time, since he met him in Cardiff, he wasn't jealous of the man. Dafydd drifted off to sleep, knowing that he had let Louisa go.

Chapter Thirty-six

In Morganton, the summer turned to autumn and the day of moving house drew near. Carrie and Granny Price were busy making new curtains, sewing lace on pillowcases and crocheting antimacassars to protect the new furniture. They were far too busy to wonder why there were no letters from Louisa. When they moved, the new house fulfilled all their expectations and Dafydd's money provided more comforts than they had ever dreamed of. The old lady still took in sewing but for her own pleasure - not out of necessity. If asked why she did it, her answer was always, "To pay for my funeral." Dafydd smiled every time he heard this for the old purse was full and still hidden in the Rosewood chest of drawers that now had pride of place in Granny Price's large new bedroom. Carrie no longer worked at Rock House, though she was always first to volunteer to help when they needed extra hands. In this way, she kept up with the gossip about the now Mrs. John Parry and her relations. Emlyn, without having to climb the hills, was able to walk to the Welfare Hall more easily and on most days he could be found with his friends in the reading room following the progress of the war. The fresh American troops decisively turned the balance in favour of the Allies and the spent German forces had to retreat. The Kaiser abdicated on November the ninth, two days before the official end of the war. The armistice was signed on November the eleventh and people throughout the country celebrated.

Nellie Evans and a few of her neighbours threw themselves into organizing a street party.

"Mam, it's winter. It could rain or even snow," said May to Nellie.

"Don't be so pessimistic. Of course it's not going to rain. And if it does then we'll have to put up with it. John will love the party."

The group of women borrowed trestle tables from Ebenezer chapel, covered them with oilcloth, organized the food, the cups of tea, and even persuaded one of the neighbours to lend them his gramophone.

There was no street party in "Gaffers' Row" since only three of the houses were built. But Carrie and Granny Price were not going to be left out of the celebrations.

"Nellie said to join them," said Carrie when they were having breakfast on the day of the party. "No one will mind. She said that there's plenty of food for everyone. Besides, we did make that bunting for them out of old scraps of material."

"I don't think I'll come," said Emlyn. "There's a nip in the air now. I'll stay in by the fire."

"I'll keep you company, Dad," said Dafydd. "It's the women that enjoy such things."

"You can come for a bit," said Carrie. "If only to see young John enjoy himself."

By the time that Daffyd arrived, most of the children had finished eating and were playing quite happily together in the street. He stood and watched a group of younger ones for a few minutes.

That limp is hardly noticeable now, he thought as he looked at John who was playing with another young boy.

"Looks like his father, doesn't he," a voice said besides him.

"Hello, May, you're right but there's a lot of you in him too."

"Come and have something to eat. We can sit at the end of that table. It's not too near the gramophone. I'm sure they've played the same record all the afternoon. The worst part is when that machine winds down!"

Dafydd smiled as he followed May to the table and sat down besides her. The contrast between the simple fare on the table in this grimy street and the feast prepared for the supper party in Louisa's elegant home didn't cross his mind. Though he did smile when he noticed that someone had placed an aspidistra in its china pot in the centre of the table.

It's over at long last, Dafydd thought. So many killed and wounded and for what?

He looked around at the happy faces and was glad that the war hadn't really touched many of them and that most hadn't suffered much. Except of course May in losing Jack and John in being without a father.

The war gave me Louisa and then took her away from me, thought Dafydd. Just as early on it took away Jack. But I couldn't have held on to her. I know that now. Jack always said that she wasn't one of us and never would be.

"Dafydd, take this cup of tea," said May as she nudged his arm. "You're far away. Forget about the war. It's all over. That's what this party's for – to celebrate. Have a piece of cake. Idwel baked it especially for today."

Dafydd managed to smile to please her as he helped himself to a slice.

After the armistice, life carried on in Morganton much as it had before. The hooters sounded in the morning to get the men to work and the women brought up their families and fought their constant battle against the coal dust. By the beginning of December, Dafydd was rehearsing for the Christmas concerts and had little time for anything else whilst Carrie was making plans for Christmas dinner. Thanks to her son, they now had a much larger house and her whole family would fit into it easily. There was even room for a few more. She knew how fond Dafydd was of young John so she thought that she'd invite Nellie, May and John to spend Christmas day with them. That evening, as she and Granny Price sat in front of the fire in their new living room, she spoke of her plans for Christmas day. Inevitably the talk turned to Dafydd and his love life – or lack of it.

"First it looked as if he'd marry Mary from Rock House. But that came to nothing because you said that he was sweet on Miss Louisa. Not that I thought that anything would come of that and it didn't. She was far too posh for us."

"I don't know what went wrong between our Dafydd and Louisa. I still think that at one time she would have had him. But it was not to be," said Granny Price with a sigh. Then she continued, " I suppose I'd better make an extra present. I can't leave John out when all the other children have their gifts."

After breakfast on Christmas morning, Dafydd told Carrie that he was going to take John the box of soldiers he had bought him for Christmas.

"There's no need for that," she said. "The boy will be here in a couple of hours. I've invited Nellie, May and John to Christmas dinner. You've been so busy that I didn't have a chance to tell you before. If you haven't got anything to do now, go and talk to your father in the parlour. It won't be long before your brothers and their families are here. Your grandmother and I have a lot to do before then."

"I've been told to come in here, Dad," said Dafydd as he joined Emlyn. "Are we allowed to sit on this new furniture now?"

"It's Christmas, son," replied Emlyn with a smile. "Besides we're having visitors."

"So I've just heard. We'll have a full house."

"The two women are showing off, that's all. Your mother will be in her element giving Nellie a conducted tour of this house and hearing her admire all the new furniture."

There was a lot of laughter that afternoon. Nellie always knew the latest gossip and her tales entertained Carrie's daughter-in-laws. John played happily with the other children and he didn't require much of May's attention.

"Go and sit in the parlour," urged Carrie. "It'll be nice for Dafydd to have someone to talk to."

"But won't his brothers be there?"

"No, they've gone up to the Royal Oak. He stayed in to keep his father company but Emlyn will be asleep in front of the fire by now."

When May opened the parlour door, she saw that Emlyn had indeed nodded off and that Dafydd was sitting on the sofa looking at some music. He looked up as May entered

"Sit here," he said as he moved to one end of the sofa. "You can't be bored with the gossip already."

"I've heard it all before," said May as she made herself comfortable. "Carrie sent me in here. She said that you needed someone to talk to."

Dafydd smiled. "It's a rest I need after all the Christmas concerts. These last few weeks have been very busy."

"So you haven't seen much of Louisa then."

"It's over, May. She's gone back to Bristol, to her own kind."

"I'm sorry, Dafydd."

"Don't be. I know now that it was for the best. I could never have been what she wanted me to be. In the beginning, she might have gone against her father's wishes but, as she saw more of the war, she began to realize that she didn't want to give up her old life. She needed to have it to go back to. She'd had her fill of horror. War weary – like a lot of us. She went home for a rest and didn't come back." Dafydd paused and stared at the flickering flames of the fire. Then, almost to himself, he said, "She loved me once. Perhaps she still does, but not enough. I think that I always knew that I couldn't have really made her happy. There was just too much of a gulf between us. There was no way that I could have married her knowing that sooner or later she would have regretted it."

"But you are wealthy now," said May.

"By our standards perhaps, but by theirs no. I could have given her a comfortable life but that was far less than what she was use to. Besides she had changed. The idealism had gone. She had seen too much. And she wasn't a rebel anymore Not that she had been much of one. Not like that Mrs. Pankhurst and her followers. No, she's tired and the fight in her has gone. It was just easier for her to conform to her parents' wishes."

"But where does that leave you?"

"Sad, as you can see. I did love her, May. I still do but I've a life to lead. God saved me when he took Jack so I'll not waste it."

As they sat quietly side by side on the new sofa, Dafydd thought of the love he had lost whilst May made plans about the one she hoped to gain.

That evening, Carrie insisted that Dafydd walked the three visitors back to their home.

"John may get tired on the way and need to be carried. He's too big for May to carry," said Carrie as she was helping Nellie and May with their coats. "You'd better go with them, Dafydd. You can put John on your shoulders."

"Who's for a ride then?" asked Dafydd as he swung John up. "Mind you duck your head for us to go through the front door."

The boy did as he was told and they set off but not before Nellie had yet again thanked Carrie for her hospitality. When they reached her house, Nellie insisted that Dafydd came in for a few minutes.

"Warm your self up before you walk back," she said as she reached over the guard and poked the fire into life.

Obediently Dafydd sat in the wooden armchair by the side of the grate and held his hands out towards the flames.

"You're right, it is cold tonight but I won't be long walking back. What do you say, John?" said Dafydd as the young boy came over to him and climbed on to his lap. He took the lad in his arms and began to sing softly:

> *When all the world is fast asleep,*
> *And stars bestud the sky,*
> *Some say the fairies revels keep,*
> *Until the dawn is nigh:*
> *They visit the earth from the realms of romance,*

To gleefully sing, and to laugh, and to dance;
They never bend the branches,
In skipping o'er the trees,
Nor crush a blade in dancing
To the music of the breeze.

Before he had come to the end of the verse, John had fallen fast asleep.

"I'll take him up to bed," whispered Nellie as she gently took her grandson.

Dafydd stood up and said to May, "It's time I went. You can all get to bed then."

May followed him down the passage to the front door.

"Thank Carrie again for a lovely day," she said as he turned towards her to say goodnight.

He looked down into her lovely eyes and yet again he caught the smell of lavender water. He didn't know what made him do it, but he bent towards her and kissed her.

"Merry Christmas, May," he whispered as he put his arms around her and kissed her again. "And a happier new year for both of us."

Epilogue

Professor Margaret Davies sat in her armchair in front of the gas fire on a cold January evening and speculated about the phone call she had received in her laboratory earlier that day. Yes, she remembered the human remains dug up in France about a year ago and wasn't that surprised when Colonel Phillips got in touch to say that he had established the identity of her finds. She was grateful for his courtesy. It was important to her to be able to follow things through to the end. Besides, being able to put a name to that skeleton for some reason seemed to make her job more worthwhile. The Colonel had said that his researcher had been able to trace a granddaughter of the soldier and that the lady wanted to be at the ceremony when the remains were interred. He'd given the impression over the phone that he'd unearthed quite a story and on impulse, Margaret had invited him to her home that evening to tell it.

"Come in, Colonel, come in out of the cold. Can I take your overcoat?"

"Thank you, there's a bitter east wind."

"Let's go into the lounge," said Margaret as she walked down the small hallway to an open door at the end.

"Make yourself comfortable in that chair in front of the fire. Can I get you a cup of tea, coffee or perhaps something stronger?" she asked as she pointed to a few bottles on the sideboard.

"I'll have a glass of whisky please, that is if you'll join me."

Soon they were sipping their drinks and swapping unimportant pleasantries. Eventually, the Colonel reached down and took a manila folder out of his brief case.

Opening it, he said, "Here's the information we have on the skeleton you found in France a year ago."

"Yes, I recollect the day well. It was freezing cold, rather like today. That east wind was bitter too. We found the usual bits of leather from his boots and I remember that there was part of a belt buckle. It was an early skeleton though. No dog tag, those fibre ones issued to the troops at the beginning of the war had long since perished. Neither was there any sign of one of those aluminium ones that were popular in the later stages of the fighting. The ones the soldiers bought themselves – out of a fear I suppose of being killed and no one knowing who they were. Sadly it's been true in so many cases. But didn't we find something else? A small tin box?"

"That's right. I've been able to piece together some of the history of that young soldier from that and subsequently trace his family to the present day. It wasn't that straight forward though."

Margaret settled in her chair and looked expectantly at her visitor.

"Thanks to you we had lots of clues." The colonel paused as he referred to his folder. "The numbers on the tin's lid, the bone structure – remember you thought that he had been a miner? You estimated his age as early twenties and he was about five foot eight tall. From all of this he should have been relatively easy to trace and in fact he was. That army number led us straight to him on the database. His name was

Jack Davies, and as you said, an ex-miner from the South Wales valleys.

"Well that's encouraging for me," said Margaret. "I remember those thickened collar bones. They are always a good indication of working with a pick or shovel."

"Yes, but our job wasn't finished. We needed to trace his descendents. As you know, it's our policy to rebury the remains in a war cemetery and if possible with the permission of the nearest surviving relative. Thus the first thing that we do is to check whether the soldier was married and if so were there any children. He did marry, just before he signed up, to a May Evans and they had a son named John in 1915."

"Do you think that he ever saw his son? He must have died in the same year as he had enlisted."

"I shouldn't think so but that was the fate of so many then. We looked for a death certificate for a May Davies but failed to find one. There were two possibilities as far as we were concerned – she could have moved out of the area or married again. Not that many young women managed to find another husband because so many soldiers didn't survive the war. Marriage was the easier option though, so we started there. We were lucky. We found a marriage certificate."

"For some reason, I'm glad that she was one of the fortunate ones," said Margaret. "What happened to the boy, Jack's son?"

"May married Dafydd Price in the summer of 1919. From what the granddaughter tells me, the boy John was treated no differently from the rest of their children. It seems that May had found a good husband. Not only that, he was quite a celebrity in the valleys - a professional singer. Later on he bought a draper's shop in a place called Morganton. The family was quite well off, and could afford to send John to

Cardiff University. Eventually he became headmaster of the local grammar school. Isn't it funny though, he was always called John Davies. He never took his stepfather's name."

"Wasn't he adopted by this Dafydd Price?" asked Margaret.

"No, it seems that his mother May, always said that as long as John carried Jack's name then she preserved some sort of link with her first husband."

"But didn't her new husband object?"

"Apparently not, Dafydd Price agreed with her. You see, Jack and Dafydd were best friends and had gone to war together but sadly only one had returned."

Colonel Phillips searched through his file and brought out some photographs.

"Jack Davies' granddaughter lent me these," he said as he handed them to Margaret.

She looked at the few cracked and faded photographs of men in uniform.

"Those two are Jack and his friend Dafydd," said Colonel Phillips pointing to two men in one of the pictures. "That's a postcard that Jack sent to May. Roses and white heather - so typical of many sent back from the trenches."

"It's funny, I've got some photos and postcards just like these," said Margaret quietly. "Not of these men of course but of my grandfather and his mates. My grandmother kept them in an old tin. But she was lucky. Her husband came back. There couldn't have been many families then that the First World War didn't touch."

"Yes, that's true. But at least we can now give Jack Davies a proper burial. There are still so many that we haven't found and as the years go by it gets more and more difficult to identify those that we do find."

The sun was shining but there was a cold east wind that February morning as a group of people stood in an immaculate cemetery on the Belgium France border. As the heavy traffic flowed passed on the nearby road, it was just possible to hear the army trumpeter playing the Last Post.

Onlookers in a passing coach saw a lady step forward and throw a handful of soil into an open grave. Unaware of the significance of the ceremony, they admired the clean rows of the white headstones and a mother was heard to say to her uninterested teenage son "Look out of the window, that's a war cemetery." A few of the passengers might have had a passing thought about the soldiers that had fought on the nearby battlefields all those years ago. If they did, it was but for a moment. There was a far more pressing topic to think about. How many euros did they have left? The bus driver had promised to stop at that supermarket on the outskirts of Calais. Beer was much cheaper in France than back home!